Still Not Over You

by

Barbara Lohr

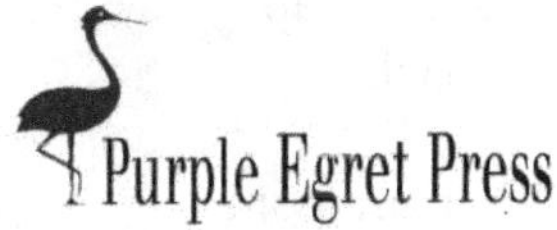
Purple Egret Press

Purple Egret Press
Savannah, Georgia 31411

Cover Art: The Killion Group
Editing: The Editing Hall

Print ISBN: 978-1-945523-08-3
Digital ISBN: 978-1-945523-07-6

Dedication

For my husband Ted,

your enduring support and fun-loving spirit.

Couldn't do this without you.

Chapter 1

Phoebe Hunicutt sat in her backyard watching the light fade from the Michigan sky. Pine trees rustled in the late May breeze while a sliver of the moon rose between the branches. She sniffed. The rich smell of spring hung in the air. Soon summer would creep softly through the dunes and doors of Michigan. Heavy jackets, wet wool and the long, cold winter would be only a memory.

Resort wear would fill the windows of the Gull Harbor stores. Restaurants would be frantic with waiting lists, and anyone who wanted ice cream would have to cool their heels outside the Swirly Top. Even Phoebe's business picked up once Chicago people poured into the summer homes. After all, women needed their hair done.

But this summer Phoebe wanted more than women's chatter and the smell of perm solution. Propping her feet on the crumbling fire pit, Phoebe sipped her iced tea and studied her toes. Maybe she'd paint them mauve to match her hair.

Whoopee do. A change in nail color. That was her summer excitement?

Today had been crazy busy at the salon. Her back ached and so did her feet. Taking another cold gulp, she captured an ice cube and let it melt on her tongue. If she weren't so darned tired, she'd wander down to the beach, only a block away. The sound of restless waves carried on the evening breeze, seductive and soothing. A short walk along the sand in bare feet? Tonight she didn't have it in her.

Setting her glass down, Phoebe massaged her neck. What was wrong? Was it the argument she'd gotten into with Sarah Mae Gary who didn't like her color one bit? "I wanted subtle. And this lime green is not subtle." Sarah had the nerve to shake a finger in Phoebe's face.

Ever since her divorce, Sarah Mae could qualify for the Wicked Witch of the West. Why didn't she switch to one of those fancy salons up in St. Joe, Michigan? No, instead she had to stay local and poke the bear. Phoebe didn't ever want to be like Sarah Mae. A touchy single lady who went ballistic over nothing. Sure, divorce was difficult. Who knew that better than her? Better to get busy than to get mad. That's what her daddy always said.

Looking around, Phoebe sized up her yard. The fire pit needed work, and her wooden chaise lounge was rotting, its green cushion splitting at the seams. The hedges were overgrown. She had more weeds than flowers, and her grass hadn't been mowed in a month. Her yard was a mess. She came home too darn tired to do much about it.

And then there was her sweet cottage. Well, *their* cottage. Brown paint peeled from the siding in strips, and the white trim looked just as bad. Buckets dotted the floor of the side screened porch to catch leaks when it rained. The whole place was falling apart. Even Fernando, the metal pink flamingo guarding the back door, needed to be spiffed up.

Phoebe was going to fix all that. The letter had been sent.

The rumble of a Harley grew louder. Maybe the answer to her letter had just arrived. The back of her neck prickled. Time to put on her big girl pants. Crossing her legs, she jiggled a flip-flop. Her ex-husband had come calling.

The property they own jointly, according to their divorce decree, was sadly in need of repair and she'd given him notice. Time for Ryder Branson to pay up.

With a *vroom, vroom,* the Harley fell silent. She didn't have to glance over at the driveway to picture Ryder's arrival. Hadn't she watched him come home for almost two years? Her ears had been tuned for that Harley coming up the drive. He'd swing one leg over, take off his helmet and hook it on the back. Then he'd run a hand through his crazy chestnut curls and unzip the leather jacket, like that broad chest needed some air.

Give me strength. After a year without Ryder Branson in her life, she still had to get up her gumption to face the man. The ground seemed to shake as he stormed toward her. "Phoebe Hunicutt, what are you trying to pull?"

She turned. "Hello to you too, Ryder." Could he see her heart galloping under her pink top?

His fine head of hair was outlined against the sky. Phoebe's fingers curled. She could almost feel those springy curls in her palm. Teasing. Exciting.

Past history.

Staring her down, his gray eyes hardened to stone and then

traveled. When his gaze skimmed her legs, she was glad she'd shaved. Only nicked herself twice this time. But those eyes? Worked her skin like a pumice stone. Arching one foot, she brought a leg up and skimmed her calf with a toe. Her ex was too busy ogling the curves to notice the nicks. Ryder's eyes bulged, along with another part of his body. Phoebe tried hard not laugh.

Remember Trixie Tatum.

The name froze the giggle in her throat. No one could hurt her like this man. Making her ex-husband pay for two-timing her? Always a delight.

She sat up straighter. Ryder flattened his hair with the heel of one hand. "What the hell do you think you're doing sending me a list like this?"

As he tugged the yellow sheet from his jeans, she smiled. My, oh my. This was getting better by the minute. "Just thought you'd like to know what it takes to keep this place running."

Ryder had the nerve to shake the paper in her face. "If you can't afford to keep the cottage in good shape, you should sell. Isn't that what I said when we divorced?" Then he turned to study their sweet cottage. Was he wondering how much the place would bring?

Anger seared her. Dropping her legs, Phoebe crossed her ankles. She'd seen Queen Elizabeth do that once on TV and it looked real classy. Not that she was anything like the queen. "That's not what the decree said, Ryder. The court decided that we owned the house jointly. You may remember that trade-off. I got to stay in the house until I wanted to sell, in exchange for you riding away with the Harley you always said was joint property."

Ryder's black boots shifted. Lightning sparked in his eyes.

Looking away, she kept talking. "Time to bankroll some repairs. The roof is leaking. The paint is peeling, and a strong wind will probably flatten that garage." When she stopped to breathe, her pulse was racing.

Folding his arms over his chest, he glared at her. "That's all? You sure?"

"Not really." Her chin went up—that "sweet heart-shaped chin," as he'd once described it. "The kitchen linoleum and the cabinets desperately need replacing."

"Desperately?" He didn't look convinced.

But he did look hot. How she hated that.

"Well, I-I think so."

Her anger melted under his gaze like a popsicle left in the sun.

Phoebe's eyes fell and Ryder followed her gaze to the ruined fire pit he'd built. He flinched.

"Damn." When Ryder fisted his hands on those trim hips, he unleashed a wave of wonderful man smells. Perspiration under a splash of cologne, with some gritty oil from that garage he had. She liked it. The weakening that turned Phoebe's body into linguini sure felt like swooning. She'd heard that word on TV. But she was not a woman who swooned. And right now? She couldn't afford it.

Grabbing a can of bug spray from the ground, she hit the button and cleared the air. While her ex went into a coughing fit, Phoebe struggled to pull herself together. Mercy, this was no time to get all googly-eyed. Those strong arms waving at the cloud of fumes? She'd once felt sheltered by them. Nine years older, Ryder had been her strength. Back when he stopped in the salon, every woman's heart rate went up. They adored him.

Right. Which was why they weren't married anymore.

Holding up the letter she'd worked on for two whole weeks, he flicked his fingers across her neatly typed list. "*Supplies and labor? What are you up to, Phoebe?*"

Well now, she thought the wording sounded real professional.

Beginning to pace, Ryder kept going. "You never answer my calls or my emails unless you want something." His thick head of hair shivered with fury. He was pissed. Well, so what? If he'd let her have the house, they wouldn't have to go through this every time she needed work done.

"You're…you're reprehensible." She'd heard that on *Days of Our Lives*. Or was it *Judge Judy*? Now *there* was a woman who knew her stuff.

Ryder hadn't seen that show. "Repre-what? What are you talking about?" His forehead wrinkled.

Did he think she was a walking dictionary? "I mean you are trouble with a capital T."

Although she hadn't asked him to sit down, he took the chaise across from her. But he kept his boots planted. The old chair was missing a wheel and he knew it. When it listed to one side, his frown deepened. "I don't have time for this, especially now, when I'm expanding in the Michigan market."

Ryder owned a string of body shops that ran from St. Joe, Michigan, up to Traverse City. He knew cars and motorcycles like the back of his hand. Stanley, his dad, had taught Ryder well. Why, he'd tell anyone who'd listen that his son could change oil when he was four. Ryder had taken Branson Motors and spun it into a string of garages. He was an entrepreneur with a capital E. That was one thing Phoebe had always admired about him, along with a few more personal parts.

No matter, she wasn't backing down on this. She loved this little cottage, and he was partially responsible for it. Full of renovation plans and crazy in love, they'd bought a fixer upper. They knew the place needed work. But their marriage had ended before the renovation even started. Basically, they'd been too busy with each other to get busy with the cottage.

She might have to negotiate. "All right, if you don't want to pay contractors, write me a check. I'll paint it and do the rest of the work." *What am I saying?*

Leaning back on one elbow, Ryder snorted.

That did it. She'd fix up the place if it took her every Sunday this summer. Jen and Carly, her hair stylists, could run Phoebe's Place for her. No way was she going to let her cute, cozy cottage fall down around her.

"I got a better plan." The scheming way he said that? Phoebe wasn't going to like this.

"I'm all ears, Ryder." Linking her arms behind her head, she let his eyes trail down over another area he used to appreciate. Phoebe kept herself in shape. Well, she tried. But she wasn't a skinny rail of a girl, like Trixie Tatum. Oh no. She liked a doughnut or two and it showed. So, what of it?

Was Ryder marrying that skinny Trixie soon?

The thought brought a sour taste to her mouth. Ryder didn't come down to Gull Harbor much since the divorce. They ran in different circles, so she had no clue what he was up to. But her imagination was filling in the blanks.

Turning, he studied the brown cottage. "We've got three bedrooms here."

"Hold it right there. *We* do not have three bedrooms. *I* have three bedrooms."

Too late, she realized her mistake. He grinned. "But I thought you said our joint interest in this rundown place was why I should pay for fixing it up?"

"My home is not rundown!" She cast an apologetic glance at the cottage. Fernando even looked offended, leaning a bit more to the side. Or maybe that was her imagination. A lot was at stake here. Phoebe better clamp a lid on her anger and think this through. She needed Ryder's financial support. Folding her hands meekly in her lap, just like Queen Elizabeth, she prepared to listen to his harebrained scheme. "Yes, you were saying?"

"As I see it, I could move in here for the summer, do the work. We can split the cost of supplies. The place is falling down around you." He delivered his proposal with a saucy grin.

Move in? Over my dead body. She pressed a hand to her heart to make sure it was still beating. Yep, still working. "How about we split the cost of the supplies and I do the work? Or better yet, *you* pay for three-fourths of the supplies and *I* do the work." Her mind whirled as fast as her heart.

Ryder sat up so fast, the remaining wheel fell clear off the chaise and rolled into the grass. "You are not getting up on a ladder to do anything on this house. You don't have the time and…" His eyes coasted over bare arms and legs, leaving a trail of goosebumps. He could still do that to her. "Let's just say you don't have the muscle for this job."

"I'm getting supplies this weekend." She lifted her chin even higher. He was treating her like a little girl. The nine-year age difference didn't work in her favor. An only child, she'd never learned how to cook. Her mama took care of that. Housekeeping? Their vacuum had given up the ghost when she rolled over the cord. But shampoo and scissors? Bring them on.

His lips set, like he knew he'd been beaten. "I'll leave a check on the table."

"You can pay me later." Made her feel good to say that. Of course, she was dead broke. What were credit cards for? Too late, she remembered hers were maxed out.

Getting up, he eyed the cottage with disgust. "You going to paint it brown again?"

Phoebe couldn't get excited about brown. "No, I want a little white cottage. Something cute."

The eyes he turned on her were twin tornadoes. "That's crazy. And girly. It'll take you two, maybe three coats of paint to cover all this brown. Pretty this place up and you'll never be able to sell it."

Ah, hah. So selling *was* on his mind. The weasel.

"Not a problem. Not selling." She'd show him. When she got finished, this cottage was going to be so girly, it would make

Ryder's stomach heave. No way was she selling.

The wind had kicked up. Behind her a couple more tiles rattled from the roof. Ryder rolled his eyes. Phoebe preferred to think her little house was applauding her decision.

"Memorial Weekend is coming up so I'll have two days to work on it. Probably knock it off in no time." Brave words that brought another eye roll from her ex.

She always worked Saturdays, but she'd have Sunday and Monday that holiday weekend. Jumping to her feet, she was already in Hill's Paint and Paper store, picking up supplies to transform her happy home. Enough lolling about with Ryder Branson. This conversation was going nowhere.

"Nothing you do makes sense anymore, Phoebe." He shoved himself to his feet.

Oh, just pour salt on the wound. "But I'm none of your business *anymore.*"

A shield slid over his eyes. She could almost hear it click into place.

"Weren't you on your way out?" Waving toward the driveway, she delivered the line as if they stood in a palatial ballroom.

"Mind if I use *our* restroom?"

"Of course not." But her mind leapt ahead. Neatness had never been Phoebe's strong suit. Last she saw, her makeup looked like it had exploded on the bathroom counter. And her clothes? At least one pair of panties had been left near the shower. She always had too much to do and not enough time. While Ryder was busy inside, Phoebe ambled over to Fernando for a little heart-to-heart.

"The man's a crazy idiot, right, Fernando?" She straightened the metal piece she'd bought at the South Haven Art Fair. "What does he know?"

Phoebe could swear the pink flamingo winked at her.

When Ryder barreled back out, he nearly knocked her over. Catching Phoebe by her upper arms, he flicked his thumbs up her biceps. Why didn't she work out more? His jaw shifted. Chests heaving, the two of them froze while their eyes met, snapped and sizzled.

Then the screen door whapped shut behind him and the trance was broken. When Ryder released his hold, she stumbled back. Face flushed, he turned and walked away.

So he was that upset about her mess?

"I try to clean things up." She stumbled after him.

"So I noticed."

Rubbing her tingling arms, she followed him to the detached garage. Big mistake. The blue paint on the doorframe must have caught his eye. He stopped so fast, she nearly ran into him.

"You and the garage still having problems?"

Smart ass. "Not my fault that door is so narrow." A new garage had been on the list when they split up.

He stared at the blue Mini-Cooper he'd given her. "So I guess I don't want to see the front bumper."

She swallowed hard. "No. But the brown's hardly noticeable."

Wheeling around, he pinned her with a crooked smile that could melt flip-flops. "Sweet Cheeks, there isn't a thing about you I don't notice. That mess in your bathroom? I liked it. Way too much." Ryder bit his bottom lip, like he wished he could take that back. He wasn't a man who admitted to weakness.

"Don't call me Sweet Cheeks." But chills rippled down her spine. She'd always loved his pet names for her. They were cute. Personal. Flustered, Phoebe combed fingers through her hair. They came away wet with perspiration.

"And I still liked it better red," he muttered, his eyes on her mauve hair.

"Here today. Gone tomorrow. Some people like change." Wasn't he living proof of that? "Besides, what you like doesn't matter. Not to me."

What were they talking about? The garage. The car. Her hair. Their marriage. The man had her all confused. When Ryder got mad, a vein pulsed in his left temple. She loved seeing that line dance under his skin. He opened his mouth twice. Phoebe chuckled when nothing came out.

Oh, he might not love her anymore, but she still had the power to irritate him. Tonight she'd had enough of his muscled manliness. Turning, she strolled away. The Harley roared to life. Her ears strained until the sound faded.

Phoebe's shoulders slumped. Oh, why did he have to come over? They could have done this over the phone. It was easier to stay mad if she didn't have to see him. Her throat swelled, the way it did when she had a bad cold. Wandering back into the yard, she took a sip of her tea but the ice had melted. She poured the drink onto the grass. Seeing Ryder had shaken her. She avoided places her ex haunted, like the Rusty Nail. That was why she'd mailed her request about the cottage.

Request? Probably more of a demand. But she'd been quiet long enough. Had avoided places and people more than she cared to admit, just so she wouldn't run into him.

And with good reason. Their conversation felt like ripping off a bandage. She thought things had healed. But Ryder's scent still lingered, and their past history washed over her. Ryder Branson was one hard man to forget. Her body had a long memory, so she probably wouldn't sleep well tonight. That big galoot had been the love of her life, the only guy she ever wanted.

Until Trixie.

Tears prickled in her eyes. Of all women, Trixie. Darkness crept from under the trees onto the patio. Dampness settled, the kind you get when you live near a lake. Grabbing her glass, Phoebe scampered inside to trade her cut-offs for jeans. Wasn't until she was making popcorn for her dinner that she found the check tucked under the toaster. Big man. Big check. Boy, it was tempting. But Ryder had made her mad. She ripped the check once, twice and then again, until it flowed like rice through her fingers and into the trash.

"Change of plans, big boy." She wasn't accepting anything from him.

~.~

Although he knew it wasn't safe, Ryder rode like a bat out of hell all the way up Red Arrow Highway. Every shop and restaurant along the way blurred in his side vision. Bending his head into the wind, he felt the powerful machine vibrating under him. Those black panties were imprinted on his brain. He remembered the times he'd slid them off. Opening up the throttle, he broke the speed limits of the small towns as he tore through. When no squad came wailing after him, he felt almost disappointed. Ryder was always spoiling for a fight. At least, that's the way it had been for the past year.

He didn't ease up until he reached the green sign that said Branson Motors. Taking his Hawg around the back, he pulled into the garage. The smell of grease and oil soothed him. He stood a moment in the cool night air and breathed it in.

This place had been his dad's, and Stanley still managed the business for him. Ryder had him driving to other small towns to check out locations for expansion. Right now his dad was talking to Mick in the glass enclosed office. Dad liked to chew the fat with the guys when they worked late. Unsnapping his helmet, Ryder pulled his Harley into the spot marked Boss Man. Usually that yellow paint made him smile with satisfaction. Not tonight.

Ripping off the helmet, he jammed it on the back and unzipped his jacket. Heat rolled off him in angry waves, along with rivulets of sweat. Licking his lips, he could taste it. He needed a shower, but he didn't want the one in his crummy apartment upstairs. No, he wanted the sweet-smelling soap and the sweet-smelling woman in a messy bathroom.

Ryder was screwed. After swinging himself off the Harley, he staggered with his first step, like someone had punched him in the gut. For a second he hung onto the leather seat, remembering

Phoebe's soft skin under his hands. Just seeing her had torn him apart. What a fool he'd been a year or so ago. Thirty years old and so full of himself back then. Disgust tasted sour in his mouth. Wasn't a day that he didn't regret his stupid mistake.

Tonight she'd looked so soft and sweet. That game she was playing with her legs? Phoebe knew damn well what she was doing. *Bring it on. Make me suffer.* His arms ached to hold her. But that brief clutch at the back door would have to do. And it wasn't nearly enough. His throbbing body told him that much.

Whatever it took, he was getting Phoebe back.

Not that it would be easy. Phoebe Hunicutt had never been easy.

Chapter 2

The next afternoon Phoebe took a break between clients. "Hey Jen, you're in charge!" she called out to the woman who'd been her right-hand girl since she opened Phoebe's Place. "I've got to run an errand."

Jen smiled with a wave of her styling comb. "Good luck with the paint."

Stepping into the sunlight, Phoebe got in her Mini Cooper. Jen had already told Phoebe she was crazy for taking this project on. Maybe she was right. Ryder had goaded her into it. Seeing him again stirred up a lot of memories. Last night she'd had crazy dreams about Ryder, and the two of them weren't painting. She woke up hot, sweaty and mad as heck.

He just didn't understand. It was hard to explain how she felt about that cottage. Or her ex-husband.

In five minutes she was pulling into the lot next to the huge red sign that said Hill's Paint and Paper. That sign was probably older than she was. Melvin Hill and his darling wife Louella had operated this place a long time. The good thing about shopping here was that Phoebe had a private account, something Melvin only did for favorite customers. He was such a sweetie. The sign had seen better days and so had Melvin, who was busy at the counter when she got there.

"Be with you in a minute, Phoebe," he said when she walked in. Not one to use "newfangled contraptions," as he called them, he was adding up the stack of supplies with a calculator. The customer didn't look fazed and was checking out brushes. Everyone in Gull Harbor knew how Melvin and Louella worked.

"No problem. I'll just look around." With a wave, Phoebe headed for the paint samples, her lime green slides slapping the soles of her feet. The place smelled like paint and turpentine, great for getting her into a project mood. Off to one side, Louella was painting a child's rocking chair. Melvin's wife was always making something for their grandkids. Repainting old furniture was her hobby. Phoebe wouldn't mind taking one of her classes, but they were always on Saturdays, the busiest day at her salon.

Standing in front of the display, Phoebe turned her attention to the tiered paint samples. She ran her fingers over the crisp cards, each holding five shades of a color. Today pink caught her eye. Did she really want a white house? Half the people in Gull Harbor had white houses with green or black shutters. Of course, some creative folks opted for yellow or blue. But not many. She fluffed her mauve hairdo. Running with the crowd had never been her thing.

Heck with Ryder and his talk of girly choices. Snatching up a card with a range of fabulous pinks, she whisked it to the window. Number 6584 was a dead ringer for cotton candy. Licking her lips, Phoebe could almost feel the sweet wisps sticky on her teeth.

When she was a kid growing up in Escanaba, Michigan, a carnival came to town every summer. As calliope music cast its spell over the town, she'd wait for the night her parents took her to the fair. Colorful lights sparkled in the sky, and the air was filled with the rattle and whirl of rides while kids screamed. Was anything as exciting as the summer fair? Dragging on her father's hand, she pulled her parents through the crowd until she found what she'd dreamed about all year. Wearing a white chef's cap, the cotton candy man whisked a paper tube along the inside of a huge cauldron. The sugary bouquet grew plump while she drank in the sweet air. When the man finally held out the wonder of pink cotton candy, her father would pull out his wallet. The wispy confection felt so light, so perfect she almost hated to eat it.

But she did. That mass of cotton candy helped her endure the long winters in the Upper Peninsula. So today? She snapped a finger against the card. Pink. Why hadn't she thought of pink earlier?

"You doing okay over there, Phoebe?" Louella called out.

"Oh, I am doing fine." The edges of the sample card bit into her palm. Louella went back to work while Phoebe considered colors for the trim.

Almost dizzy with excitement, Phoebe slid her eyes down the display until one color practically waved hello. Turquoise. Oh my. Like the pink, turquoise was such a happy color. Phoebe could savor morning coffee on the porch, sunlight falling through the screening framed with slats of turquoise. Feeling as if she held the winning Powerball ticket, Phoebe strolled toward the counter, the cards clutched tight in her hand.

She was going to have a slam-bang wonderful summer. Sure,

her friend Diana was getting married, and Carolyn was jetting off to Santa Fe to spend the summer with Brody, her new honey. Whatever. Phoebe would have her own thing going. This would be a summer worth remembering.

The customer left, laden with heavy cans. Melvin pushed aside his calculator, his gray moustache opening into a smile. "What you got there, Phoebe?"

"My most precious dream." Laughing, she folded the cards back to the shades she'd chosen and held them out.

"Well, that looks right pretty. Like something Lou would pick." Melvin waved both cards at his wife. "Looky here, Louella."

Setting down her brush and wiping her hands on her paint-stained smock, Louella sidled over. Her eyes lit up when she saw the colors. "Fixing to do a table, are you?"

"Don't I wish I had your talent? No, my house!" The words exploded with delicious excitement. The three of them smiled at each other, kindred spirits.

"You'll have the prettiest place in town, that's what," Louella assured her. "They'll be begging you to be on the Gull Harbor house walk next year."

Heads together, they talked about how much paint she'd need. Phoebe was sure glad she had an account here. Mercy, paint was expensive. She decided to start with six gallons. "Eggshell finish, gloss or matte?" Melvin was already reaching for the cans.

"I have no idea. Whatever people use outside." While Phoebe watched the machine jiggle her paint, she knew her most precious dream would drive her ex-husband bananas. That is, if he even got to see it, which she doubted. But Ryder might get curious when she didn't cash that check. She'd worry about that later. All the way back to the salon, she belted out "Fun, Fun, Fun," her favorite summer song. She would have fun. These cans of paint guaranteed it.

After her final client had left, she asked Jen to lock up and dashed home. Dressed in her old jeans and a T-shirt, with her hair tucked safely under an orange bandana, she got ready to paint. Evenings were long in the summer, thank goodness. She might need all the daylight she could get. Spreading old newspapers on the ground, she painted a sample patch on the siding outside the kitchen. " Bright and beautiful." She turned to Fernando. "Hey, this paint almost looks like you." Happily humming, she made the patch bigger, just to get the effect. She could hardly wait for the weekend.

~.~

Memorial Day weekend arrived. Phoebe's schedule was packed until three o'clock that Saturday. Women with weekend plans had booked cut, style and color appointments to start their summer off right. She knew just how that felt. Like her, Jen and Carly had arranged their schedules so they'd be out by three. While they finished with their last clients, Phoebe made sure the shampoo bowls were spotless, and the break room refrigerator was stocked with pop for Tuesday. She might be messy at home but here? Phoebe wanted to set a good example. When Merilee Curtis pulled away in her classic Mustang, Phoebe locked the front door and flipped the sign to Closed. All three exited through the employee side door, and Phoebe set the alarm.

"You two girls have a great time now," she told them. Phoebe could hardly wait to get painting.

"Don't work too hard, Phoebe," Jen called out, sliding into her Bronco.

"With any luck, I'll have that sucker done by Tuesday," Phoebe called from her open window, starting the Mini Cooper. The trim could wait, but she was going to knock off the siding over the next two days.

When she got home, she quickly changed clothes. Then she opened one of the cans of pink paint and began near the back door. Around seven, she made a turkey sandwich and then it was back to work. Mosquitoes bit her neck and arms. But the fireflies also came out. How she loved their tiny lights blinking as they flitted around the yard. Made the time go faster while she worked.

And she loved to imagine how amazed Ryder would be, if he ever saw it. After a hot shower, she fell asleep, muscles sore but content.

Rain on Memorial Day weekend was practically a tradition in Michigan. But Phoebe had been hoping this year would be different. No such luck. On Sunday she was awakened by the staccato beat of rain on the roof. Outside her window, lightning split a dark sky. A sky that should have been sunny. "Oh, no." Scrambling around, she slipped on jeans, T-shirt and flip-flops. As she scurried through the cottage, the whole place smelled like the paint she'd rinsed off her brushes the night before. Maybe next time she'd use the hose outside instead of the kitchen sink.

Pulling aside the white curtain over the back door, she watched rain pour from the eaves. The newspapers spread out where she'd stopped painting were soaked. Then she checked the side porch. The french doors were almost swollen shut and needed a good push. When she finally got them open, damp air bathed her face. Rain pinged into the aluminum bowls set up around the porch under all the leaks. There'd be no painting today.

Slamming a mug into her coffee machine, she waited for the water to heat. Turning on the morning news didn't help. The weather map showed a front of rain moving across Lake Michigan from Chicago. The coconut almond mocha coffee didn't even lift her spirits while she watched TV. Finally she clicked it off.

After she moved the paint under the eaves along with her brushes and rags, she sat down to have breakfast. Okay, so she'd regroup. Time for one of her comfy cottage days, as she called them. Those were days when she curled up with a book. She had a great romance to finish before their Wednesday book group meeting, a standing monthly appointment. Not too long ago, Sarah, one of the members, had lost her husband Jamie, a Marine deployed to Afghanistan. The book group quickly became a support group for their friend.

Instead of sitting there watching the rain, Phoebe decided to drive to Mandy Klavis' bakery for some raspberry kolaches. Only three left when she got there and she took them all after chatting with Mandy. After all, she had to plan for Monday too. The calories would go straight to her thighs. She could practically feel them bulge with every sweet bite. Phoebe would've driven into The Full Cup. Sarah always had a comforting ear. But this weekend? Phoebe was rushed. Mandy's bakery was way closer. Content with her book and a kolache, she curled up on the porch until the chilly air drove her inside. The rain continued into Monday. She got soaking wet dashing out to the driveway for the paper. After finishing the newspaper and her book, she had nothing to do. Her good friend Diana was getting ready for her wedding, and Carolyn was preparing for her return to Santa Fe.

On days like this she hated being twenty-two and single. Last summer she'd driven out to Sturgis for the motorcycle rally with her cousin Rosie from Escanaba. Rosie was a motorcycle nut and they'd had a good time. Of course guys had checked them out. But in the middle of the crowd, Phoebe felt alone and out of place. The rally reminded her of Ryder, and she'd come home feeling bad.

Self-pity never fixed anything.

While the rain poured down in gray sheets, she made herself a cup of peach tea and roamed the small house. Standing in the doorway of her bedroom, she studied the daisy wallpaper. Ryder had always hated it. But they'd been too busy during their short marriage to change the walls of a room they used, well, quite a bit. Taking a mouthful of the fragrant tea, she swirled it in her mouth and swallowed. Maybe it was time to get rid of painful memories. Why not paint the bedroom pink?

Pleased with her decision, she gulped the rest of the tea and set to work. Why hadn't she tackled this a long time ago? This bedroom held memories. The kind that could bring tears, if she let it. No more. She'd show Ryder she was moving on, not that he'd ever see this room.

Phoebe set to work. At least she could use a roller for most of the job. Outside, the uneven wood demanded a brush. Putting on an old pair of jeans and T-shirt, she tied the bandana over her hair and set out her supplies on newspaper. Just as a precaution, she draped an old spread over her bed. She sure didn't want to leave paint splashes on her quilt. Stripping the wallpaper would take too much time so she'd just paint right over it.

The first swath of paint was a strike for independence. She'd free herself from a painful past. But by the second swish of her roller, her traitorous mind had recalled a certain Fourth of July. They'd told people they were going to the parade in town. But they never made it. Boy, they sure took a lot of teasing for that one. Lost in dreams of what they actually *had* done that day, she stopped painting. A heated daze made her body swell and throb.

Oh, Ryder. Oh, honey. The splat of paint onto the old spread brought Phoebe to her senses. Horrified, she flexed the hand that now wore pink ribbons of paint. *We'll have none of that, Phoebe Hunicutt.* No lusting for the ex who broke your heart. That is *not* allowed.

Back to work. *Swish, swish.* She delighted in the sucky sound as she buried her past under the bright paint. Things were going well until she got to her bed and the curly metal frame. No way could she move this sucker. The box spring squeaked when she climbed up after setting the paint tray on her nightstand. Trying to balance, she widened her stance as she painted. Maybe it was the rhythm that got to her. When the bed kept squeaking, she accidentally fell into a Christmas reverie so powerful, she had to grip the frame to stay steady.

Oh, Ryder. Their first Christmas Eve had been so special. How they'd laughed while they got creative. And then *really* creative. Shocked, she stared at the pink heart she'd traced on the wall with the tip of her roller.

Phoebe Hunicutt, you should be ashamed.

But she wasn't and that was the problem.

Clutching her sticky paint roller, she continued with the wall, relieved when she'd passed the bed frame. But her eyes drifted back to the bed from time to time. She couldn't help it, and this was all Ryder's fault. Why did he have to stop in after she'd sent him that letter? Couldn't he have phoned? The darn rain kept pounding on the roof. Just thinking of all those disappointed children huddled in the neighboring cottages—well, that's what made her cry. Really, it was the thought of those poor children who could not enjoy the beach today. Her sympathy for them brought tears.

Sure. Right.

She was pathetic.

After an hour or two, her neck started to hurt. Time for a break. So she stopped to watch two, well, maybe five segments of *Days of Our Lives* on her DVR. Her customers loved watching the show too so she usually had the TV on in the salon. Would Abigail recover from her surgery? Does Eric have feelings again for Nicole? Grabbing her tissues, she sat riveted to the huge screen her parents gave her last Christmas. Maybe love never worked without a few bumps in the road. Not on TV and *not* in her life.

Watching TV seriously cut into the painting time. When Memorial Day weekend was over, Phoebe had only finished two walls of the bedroom. That wasn't enough, not by a long shot. She had more paint on her T-shirt and jeans than on the wall, and her arms ached from working that roller. Leaning in the doorway of her bedroom Monday night, Phoebe licked kolache crumbs from her fingers. The pink really perked up the room, well, those two walls at least. But it would need two coats. The outlines of daisies peeked through, looking like yesterday and reminding her of the past. And Phoebe didn't want to dwell on her yesterdays.

Waking up on Tuesday was so hard. Phoebe burrowed deeper under the quilt. She'd left the windows open to air out the bedroom, but the smell of paint lingered. Paint. Her aching shoulders reminded her. When she pried her eyes open, the pink walls smiled back. Phoebe wore a grin all the way into work. But listening to Jen and Carly chatter with customers about their weekend, she felt cheated.

"How about you, Phoebe?" Jen asked her, scissors snipping at Greta's perky hair-do. "What did you do this weekend?"

Dabbing color on Alice Kennedy's gray roots, Phoebe said, "Worked on my project."

"What kind, Phoebe?" Alice peered at her in the mirror.

"My cottage needs a fresh coat of paint." Wow, she sounded like she could actually handle that.

"You painted in the rain?" Jen's scissors stopped.

Swirling her brush in the hair dye, Phoebe shook her head. "Of course not. I painted my bedroom instead." No need to mention that she hadn't finished it.

"You be careful up on the ladder," Alice said, a note of warning in her voice.

"Well, of course, Alice." Hadn't she been taking care of herself forever? She'd always been a wild child. How shocked her parents had been when she took off on the back of Ryder's motorcycle to set up a shop down here.

When their short marriage ended, she had to get used to being alone. That hadn't been easy. Heart-broken and reeling, she'd been grateful to have Phoebe's Place. Her parents had tried to get her to come home to Escanaba. But she wasn't a quitter. She'd built up a nice business and no way was she leaving. Besides, she didn't want to be pestered with questions. Being unfaithful was unheard of in her family.

Why would Ryder even look at another woman? The only logical answer echoed in her heart. *You weren't good enough.*

"Ouch." Poor Alice jerked. "Phoebe. Really."

"Sorry, so sorry. My fingers slipped." *And so did my thoughts.* She'd given Alice's hair a sharp yank.

With a twitch of her shoulders, Alice settled back down. "You excited about becoming a grandmother, Alice? Kate seems to get bigger ever day." Finished at last, Phoebe set the bowl aside and handed Alice the latest Hollywood magazine.

Alice's daughter was married to Cole Campbell, hot city planner, and they were pregnant. Taking the magazine, Alice chuckled. "I can't wait to see that baby."

"I'll just bet." Pregnancy must be like a Get Out of Jail free card. For nine months, you could eat anything. Would Phoebe ever have that freedom? Her eyes misted while Alice rattled on.

"Oh, I get so jittery just thinking about Kate having that baby. Of course, Natalie is like my own granddaughter, but I have to share her with Marie McGraw. This baby will be all mine. It's a boy you know. Sean." Alice got this dreamy look on her face, the magazine lying unopened in her lap.

When Kate married Cole, he already had an eight-year-old daughter Natalie. In some relationships a stepdaughter might be trouble. But not Natalie. The little girl had even helped Alice recover from a stroke. Oh, Phoebe supposed there were some jealous moments because after all Natalie already had a grandmother. A long-time resident of Gull Harbor, Marie McGraw was the mother of Cole's first wife, Samantha McGraw. But that was another story.

After getting Alice settled, Phoebe dashed to her purse for some aspirin. Her shoulders and her neck were starting to ache. This was going to be a long day.

At least coming to the salon kept her away from that bedroom. Those memories yesterday? They kept replaying in her mind like her favorite movies. The ones that would make her mother faint if she ever knew Phoebe had seen them when she was only twelve.

Chapter 3

Of course at book group that week, all anybody talked about was the wedding. The camping honeymoon also came up. No one could picture Diana in a tent, and they teased her unmercifully.

When they finished discussing the wedding, they moved on to Carolyn's trip back to Santa Fe. Everyone agreed Carolyn wasn't going back for her grandmother. Oh no, she wanted to check on the chemistry she'd had with Brody Wolf while visiting with her grandmother in the spring. He may have been her student years ago, but now that Carolyn was thirty-two and Brody, twenty-eight, their chance meeting could lead to something more. At least, they all hoped it would.

After dropping Diana off on the way home, Phoebe felt restless. Maybe it was all that chocolate. When she got home, the sound of waves lapping the shore carried on the night air. Going inside, she plunked her purse on the sofa, grabbed a flashlight and took off for the beach. A walk might work off these jitters.

The lane was dark and silent, its sandy surface shifting underfoot. Somewhere in the darkness, an owl hooted and the pine trees whispered overhead. But night sounds and darkness never bothered her. To a girl who grew up in the woods of the Northern Peninsula, this all felt familiar and comforting.

Although some cottages had their lights on, nobody was around when she reached the beach. With her flashlight lighting the way, she took the steps down to the sand and kicked off her huaraches. Clicking off the flashlight, she left it with her shoes, wanting to disappear into the darkness. What a beautiful night.

When she reached the water, the moon cast a blue light over the lake. Whitecaps formed ruffles that fluttered to the shore, and she welcomed the chilly breeze. The night air might counter the sugar and caffeine in her system. Maybe then she'd be able to sleep tonight.

She hadn't said anything to the book group about Ryder. Her friends would want to know every detail, and the encounter with her ex had left Phoebe shaken. Although she might talk about her plans for the cottage with Diana or Carolyn, she wasn't ready to open up with the entire group. The situation felt too private and too unsettling.

Her feet sank into the dry sand, and she jammed her foot on a twig or two before reaching the shoreline. Turning left, she walked toward the lights of Gull Harbor, glittering in the distance. No lights beamed across the dark water. All of the yachts and sailboats were probably snug in their Gull Harbor berths by now.

Feet splashing along in water that still wasn't swimming temperature, she set a brisk pace. But Phoebe couldn't outwalk her racing thoughts. Life was moving on for her friends. Sure, they'd all met setbacks, but couples were forming and families too. Her life wasn't supposed to end up like this. Every time she talked to her parents, her mother would ask, "Are you dating anyone?"

"Mom, even if I were, I sure as heck wouldn't tell you. All of Escanaba would know." They'd laughed together, but it wasn't funny. In fact, it hurt. Her mom came from a different time. A time when girls married younger and became mothers earlier.

"How are you doing, sweetheart?" her dad would ask after Mom had surrendered the phone. Her father wanted to kill Ryder when Phoebe's "perfect marriage" ended.

The end. Sometimes she still couldn't believe it. Oh, she didn't blame her parents for their concern. After all, she was an only child and somehow she blew it. Had they even finished paying for the wedding?

The dark night closed around her. Maybe this walk had been a bad idea. Turning, she headed back. To shake her funky mood, Phoebe broke into one of the beach tunes her parents used to play. They had a great collection and would even dance in the kitchen sometimes. Although she couldn't recall all the words, the singing sure made her feel better. Pretending she was wearing her scandalous green bikini, she pranced her way up the shore.

Her feet left pockets in the damp sand as she swung her hips. Hadn't she studied Beyoncé's dance moves? With a hip here and a provocative glance there, she worked it out. By the time she reached the stairs, she had it just right.

This summer, Phoebe was going to fix her house and her life. And this shoreline? Maybe she'd start right here. Dumping the sand from her shoes, she pulled them on and grabbed her flashlight. Looking back at the sandy stretch, she pictured it full of hot guys who wanted to have fun.

Uh, scratch that. Hadn't she'd gone that route already? *Single and ready to commit.* She was only interested in men who wouldn't fool around on her. One hand on the railing, Phoebe started to climb. If these stairs didn't shape her up this summer, nothing could. In the past, she'd just paint a mental picture of whatever it was she wanted. From prom dresses to her salon, she saw it in her head before it became a reality in her life.

Except for Ryder. No, she'd never seen him coming.

~.~

Getting ready for Diana's wedding a couple of days later, Phoebe did a little spin in front of her full-length mirror. The soft ruffles on her pink party dress made her feel fun and flirty. That's just what she wanted this summer. Slipping into her silver sandals, she tried out a few dance steps. Oh, she doubted that she'd dance today but after this wedding? She had the whole summer before her. Lots of trips down to the beach in her green bikini. That is, in between her sessions painting the cottage.

The parking lot of the Gull Harbor Care Center was packed when she arrived. Her slings sinking into the grass, she hurried to the back of the facility where the ceremony would take place. Scooting down one of the rows of chairs, Phoebe sat next to Carolyn, who squeezed her hand. Today she was surrounded by people who cared about her and it felt good. A June breeze carried the scent of summer, mingled with the smell of the white carnations and roses decorating each row. White streamers fluttered from the gazebo and the opening to the tent where the reception would be held.

Will looked so handsome as he waited for Diana. They made a beautiful couple. When the traditional wedding march began, everyone's attention swung to the back. The guests smiled when Maisy walked down the aisle with hesitant steps in a long glass green dress. Thirteen and she was still trying to find herself. Hopefully the summer would help. Will and his family could provide the stability the girl needed.

When Diana started the short walk, all whispering stopped. She was a Grace Kelly knockout. Secondhand Rose, the consignment shop along Red Arrow Highway, had produced the dress. The modest scalloped neckline was repeated on the floor length skirt that rustled as she walked toward Will. Although the dress looked sweet in the front, that dip in the back told an entirely different story. That morning Phoebe had styled Diana's hair. Now the sun gleamed off the long curls cascading from a beaded headpiece.

Chicago people brought their barely-worn designer clothing to Secondhand Rose, so the stock was usually pretty upscale. The shop had been sold recently, and everyone wondered if the new owner would change things. But Phoebe couldn't worry about that now. Smoothing the ruffles on her own dress, she squeezed Carolyn's hand and waited for the service to begin.

When the minister stepped forward, the music faded away. Taking a deep breath, Phoebe listened to the couple recite their vows. She tried to stay in the present. Really, she did. But she couldn't shut out the memory of how handsome Ryder had looked on their wedding day. How certain she'd felt, hearing him promise to love her forever.

After the ceremony the guests congratulated the bride and groom before settling at round tables inside a white tent. The food was wonderful but Phoebe wasn't hungry. When the dancing started, Phoebe grabbed her handbag. The song was way too romantic. Watching Will guide his bride around the dance floor, Phoebe saw his lips touch Diana's forehead and a lump formed in her throat. What was wrong with her? Seeing Ryder had stirred up way too many memories. How relieved she was when that first dance ended. "Have a great trip," Phoebe whispered to Carolyn, passing behind her chair on the way out. "Bring Brody to see us, okay? You know, a longer visit this time."

"Oh, Phoebe. I will," Carolyn said.

No more weddings for her this summer. Stopping at Clancy's, she picked up a quart of chocolate almond ice cream. Once she'd slipped out of her dress and into her cut-offs and a T-shirt, she popped *La-la Land* into the DVD player. During the first half of the movie, Phoebe polished off two bowls of the ice cream. She allowed no guilt whatsoever.

After all, tomorrow she was going to paint the place pink.

~.~

Spreading Sunday's newspaper under the eaves, Phoebe decided to start at the sample she'd painted earlier. Rooting around in her musty garage, she found the old ladder left by the former owners. Ryder had always talked about taking it to the dump but never got around to it. Man, it was heavy. Maybe she should have considered a new one when she was at the paint shop. Too late now. Straining every muscle in her body, she managed to drag it across grass still damp with morning dew. When she reached the side of the house, she had to stop to catch her breath.

But she was burning daylight, as Ryder used to say. Heaving the ladder upright, she rested it against the gutters. Her arm muscles screamed, and the gutters screeched and dipped under the weight. She sure hoped they'd hold. When it rained they leaked and, clogged with leaves, the downspouts overflowed. Another project for her to-do list. But she wouldn't think about that now.

Then she went into the garage to haul out the paint. It took a while to get everything set up. She'd picked up one of those paint can hooks at Melvin's. Holding her breath, she inched up the ladder with that gallon can. It took some doing, but eventually she had it hooked securely on a rung where she could reach it. Brush in hand, she began to paint, starting at the top. Since she was going to do the trim later, it didn't matter if paint dripped. Wasn't that all a part of the creative process?

The sun beamed through the trees, and the soothing sound of waves came in the distance. Soon Chicago people would fill the rental cottages, some docking their boats in the marina. By that time her place would look wonderful, and she'd be ready to enjoy the summer. Maybe she'd buy a new swimsuit, one that was even more daring than her green bikini, if that were possible. This was the summer for shameless.

If Carolyn and Diana could find a man, so could she. Spirits rising, Phoebe wielded her brush. But she could almost hear the dry siding slurping up the paint. Six cans might not do it. She'd worry about that later and kept painting. The faster she worked, the better she felt. At times, the ladder seemed to sag under her weight. No matter. She'd show Ryder. Phoebe was doing this all herself.

Take that, Ryder. Her brush flew, flicking paint back in her face. Thank goodness she was wearing goggles. Oh, yes. She was a woman who knew what she was doing. If Ryder ever saw the place, he'd be impressed. No more Sweet Cheeks for her. She was a girl who knew what she wanted and how to get it.

Hear that, Ryder? Another vicious swipe.

Holy moly, she leaned back to appreciate her work. This pink paint made the whole place pop. Why hadn't she done this earlier? Oh right, Ryder had thought the brown was "serviceable." It would hold up well, whatever that meant. Sometimes she felt glad she had no man in her life. They had their own opinions, and he could just keep his. She was going to girly up the place, no matter what Ryder thought.

But this painting was harder than she expected. The brown kept popping through the pink. Darn it. She'd have to do a second coat, which meant more charges at Melvin's. But she wouldn't think about that now. As the morning passed, her arms started to ache and her neck hurt. By the time noon came around, she was wishing she owned a one-floor cottage. How did the place get so big?

Moving the ladder became a major event. Her side hurt. After reading all those magazines at the salon, she figured she either had a hernia or appendicitis. Then her shoulder chimed in. Yep, torn rotator cuff too. She just knew it. Taking a break, she grabbed a can of pop and took a seat on the porch to consult with Fernando. "What do you think? My side is killing me. Appendicitis, right?"

Let's remember, amiga mia, I'm not your doctor. I'm your therapist.

"Okay, cut the attitude. Sometimes you can be so uppity. Geesh."

The flamingo's expression never changed.

Then it was back to work for another hour. Phoebe's side stopped aching, but her shoulders were killing her. Wielding a paintbrush took a lot more muscle then styling with her scissors and comb. The ground was so spongy from the recent rain that the ladder finally got stuck and wouldn't budge. Climbing down, she had to think about this.

After stopping for a peanut butter and jelly sandwich with two ibuprofen, Phoebe surveyed her progress. This was really going to happen. *She* would make it happen. Taking the ladder in both hands, she heaved it up and scooted it over. Pumped up with sugar, she tromped up that ladder like a fireman. Picking up her brush, she threw herself back into her project. But when she got to the top, the ladder felt crooked. Throwing her weight to the other side, she tried to balance it.

Shifting didn't help. In fact, the ladder tilted more. Paint slopped from one side of the bucket. Stomach lurching, Phoebe clutched the sides of the old wooden ladder. This wasn't looking so good. As the tilting continued, her paint can flipped off. She was going down. Panicked, Phoebe grabbed at a gutter but it ripped off in her hand. Falling faster, she wound both legs around the ladder and closed her eyes.

When she hit the ground, pain ripped through her body. In the middle of her blood curdling scream, Phoebe heard something snap. Flat on her back, she stared up at the trees spinning overhead. The heavy ladder had landed on top of her and wouldn't budge. She wasn't going anywhere, and panic clawed at her throat. The wet grass soaked through the back of her shirt. Why didn't she carry her cell phone with her? Every time she tried to move, the pain dug deeper, like it was there to stay.

She would not cry. She just would not.

Squirrels chattered in the trees as if even they were concerned. Somewhere a phone rang. Was that hers? She might be here for a while, at least until the mailman came. But the mailboxes were out at the road. Maybe a family would pass by on their way to the beach. Her panic mounted, almost shutting out the sound of the Harley rumbling up the drive.

Perfect. The last person on earth she wanted to see. And she'd been feeling so I-am-woman-hear-me roar until now. The sound of the engine cut out. "Phoebe?"

"Over here." She tried to wave an arm. "I'm on the ground."

His boots drew closer. Ripping off her painting goggles, she twisted to meet his eyes.

"Phoebe...what the hell?" Taking in the situation, Ryder's eyes grew round. Was he going to laugh at her? Pink paint had splattered everywhere. The gutter was twisted on the ground. She was a total mess.

"Please help me." Her roar had become a whimper.

Whipping out his phone, Ryder punched in some numbers.

Phoebe knew from his expression that something was seriously wrong. "Just give me a moment, darlin'. We'll have this fixed in no time. I'm here and everything is going to be okay."

Ryder had always liked to be in charge. Back when they were married she'd liked that. Was she a total wimp to feel comforted by his take-charge attitude now? The pain wouldn't quit and she was in no position to argue. "My leg, my leg," she moaned.

She'd never seen Ryder so upset. He dropped to his knees next to her. Her bandana had slipped over one eye and he flipped it off. "I know, darlin'. I know it hurts."

"My shoulder too, Ryder. This ladder's so heavy."

Sitting back on his heels, he sized up the situation. "Now, what I'm about to do is going to hurt but just for a second. I think."

"You think? That's not comforting, Ryder."

"This ladder has to come off, but I'm not a goddamn EMT. They're coming."

"Okay, okay. Just do whatever you want to do." Phoebe prepared to grit her teeth.

He lifted a brow. "Whatever I want to do?"

"I mean when it comes to the ladder." Did she really say that?

Working slowly and gently, he lifted the ladder and tossed it to the side like a toothpick. "Damn thing. I thought we got rid of this."

How many times had he dragged this ladder out to the road for the trash? He'd been so mad when he found it back in the garage. "You're too stubborn for your own good," he'd tell her.

That sure applied today. He'd told her not to do any painting.

Hadn't he left a check for all that? Covering her eyes with her hands, Phoebe wanted to die.

"The EMTs should be here soon." Ryder cradled her head in his lap. The sun slanted through the trees. Everything felt cozy and warm. Maybe she was dying.

Then the wail of a siren split the summer air.

Nope, she wasn't going to die. But right now? She wished she had.

Chapter 4

What could be worse than being at the mercy of a man she'd kicked out a year ago? Stretched out on a bed in the ER of Memorial Hospital, Phoebe stared at her white cast. The past hours had been a nightmare. She felt so stupid. But Ryder hadn't said "I told you so." At least, not yet. The staff told her how lucky she was that Dr. Swanson was on call. An orthopedic surgeon, he had come in to set her leg. Feeling woozy, Phoebe didn't remember much about it.

But she wasn't feeling lucky. Lucky would have been not having this happen. Lucky would not be not sitting here with Ryder, who was looking a little pale himself. Poor guy. He probably had a million other places he'd rather be than this blindingly bright ER. Overhead lights bounced off a lot of serious looking stainless steel equipment. And all that tubing on the walls? She didn't even want to go there.

"I'll be right back." Ryder got up with a distracting stretch of his muscled arms. "Want anything?"

"No, I'm fine." Her eyes went to the cup of crushed ice on the tray.

"Are you thirsty?"

"A little." Was that her voice? So tiny and weak.

When he handed her the cup, she thought he might try to feed her the chips and grabbed the spoon herself. "I've got it."

Backing up, Ryder held up his hands. "Okay. Okay."

"Hey, I'm sorry, Ryder." But he was gone and Phoebe felt terrible. After all, she'd still be sprawled in the grass under the darn ladder if he hadn't come along.

A pretty blonde nurse bustled in. "Dr. Swanson should be here any minute to check on you. You'll like him. He's an excellent surgeon and cute too," Blondie told her with a wink as she left.

"Terrific." Phoebe stared at the empty doorway. The anesthetic hadn't worn off and the room felt like it was moving.

Before long, an attractive man in a white coat swept into the room with Ryder right behind him. "Hello, I'm Dr. Swanson." Giving Phoebe a quick smile, he turned to Ryder. "How's the wife doing?"

She pointed to herself. "Me? I'm not his wife and I'm fine. I was just painting, you know. Should have gotten a new ladder, I guess, but no. Got right up there and..." Ryder was looking at her like she'd lost her mind and so was Dr. Swanson.

Mercy. She was blabbering

The doc smiled like a father whose daughter just put her face in her birthday cake. "The anesthetic," he said to Ryder, who had the nerve to nod.

Okay, maybe it was the anesthetic. Maybe it was Dr. Swanson's amazing good looks muddling her mind. Dr. Swanson was a Dr. McDreamy. A surgery mask hung from his neck, and his hair was matted from the cap surgeons wear. She'd seen this all on TV. He even managed to wear those white booties without looking silly.

While Phoebe tried to straighten out her mind, Ryder shook the doc's hand. "Thanks for helping us out." Cripes, he even sounded like a husband.

Phoebe cleared her throat. "He's not my husband. He's my ex."

For a second the poor doctor looked confused. "Oh, I see." But it was clear he did not. For the next ten minutes he talked to Ryder as if she wasn't even there. Pain pills were handed over. Snatching them from Ryder's hands, Phoebe set them on her tray. She wasn't one for a lot of pills, but the insinuation that Ryder would be in charge of anything infuriated her.

Finally getting the message, Dr. Swanson gave her his full attention. "Stay off your feet at first. The nurse will bring some crutches and show you how to use them."

"I can show her," Ryder said. Oh, he sure could. How well she remembered that July 4 when he'd had a few too many brews down on the beach. Ryder had tripped on the steps carrying their cooler back up to the house. The cast had slowed him down for the rest of the summer.

Now the cast was on the other foot. Well, person. Technically, it was her right femur. She wouldn't be doing any painting anytime soon. Tears welled behind Phoebe's eyes. No way would she let Ryder see her cry. Dropping her head, she picked at the paint splattered on her arm.

"Excellent. You can handle the crutches, and let me know if you have any questions." Dr. Swanson edged toward the door.

She waved good-bye to Dr. McDreamy-Swanson. And then

they were alone. "Do you feel ready to go home?" Ryder asked.

"Absolutely. When can we leave?" Said boldly but how was she ever going to handle this?

"Soon. They said soon." Sure enough, Blondie reappeared with a pair of crutches.

After a quick crutch demonstration, Phoebe was trundled off to the exit in a wheelchair. "I'll just wait right here with your wife, Mr. Hunicutt," the pretty nurse said when they reached the front entrance, batting her lashes at Ryder.

The nurse nearly ran into him when Ryder stopped and pivoted. "Name's Branson, ma'am." He was all business today.

"Of course." Practically purring, Blondie beamed up at him.

"How did your truck get here?" Phoebe asked. Ryder had insisted on coming to the hospital with her in the ambulance.

"My dad drove it down. Mick took him back to the shop."

"Aw. Stanley's so sweet." Phoebe had been crazy about Ryder's father. Losing him almost hurt as bad as losing Ryder.

"Right. And he's plenty concerned about you. I'll be right back." Ryder held up a finger as if he was afraid she'd scurry off. Glancing down, she knew her scurrying days were over for a while.

"That man is so sweet." The nurse's eyes followed Ryder while he loped across the parking lot, sun beating down on his broad shoulders and casting a copper glint to his hair. Uncomfortable as all get out, Phoebe fidgeted in the chair.

"So how did you break your leg?" the nurse asked, the sexy purr gone.

"I was up on a ladder, painting my house."

Her lips formed an O. "You kidding me? Why would you do that when you have…" She nodded toward Ryder, now getting into his truck. Obviously Blondie wasn't a woman who took things into her own hands, not a paint brush at least.

"I don't *have* him." Not that this was any of her business. "I like to do things myself."

"Oh, well. He sure acts like he's your husband. But he's not, huh?" She moistened her lips.

Phoebe snorted. "Nope. And he's all yours. Open season."

Although the nurse didn't seem to find that funny, Phoebe was still chuckling when Ryder pulled up in the pickup. Jumping out, he came around, opened the passenger door and adjusted the front seat. Then he turned to her, holding his arms out like a forklift.

"Stop." Phoebe tried to push him away. "I can do this myself."

"Isn't that how this whole thing started?' Ryder muttered. But he stepped back.

Pushing herself up, Phoebe began to sweat. This might be harder than she figured. "Hand me those crutches, please."

But Blondie was still transfixed, holding Phoebe's purse and crutches while she stared at Ryder. Phoebe had to grab the crutches from her hands, fit them under her arms and swing herself over to the SUV. The two steps felt like a mile. Watching her all the way, Ryder seemed to be biding his time.

"Has your truck always been this high?" Helpless, she stared at the black leather seats, about shoulder level. Ryder didn't say a thing.

He was going to make her ask for help. Or not. When he

scooped her up, she squealed. Blondie stepped back and Phoebe felt strangely satisfied. After getting her situated in the front seat, he snapped her seatbelt shut. Then he tucked the crutches into the back seat and nodded to the nurse. "Thank you ma'am." Blondie got the message. Reaching up, she handed Phoebe her purse. Then she stepped back and waved goodbye.

For a second Phoebe fell back against the headrest and closed her eyes. The truck must have been in the sun but she welcomed the warm seat. The smell of leather and Ryder's soap lulled her. Her eyelids felt so heavy.

"You cool enough?" Ryder asked, slamming his door shut behind him.

"Kind of." She fanned herself with a hand that felt like a wooden paddle.

All the exciting plans she'd had for the summer had been ruined. There would be no strutting down the beach looking for Mr. Right. No running through the shallows before diving into the waves. No picnics watching a fabulous sunset. The cast had made a lot of her former plans impossible.

By this time Carolyn was in Santa Fe with Brody, facing an exciting summer. Diana was still on her honeymoon. Kate was very pregnant and Chili was busy at Ignacio's produce store. Sarah had her hands full with the boys. Who would help her? Her parents couldn't leave the Christmas tree farm untended. Some pranks had been pulled in the past. Anyway, she didn't want them clucking over her.

Hands fiddling with the knobs, Ryder was all business. Closing her eyes, she tried to pretend this was two or three years ago. Back then she'd been tickled pink by everything he did. Every arch of his brow, every shrug of his shoulders, every touch from those sensitive but large hands shot her to the moon.

She'd been in the luminescence.

One of her customers had used that term one day, referring to the beginning of the relationship—the time when the man can do no wrong. That's before the woman remembers she has her own checkbook, and she really doesn't like sharing a bathroom.

Back then Phoebe had been just plain crazy about the man.

But that was then. "I'm fine now."

"Glad to hear it." Ryder pulled away from Memorial Hospital. "Don't suppose you want to tell me what you were doing up on that ladder."

"You're not my father, Ryder."

His lips flattened into a thin line. "Don't even bring up your dad. He'd have a fit about this."

He had a point. "I was painting my house. Didn't I tell you that was my plan for the summer? Fix up the place."

"Well if you took a look at the check I left on your kitchen counter, you could have hired someone to do the work." That twitching muscle in his jaw said it all. He was steamed.

"I ripped it up." Her voice was a whisper and Ryder bent his head to hear.

"You ripped it up. Whhhhy?" Throwing back his head, he roared like an angry lion. Kind of resembled one too, his hair all wild and woolly. Blondie would like this look. Phoebe was over it.

Looking out the window, she saw Highway 12 streaming past. Mario's Italian restaurant, Skip's Other Place, all the shops and places she knew like the back of her hand. The tourist season would be starting soon and these parking lots would be packed. She'd be stuck at home. "In case you missed the memo, I don't want your help. I'm fixing the cottage up just the way I like it. Myself."

"And in case you missed the memo, I still own half the place."

"But I have custody…"

He glowered at her in the mirror. "What are you talking about?"

Custody. Habitation. Divorce. All angry words. She closed her eyes and tried to breathe in so she'd make sense. How she wished the house was all hers and hers alone. The screened porch came to mind. That was her peaceful place where she could curl up on the futon with a book or an electronic reader in her hands. A summer breeze would cool her, while tree branches rustled overhead, an acorn dropping onto the roof now and then. Her muscles relaxed and her mind cleared. Eyes flagging, she felt like she was all alone, drifting on an inflated raft. The sun smiled down on her.

"Take a little rest now, Sweet Cheeks."

The words came to her through a fog. "Don't call me…" She must have drifted off. Did she imagine that pat on her hand?

In her dream she was splashing along the shore, the waves lapping over her toes. She could taste the lake breeze on her tongue, feel the sun on her shoulders and smell the coconut sunblock.

Next thing she knew the passenger door was opening. A gust of warm air hit her. She struggled to sit up, licking her dry lips. Wearing a smile that used to melt her clear to her toes, Ryder held out a hand.

"No, really. I can do this."

Stepping back, Ryder looked like he was waiting for her to fall. Phoebe sucked in some fresh air to clear her head. Turning slightly, she scooted down on her stomach, reaching with her good leg for the ground. Pretty gutsy or pretty stupid. Sometimes it amazed her how she could be both at the same time.

"Guess it's easier to slide out than it is getting in," Ryder said, watching her maneuvers.

"Right. You should know all about that." What was she saying? Smoothing a hand down her paint-stained T-shirt, she caught his hurt expression. What was wrong with her? What if he hadn't happened along? "Could you hand me those crutches please, Ryder?"

His face taut, he opened the back door and grabbed them. But he'd paled beneath his tan, as if she'd just backhanded him. Guilt splashed over her like a cold wave on a windy day. He handed her the crutches but didn't meet her eyes. Reaching in, he snagged her purse.

"Sorry, Ryder. If it weren't for you, I'd still be stretched out on the ground." He was studying his boots, her handbag on his shoulder. "Could you just help me get inside? Then you can head on your way. By the way, you look nice with my purse." She'd insisted that he bring it since her wallet had her insurance card.

"Thanks." He glanced down with a twisted smile. They'd

bought that leather shoulder bag with the fringe at the Sturgis motorcycle rally. He'd paid for it, and she couldn't recall when a gift had pleased her so much.

As Phoebe made slow progress to the house, the beautiful day almost broke her heart. Sunshine poured through the trees, and the birds hopped from branch to branch. They moved so freely, but she sure wasn't. Glancing at the yard, she tightened her hold on the crutches. What a mess. Pink paint had splashed all over the brown siding as it fell. The ladder was caught in a bush, where Ryder had heaved it. And to top it off, she'd done a terrible job with the small area she'd painted. While they were at the hospital, it must have showered. The rain had taken some of the paint with it. Pools of pink floated in her weed strewn flower beds.

She just couldn't deal with it. Not now.

Chapter 5

Phoebe still kept a key under the flowerpot. Ryder unlocked the back door. The house had that familiar, closed-up smell to it. When he inhaled, the kitchen brought back so many memories. But today he didn't have time for them. Phoebe thumped her way to the french doors. She'd always had trouble opening them after a rain because they swelled shut. Putting one hand flat on the door, she bent her head.

"Here, let me." In two shakes, Ryder had the doors open. The breeze felt great and Phoebe swung herself onto the porch like it was no big deal.

Ryder studied the rattan chairs. "Remember when we bought these?"

"Yeah. My lucky day, right?"

She'd called Ryder from the antique store, all excited. He told her to go ahead and buy the set. After work he stopped at the shop with his pickup. Now she lowered herself onto the futon, and he took one of the chairs.

"So do you have these bowls out here all the time?" he asked. The porch was a mess. The paint wasn't the only thing that had to be addressed. All around them, dripping water hit the metal bowls. The rain may have stopped but water still drained from the roof.

"Yeah, I like the look." Phoebe's chin came out and he felt warned.

Glancing up, Ryder studied the tongue and groove ceiling. "That roof should be replaced. The water is going to ruin the wood." He'd put that ceiling in himself, and it killed him to see water seeping through his neatly turned joinings.

Grabbing one of the throw pillows, she jammed it beneath her head and lay back. "I'll get to it, Ryder."

Ryder rested an ankle on the other knee. "I've been thinking."

"About what?" Phoebe's face flushed. The slightest comment seemed to set her off.

Shifting in the chair, he cleared his throat. "You're going to need help. And that was before you did...this." He waved a hand toward the cast.

She heaved up on one elbow. "I didn't do this on purpose, Ryder." Phoebe's eyes turned from hazel to green when she was mad. Right now? Grass green.

"Oh, I know you didn't mean to fall off the ladder, Sweet Ch-...Phoebe. Anyway, your folks are way up in Escanaba."

"And I don't want them down here, fussing over me." She glanced around, clearly exhausted. "Besides, what needs to be done here is more than they can handle."

He looked up at the ceiling again. The water was still dripping. "The place does need a lot of work, more than you can ever give it. Why don't you let me line up the guys?"

Phoebe reared up. "Over my dead body. Somehow I will do this, Ryder. Once I'm rested? *I'll* hire people..."

This was ludicrous. Phoebe could hardly get the words out and fell back on the cushion. She couldn't do it, and unless her business had picked up considerably, she wouldn't be able to fund all the repairs he now knew were needed.

"You're not being reasonable. Let me do it. When the Chicago people start streaming into Gull Harbor, they'll sign up all the contractors like this." He snapped his fingers. "I can pull some strings. You think you can call and crews will come running? I don't think so."

Phoebe's face reddened. Then right before his eyes, she folded. Just melted onto the futon as if all the spunk had been drained right out of her.

"Fine, Ryder," she said softly. "If that's what you want, that's the way it'll be."

Who was this woman? He was getting concerned. Somewhere a chainsaw rattled and she jumped. Ryder waited until she settled.

"It's not just what I want," he finally said slowly. "It's what I'll do…for you."

Tenting a hand over her eyes, she blocked him from her vision. "Fine. Please close the back door on your way out."

That just about did it. He'd spent the entire day taking care of things after she'd practically killed herself, and now she wanted no part of him? The cushion squeaked when he jumped up. With two strides he was back in the kitchen.

She'd never been a great housekeeper, and he never faulted her for it. But he wasn't leaving the place like this. He emptied the dishwasher, put everything in the cupboard and then wiped down the counter.

"See you later," he called out right before he slammed the door.

When Ryder got back to the shop, he parked in back and stormed inside. All the way up the Red Arrow Highway, he'd been madder than hell. Took some turns faster than he should have and slowed down only after he narrowly missed hitting a deer. Anger throbbed in his head.

And he was mad at himself. If it weren't for him and a stupid mistake he made, she wouldn't be in this jam now. He wouldn't have to sit there and watch Phoebe suffer. Oh, she may be proud. That was one thing. He'd always admired that in her. But that house needed him. Hell, she needed him.

At least, he hoped she did. He sure as hell needed her.

"So how's everything at the hospital?" Stanley asked when Ryder slammed into the inner office. "How's our girl?"

"Fine, I guess." He hated to fill in the blanks. "She's at home now."

Stanley's stormy look told Ryder this was all his fault. Phoebe was his father's favorite. He'd taken the divorce almost as hard as Ryder. Leaning against the glass counter, Ryder stared out at the traffic on Red Arrow.

"She always was stubborn." The satisfaction in Stanley's voice irritated Ryder no end.

He glared at the man who'd started him in this shop. Where would he be without his father? Heck, Stanley had supported this expansion he'd embarked on. For years his dad told him how proud he was. "You're taking this business to the next level, son.

I'm proud of you." Usually a shoulder clap had accompanied those words. Not anymore.

His father hadn't approved of him since Phoebe kicked him out. Now instead of a compliment, his father was more apt to say, "I'm glad your mother isn't here to see this."

Well, damn. So was he. His mother would have read him the riot act. "Phoebe didn't want to accept my help with the cottage. I told her I could line people up to do the work that needs to be done. She's giving me a hard time."

The dry chuckle came from Stanley's gut. "Oh, that's not what steams you the most, Ryder. You'd like to give her a heck of a lot more than *help*." His father heaved out that last word with suggestive intent.

When Ryder kicked the corner of the counter with his boot, it hurt like hell. He should know that by now. Lately he was all aches and pains. This being over-thirty stuff sucked. The contentment had vanished from his life. Success meant nothing to him anymore. "I'm going to hire the right guys and stop by to supervise. The day after, and the day after that. Somehow I'll get her to accept my help." His eyes swerved to Stanley, who wouldn't look him in the eye. "I'm counting on you to hold the fort."

His father looked skeptical. "What's your plan?"

"I'm going to hire contractors to do the work. There's a difference."

"There sure is." Stanley was not looking happy. Ryder stomped upstairs to his apartment before his father could say anything else.

~.~

And to think that she'd done this to herself. As Phoebe sat at the kitchen table the next morning, nothing seemed right. She hated the red plaid wallpaper she'd once thought was so cute. That was so yesterday. But what could she do about those walls now?

Shifting around to face the porch took too much effort. This cast was a killer. Maybe she'd pour herself some orange juice. The refrigerator looked big, harvest gold and far away. Every step in this tiny kitchen felt like a mile. Her growling stomach reminded her that she hadn't had breakfast yet. What she'd give to have her old morning routine back, the one without a cast on her leg. And she'd hardly slept a wink.

What was she going to do about her salon? Time to make a call. Phoebe's Place opened at ten. Jen and Carly should be there by now. They both knew how to open up.

Jen answered on the second ring. "Hey, stuck in traffic?" That was their favorite joke. They all loved living in Gull Harbor because there was no traffic, unlike the snarls along the Dan Ryan in Chicago.

"Not exactly. But I'm not coming in today." As quickly as she could, Phoebe filled Jen in. "I'm sorry to drop all this on you, Jen."

"Don't even think about it. We'll be fine. Do you need me to come over?"

"No, of course not. It's just my leg." Oh, she sounded so confident. That was her. The person who took care of others, like Diana when she suffered those burns from hot oil. Phoebe had been right there to help with her hair and a lot of other stuff.

But Phoebe wasn't good at taking help. She just liked to give it.

Jen and Carly would have their hands full running the shop. In the background she could hear Jen rifling through the pages of her schedule. "Let me see. I'll call all your customers and reassign them to Carly and me."

"Will that be all right? I hate to load you down. After all, it's summer." The time of year when they usually took off early and headed for the beach.

"Don't be silly. It'll be fine." Jen almost sounded insulted. "Everybody knows us. We'll just tell them what happened. You'll probably get a slew of cards. Why were you up on that ladder anyway?"

"Painting my house." Propped up on a kitchen chair, her leg hurt like the devil.

"What? Look, there are plenty of guys around here who would paint for you," Jen scolded. "You're not a painter, you're a hairstylist."

"Point taken." Phoebe studied her chipped manicure. Not even ten o'clock and already her day was going downhill. "Do you think Clancy's will send out some groceries if I call?"

"If they won't, I'll be glad to pick them up for you. But I won't paint the house. That's where I draw the line." The implication was clear. What Jen really meant was, that's where *you* should have drawn the line.

"Oh, Ryder's going to take care of that."

Silence rang over the phone. "Have you seen Ryder?"

"I most certainly did. He found me after I fell."

"Wow. What luck. The hottest man rumbling down Red Arrow

Highway," Jen murmured.

A shooting pain zipped up Phoebe's leg and went straight to her heart. "What did you just say?"

"Ah, the most rotten man along Red Arrow Highway. So he..." Jen waited. She wanted details.

"He took me to the hospital and helped me. Really, he was great."

"I'll just bet." Jen let the pause play out. Phoebe could only guess what her employee was thinking. Of course both Jen and Carly sided with Phoebe, but there was no denying that all women found her ex irresistible.

"It's not like that. He's going to line up the contractors to do the work."

"Oh. Well." The sly enthusiasm had left Jen's voice.

Frustration bubbled inside Phoebe. The rumble of a Harley cut into the conversation. "Gotta run, Jen. Talk to you later. Let me know if any problems come up." Phoebe ended the call.

Well, hells bells. Why hadn't she gotten dressed? Here she was in her pink flamingo sleep shirt without time to even splash water on her face. Would he have the list of contractors all lined up? Her head ached from hunger, but she was determined to get her mind around this house project. She picked at some of the pink paint dots still on her arm. Maybe painting wasn't her thing.

What did she care? Ryder had seen her looking a lot worse. But she had her pride and this wasn't her finest hour. Her house was falling down around her, and she was totally helpless to pull it back together. But she was not going to let Ryder see that, no way, no how. Somehow she was going to clean up, do her hair and change into something so sexy, he'd eat his heart out.

But that would be later. Right now, he was here and she was a mess.

A rap came on the door.

"Door's open."

"Hey, good morning." Ryder stepped inside, a paper bag in one hand. She sniffed. A scone from the Whistle Stop Cafe?

"Morning, Ryder." If only he didn't look so fine, freshly scrubbed and smelling so darn good. All soap and all man, his hair still damp from the shower.

"How are you feeling?" He said it as if he really cared.

But never would she be taken in again. "Fine. I guess."

He handed her the bag. She peeked inside. Yep. Whistle Stop. Phoebe melted. "Gee, thanks, Ryder."

"Don't mention it." Ryder's eyes swept the area. "Have you had coffee?"

"Not yet. But I will." Lurching to her feet, she grabbed her crutch and headed for the counter.

"Are you in much pain?" He came close, too close. The scent of his tangy aftershave teased her nostrils.

"A little." Removing the water tank from the coffee machine wasn't easy. Finally she got it off, set it under the spout and turned on the water.

Ryder regarded her with cautious eyes. "Did you have any trouble sleeping?"

"Kind of."

"Have you taken your pain pills, like Dr. Swanson said?"

"Not yet. Why all the questions?" *Who made you the boss?*

Staring down at her, he took her upper arms gently in his hands. Even though spidery feelings were dancing up her skin, she would not look up. She just wouldn't. "You have to rest and you can't if you're in pain. Are you worrying?"

Sure. Worrying about this tingling in my arms. Lost in thoughts she should not be having, she wrenched out of his grasp and grabbed the first thing she saw. What a shame that it happened to be the full plastic container. With a crash, it hit the floor and water shot everywhere.

Ryder knifed a hand through his hair. "Darlin', let me help you, okay?"

Her eyes filled. "I'm not your darlin'. And I'm fine." The water had drenched her night shirt.

"Right." One glance at the wet flamingo on her chest and Ryder looked away. His jaw clenched. He must be mad as all get out. Picking up the container, Ryder refilled it. Thank goodness it didn't break. She needed coffee so bad. While he got the machine going and wiped up all the water, she sat and nibbled on the scone. Never had this flaky delight tasted better. The chocolate chips folded into the pastry exploded in her mouth. Chocolate should definitely be included in the food pyramid.

"Where are your pain pills?"

"I left them in the bathroom," she managed over a full mouthful. Yep, crumbs spewing from her lips, she was a hot mess.

By the time Ryder returned, the blue light on the coffee

machine was winking. With ease born of familiarity, Ryder slotted a container of Hawaiian coffee into the machine, slid her flamingo mug under the spout and pushed another button. Then he studied the instructions on the vial of pain pills. "You didn't take one this morning?"

Shaking her head, she took another bite. "Chocolate is good for pain, right?"

"Not really." Ryder shook a pill into his palm and poured a glass of water. "Here take this."

So she did. He turned his back to her while she gulped, as if he couldn't stand the sight of her. Setting the prescription back on the counter, he said, "I'll be right back. Have your coffee. Do whatever. Just give me a few." And he was moving toward the door.

Ryder couldn't wait to get out of here. How amazing that she could still feel disappointed. "Sure, see ya." With a flutter of her hand, she dismissed him. He'd brought her a scone and got the coffee working. For this morning, that was more than enough.

Holding the door open with a shoulder, he stood his ground. "Phoebe Hunicutt, formerly Phoebe Branson…" That still bugged him and she loved it. "I *will* be right back."

"Sure you will. Whatever."

His cheeks flushed. *Cut him some slack, Phoebe.* "Sorry I'm such a witch this morning, Ryder."

"Apology accepted." He still looked steamed.

The coffee had finished trickling into the mug, its rich scent filling the kitchen. Coming back into the room with two strides, he grabbed her full mug and plunked it on the table in front of her. Then he took creamer from the refrigerator and a spoon from the drawer and slapped those on the table too. Man, he was mad. She went back to her scone, wishing she'd brushed her teeth and was sitting here in something beside a wet sleep shirt.

Then Ryder was gone. Enjoying the sounds of birds in the trees outside, she closed her eyes. If only this were a normal summer day. The kind of day when she could take a quick stroll on the beach before heading down Red Arrow Highway to work. But it wasn't. So she'd better suck it up.

Time for a talk with her therapist.

Chapter 6

Jamming her crutch under her right shoulder, Phoebe grabbed her mug and the white bag with her left hand and made slow progress to the porch. Dropping the bag onto the coffee table, she collapsed on the futon sofa to enjoy the rest of her scone. In the process, coffee splashed from the mug and splattered her flamingo night shirt. Perfect. This was going to be a slow recovery.

The morning dew glistened on Fernando's bright pink surface.

"What's Ryder doing here?" she grumbled to her lawn ornament.

Could it be that he's concerned about you?

"No. He just wants my cottage." She took a sip of coffee.

He could have called, Phoebe. And why the scone?

"He's just buttering me up." She crammed the last bite into her mouth.

When it comes to Ryder, you're so suspicious.

"And with good reason. Remember Trixie?"

But of course he did. Hadn't she poured out her heart to Fernando night after night? "Catch you later."

Next stop was the bathroom. Never had this hallway felt so long. Her leg ached and her eyes felt gritty from lack of sleep. Once she got into the bathroom, she set her coffee on the edge of the sink. Balancing on one leg, she leaned against the sink for support. Her mother had taught her how to "spit shine" herself. Grabbing a washcloth, she filled the basin with warm water and got to work. It wasn't a shower but it was something.

Twenty long minutes later, she was feeling much better in a fresh T-shirt. But shorts were out. No way could she ease them over that cast. Heck, she couldn't bend over that far so she settled on her short denim mini-skirt that zipped up one side. The skirt had always shown off some of her best assets—her legs—and drove Ryder crazy. Forget that. He could barely look at her this morning.

Getting dressed had exhausted her. In fact, she felt too tired to put on any makeup or style her hair. Of course Ryder hadn't returned. What had she expected? Thumping back out into the main room, she continued to the screened porch and collapsed on the futon. Fernando was busy watching the birds at the feeder.

If she was going to make it through the next couple of months, she had to focus on the bright spots in her life. She had Jen and Carly to run the salon. She could order groceries from Clancy's. And if Ryder didn't come through for her, she would line up contractors herself. They'd give her a new roof and paint her house. Her jaw ached from gritting her teeth. Phoebe might have to beg her dad for some money, but she'd do it. Grabbing one of her small yellow pads and a pen from a side table, she went to work. Seated at the table on the screened porch, she was making a list when the kitchen screen door whapped shut. "Who's there?"

"Phoebe? You out on the porch?"

"Ryder, is that you?" Amazement shot through her, followed quickly by guilt. He always said she underestimated him. Well, it looked like she'd done that again. Fernando had that infuriating I-told-you-so expression on his face. After some suspicious rustling in the kitchen, Ryder appeared, holding a white takeout box. When he flipped it open, her stomach sat up and waved hello. Sunnyside eggs and hash browns from Rosie's in town.

"Is that for me?" Setting her pen down, she could hardly believe it.

"Of course it is. I told you I'd be right back." He waved her back to the table. "Now don't get up. You can eat this right here. I'll get you a glass of juice."

All this for her? "I'm out of juice."

"Make a list." His eyes flitted to the yellow pad and he smiled. He used to tease her when he found those little yellow pads all over the house. "And I'll make mine."

After handing her a plate full of goodness that smelled wonderful, he disappeared into the kitchen and came back with a cup of coffee for himself. "Oh, Ryder, this tastes so good. Thank you." Still surprised that he'd returned, Phoebe forgot to be irritated by the way he made himself at home.

So he really was going to help her line people up? And here she thought that had just been an empty promise. The sunny side eggs had never tasted so sweet, especially when she mixed the yokes in the crispy hash browns. And it sure looked like he'd gotten a double order. While Ryder looked around and made his list, she ate. At first, she felt perfectly content. The pain pill must have kicked in, and for a second she even forgot her broken leg. Then she got restless.

Sitting on the porch with Ryder brought an unwanted flood of memories, most of them bittersweet. Phoebe couldn't even look at that futon without blushing. Good thing this cottage was secluded by honeysuckle bushes. But today felt disjointed and wrong. They weren't happy newlyweds anymore. No, today they were unhappy exes, dealing with the stuff that came with divorce when you couldn't sever all the ties. She hated that part.

The sound of waves breaking on the nearby beach made her think of the times she'd slip into a bathing suit, grab his hand and tug him down to the water. Short swim and they'd come back up, wet and refreshed. Sometimes they never got around to dinner.

But that was all in the past. Pushing her empty plate aside, she reached for his list. "Now what exactly do you propose we do?"

Leaning back, Ryder linked his hands behind his head. Her mouth went dry to see his biceps plump. When he pursed his lips, she reached for her coffee. Warm or not, she needed something. Then he turned those gray eyes on her. This was so ridiculous, but she started to tremble, like he was that big bad tornado and she was Dorothy in *The Wizard of Oz*. "First of all, the roof. I can't believe that you were even thinking of painting anything without fixing the roof first."

Hearing that you-are-such-an-idiot tone in his voice, she shrank. Any dreamy images flitting through her mind vanished. Frowning, he lowered his arms. Ever so slowly, he sucked in a breath. "Sorry, Phoebe." At least he wasn't using darlin' anymore. "I just mean that it makes sense to replace the roof. The man can lay the shingles right over what we've got now."

When he used that "we," her head felt like it might burst. Was Ryder going to be this bossy all summer? Who would work for this man? Well, okay, she could be pretty bossy herself.

"All that sounds fine, but..." Now that she'd eaten, she was feeling drowsy. "Who do you plan on getting to do the work?"

Ryder knew every contractor in the area. He'd get it done and for the right price. But the way he was going about it? She hated it. The cast on her leg reminded her that she had no choice.

"How much do you figure this is going to cost?" Phoebe held her breath.

The figures he threw out sent her stomach on an elevator ride. "We're splitting this, right?" she asked.

"If that's what you want, Phoebe. Yes."

"Just asking. That'll be fine." Somehow she'd get the money. That was the only way she'd still keep some control of *her* house. Maybe her father would give her a loan, although she hated to do that again.

"Now about the color for the roof, I think we need a dark shade," Ryder began, the authority in his voice grating on her nerves.

"Turquoise. I want turquoise," she mumbled, sleepiness taking over. If she could just lay her head down, just for a second. Then everything would be fine. So she did. Right on the red-checked oilcloth. The last thing she remembered was the horrified look on Ryder's face.

When Phoebe finally came to, she felt ever so much better. Squirrels chattered in the pine trees next to the screened porch. And it sure looked as if the birdfeeder had been filled. Sparrows were having a heck of a time, scattering the seeds everywhere. Feeling fuzzy, Phoebe stretched. The weight on her right leg brought it all back. The cast. And all the frustrations caused by her broken leg. At the top of that list was Ryder Branson.

Glancing around, she realized she was stretched out on the futon, her favorite quilt settled lightly over her. The smell of peanut butter teased her. A sandwich sat on a paper plate on the coffee table, eye level, along with a frosty glass of lemonade. She heaved her body up on one elbow.

She wasn't going to question this. She wasn't going to get riled. No sir. "Thank you, Ryder." She may have to practice those words.

After she'd munched her way through a peaceful lunch, she pushed the plate aside. That's when she saw the note tucked under one of her magazines. "Gone to check out roofing tiles and materials. Stay where you are until I get back."

Sure. Right. Like I'm going anywhere. Crumpling up the note, Phoebe pushed herself to her feet. Her leg screamed with pain. For a second she had to stand there and just take it. Sure, she whimpered a little. Then she grabbed the crutch from the end of the sofa and shoved it under her right arm, which was beginning to feel sore and chafed. Somehow she made her way into the bathroom. When he got back, at least she'd look presentable.

~.~

Stanley was out back when Ryder stopped in early that afternoon. Mick was handling customers at the front counter. Ryder's dad liked the garage part of the business. He liked to get down and dirty with the oil and the grease. Right now he was studying a Harley with one of the mechanics. Parts were spread out on the floor, just the sort of job Stanley liked. He loved to put things back together. The old man looked up. "How's it going? You look like hell."

"Thanks a lot, Stanley. I needed that." Ryder preferred not to call his father Dad in front of the other workers.

"How's Phoebe doing?" His father drew closer.

"Ornery as usual, but she's not any worse."

"Broken leg. It'll take time." A chuckle deepened the creases in Stanley's face. "That girl. Climbing a ladder to paint her house. Imagine that."

"It was stupid, okay? And it's *our* house."

"It's gutsy, son. That's Phoebe all right. Gutsy."

For his father, Ryder's ex-wife still walked on water.

This was damned annoying so he moved along. "When you think of roofers, who would you hire? I need someone who could schedule the job within the next two weeks."

Running his fingers through hair matted down by his helmet, Ryder paced. He wanted to get this job over and done. Being around Phoebe was killing him. She'd looked so sweet and sexy in her flamingo shirt that morning, especially after the incident with the water. Wet, that shirt revealed way too much. He could practically smell and feel the warmth of her bed. Ryder had felt all thumbs putting the coffee machine back together.

Right now, she needed his help. He had to stick to business and leave it at that. "I promised Phoebe I'd line up some guys to do the work on the cottage. We're starting with the roof, not the siding."

Pursing his lips, Stanley made one of the rude noises he'd taught Ryder growing up. Drove his mother crazy. "I thought you were making yourself useful?"

Ryder picked up the paperwork for the parts that had come in yesterday. "I am. I'm coming up with a list of contractors. The roof's leaking, and the place needs painting inside and out. The kitchen linoleum crackles when you walk on it. Who would you get for the roof? First things first."

"Sounds like a real opportunity."

Ryder turned to meet Stanley's scheming smile. Like always, he started right in. "So you're going to hire some hunky contractors to come in and do that work for Phoebe? She's going to turn those big green eyes on the workers, so grateful that they're helping her out. And Phoebe..." Here his dad started stabbing the air with one finger. "Phoebe is going to be so grateful that they've helped her out of the predicament caused by her mean husband."

"Hey, I'm not mean. And I'm her *ex*-husband." Almost pained him to say it.

By this time he was nose-to nose with his dad. "You're not using your head, son. This here's an opportunity. A mission where you can distinguish yourself."

Damn. His father was a Vietnam Vet and everything to him was a strategy or a mission.

"Yessir," Stanley continued. "Looks to me like this has dropped into your lap, and you can make something of it. Phoebe's a strong-minded woman, but right now she's vulnerable. You have to strike while you have the opportunity."

All they needed was a war map on the wall. "She's stubborn, but you might be right." Picking up a ballpoint pen, Ryder started clicking it in his hand.

"She wouldn't let you near her for a whole year."

"Hey, I tried, okay?" Now, this was starting to embarrass him. He tossed the pen aside. "Calls, texts. Heck, I even wrote a letter."

Amazement broadened his father's features. "You did? What did Phoebe say?"

"Nothing." It pained him to admit his failure. "She wouldn't talk to me. Wouldn't believe me when I said I was sorry."

"You think that's going to do it?" Stanley made a rude noise again. "I don't blame her. You lied to her with that strumpet."

That was his father's favorite name for Trixie, and Ryder smiled to hear it. But there was nothing funny about this situation. That one hop in the hay had cost him big time. Stupid didn't begin to cover it.

"You have a chance here to prove to Phoebe that you've grown up, matured."

Ryder reared back from his father. "Hey, I *am* mature, goddammit."

"Then act like it." Pulling up the sagging jeans that he insisted on wearing, his dad frowned at him. "How many years are you going to waste? You know you want her back, you sorry sack of cow pucky. Prove it to her. She hasn't married anyone else, has she?"

That thought could give him dry heaves. "No, not yet."

"Not yet. But a woman like that? You can bet she's had her chances."

"Probably. I suppose so." Yep, dry heaves coming right up. "Thanks for reminding me."

"Instead of lining up men to waltz that girl down the aisle, work this chance to get back in her good graces…"

Good graces. Hell, Ryder lay awake at night thinking of a lot more than Phoebe's "good graces."

His father was ticking a finger in front of his face like a damn clock. "I can read your mind, boy, but first things first. For *starters*, think good graces."

By this time, the boxes of stock and pile of paperwork had been forgotten. "I see your point. No way do I want any of the crews to know Phoebe is living alone. Hell, they'd all be howling around that cottage like tomcats." Drumming his thumbs on the glass counter, he thought it over. Not a pretty picture.

"Not at all. You can't blame her for kicking you out."

"I acted like an idiot."

"You acted like you were still in high school, with girls drooling over you. Why you had the finest woman…"

"Stop, Dad. Please." Ryder hunched over. Each word felt like another slam to his gut. His father was right. Thirty was early to go through male menopause from what he read, and he'd looked it up online. But that's about what happened. At the time, he was going to hit thirty and trying to prove he was still a chick magnet. So stupid and immature. He knew that now. "So where does that leave me?"

Stanley rocked back on his heels. "Well son, I believe that leaves you up on the roof."

Chapter 7

The thumping overhead had given Phoebe a headache. This was the third day that Ryder had been working on the roof. And he was probably right about the shingles. At first she'd been disappointed. The grayish blue tiles might be close to turquoise, but not really. When he showed up with a sample, she'd promptly googled "turquoise roof." But any tiles that even came close were ceramic or clay and made in Santa Fe.

"So pretty." She'd stared at the screen for at least ten minutes while Ryder ranted about the cost. Finally, she clicked off the pictures. "I guess you're right."

He didn't look happy. "Look, Sweet Ch...Phoebe. I'd like to give you what you want. Really. But..."

"If you grab your hair any tighter, Ryder, you're going to pull it clear out of your head." And that would be a shame. He'd always had such great hair. Phoebe knit her twitching fingers together in her lap. They settled for the blue gray.

Why had she ever agreed to this arrangement? Oh right, she didn't want to hit her dad up for money. Again. After the divorce, her parents had pleaded with her to come home. She'd been such a mess back then. But she'd built up a business in Gull Harbor. No way was she going back to the Upper Peninsula where winter stretched into May. Instead of crawling back home like a wounded animal, she threw herself into building her salon with marketing plans, a new sign and extended hours.

All that had worked. For a while.

Dating? She had no time or heart for it.

Munching cinnamon toast at the porch table, Phoebe considered her summer. The plans had changed. The white cast glared up at her. There'd be no slipping down to the shore to dance along the sand. No running into the Swirly Top when she felt like a chili dog or a twirl cone. She was tied to the house and her ex. Jen and Carly were running the salon with disturbing efficiency. This was not what she'd pictured, not at all. But at least she had this porch.

And me. Fernando was giving her the eye.

"And you." If Ryder overheard her talking to her yard art, he'd think she'd lost it.

Licking the cinnamon from her fingers, she settled back. Everything was beginning to bloom. Blue hydrangeas were budding in the unweeded beds circling the house. Hollyhocks struggled to rise in the garage border. Black-eyed Susans perked up their sassy heads along the driveway. Oh, the yard was far from tidy, but the flowers sure would be pretty once everything got going.

The yard might help soothe her. Lately, she felt so jumpy. Having Ryder around was like having a rash you couldn't scratch or it might spread. Call her suspicious but she still questioned his motives. Was he bent on proving how much work this cottage involved, hoping she'd agree to sell? Her chewing slowed. The toast turned to a dry ball in her mouth when she thought of all the calls and whispered conversations that were going on. They had Trixie-that-Bitch written all over them.

Her thoughts ran wild, taking her for a pretty scary ride. Maybe Ryder wanted to get married and needed his down payment from the cottage. Why else would he do this? He was probably going to marry Trixie—or some other bimbette—and set up house with his new wife. Right now he was living over Branson Motors, not exactly home sweet home for any new bride.

Yep, he no doubt wanted her to sell her home.

The realization splashed over Phoebe like scalding coffee.

She took another bite of the cinnamon and sugar toast. Divorce was one thing but Ryder getting remarried? She had trouble wrapping her mind around that. When she studied the rattan furniture, her stomach lurched. Ryder might want half of all this too. Her thoughts darted from one fear to another, matching the rhythm of the rat-a-tat on the roof. Finished with the toast, she dusted the crumbs from her fingers and swiped one eye. The cinnamon must be making her tear up. That had to be it. She sniffled, dabbing at her nose with a napkin.

Why did she always miss the obvious? Ryder used to tease her about that. Why else would he drive down here every day? Heck, he'd even insisted on coming Saturdays. She'd put her foot down— well, her cast—when he suggested Sundays. Phoebe needed one day without him.

Phoebe hadn't heard any rumors that Ryder was getting married. But he was more a Rusty Nail guy than Mangy Mutt.

Kate's husband Cole and the rest of the guys probably never visited the Rusty Nail much. The popular watering hole was way up past Stevensville. Convenient for Ryder but not for most of the Gull Harbor guys. The fact that Ryder had met Trixie there really hurt. After all, that was where he'd come onto Phoebe, all sweet huskiness and coaxing eyes.

Giving one last sniff, Phoebe wadded the napkin into a ball. She had to get over this. Over *him*. Good-bye and good riddance. If he married someone, Trixie or whoever, so what? She had to keep this place. Their cottage, *her* cottage. Old tiles flew off the roof, breaking the stalks of her hydrangeas before they even had a chance to bloom.

Grabbing her crutch, Phoebe managed to stand up. After gaining some balance, she thumped her way out of the porch, sheltered under one of the pine trees and glanced up. "Hey!" Another tile came sailing toward her and she ducked. Cripes, she could get hurt. "Hey you up there!" No break in rhythm, just more tiles winging toward her like Frisbees.

Tucking two fingers into her mouth, Phoebe whistled. Okay, the whistle wasn't particularly ladylike. Her mother had told her that a dozen times, but what did she care? It worked. The hammering stopped. She listened for the crunch of his boots. Finally, Ryder peered over the roofline.

Holy Hotness, Batman. Sweat shone on his arms as if he were a newly glazed doughnut. The red bandana around his head was stained with sweat. Sculpted muscles rippled when he lifted a wrist to swipe his forehead. "Everything okay down there?" Twisting, he slipped a nail gun into a loop on his jeans. The weight made the waistband sag. Her pulse kicked up at the sight of paler skin below the sleeveless T-shirt, not that she was staring or anything.

Hanging onto the crutch for dear life, Phoebe struggled to remember why she'd whistled. Her mind wouldn't work. Maybe she'd just had a stroke and didn't know it. When she opened her mouth, nothing came out. Panic seized her. Just what she needed. A stroke, just like her great Uncle John while he was waiting in line at the bank years ago up in Escanaba. Wasn't stuff like that hereditary?

"Phoebe?" For a second it looked as if Ryder was heading for the new aluminum ladder he'd bought. He was probably going to take that with him too when he and Trixie outfitted their new home.

"Stop!" Whew! She could talk after all. That was close.

Hands on slim hips, Ryder stared down. "Phoebe, I'm burning daylight here. What do you want?"

"Doughnuts," she whispered, not able to tear her eyes from the sheen of his skin. Phoebe knew just how that skin felt against hers. Squeezing her eyes shut didn't work. The darn image appeared inside her eyelids, so she opened them again.

Ryder cocked his head to one side. "What's that?"

"Doughnuts!" she roared, throwing her arms wide and nearly losing the crutch. "I want some doughnuts."

The roar ended on a pathetic whimper.

Ryder's mouth fell open. "Doughnuts?"

"Yes! I want some! I do." Her voice was a primal cry.

Longing took her captive. Swaying in the morning sunlight, her body craved way more than pastry. But for now? A doughnut or two would do.

What has gotten into you? Fernando looked offended.

"Hormones." But her flamingo therapist would never understand. After all, he was male.

"What did you just say?" Ryder still stared down at her in all his hunky hotness.

"I want doughnuts." She hated being helpless.

Before she could think PMS three times, he was down that ladder and headed for the truck. Tossing his keys in the air, he moved those hips with hypnotic rhythm. "Be right back."

Watching the truck roar off, spraying gravel and sand in its wake, she wanted to kill Trixie. Ryder was the kind of guy who recognized a woman who needed a sugar fix. He'd always been like that. A lot of times, he'd joined in her feeding frenzy, whether it was caramel popcorn or double-stuffed chocolate cookies. Luckily Mandy Klavis' Lithuanian bakery wasn't far away. Their favorite treat was a braided cheese Danish with chocolate chips tucked inside. When he brought it home, they'd nuke it in the microwave for fifteen seconds to revive the melted sweetness.

That wasn't all they nuked after the pastry.

But today? She wanted doughnuts. The cake kind. Ryder knew just what she meant. No need to draw a diagram. Limping past Fernando back onto the porch, she continued to the refrigerator for a glass of apple juice. Then she settled at the porch table to wait. Ryder was back in a flash, roaring into the driveway just like that ambulance. He jumped out, carrying a crisp white pastry bag. From the glaze crumbs clinging to his lips, she knew he'd done some sampling on the way back. When he shouldered the porch door open, her tongue swept her lips in anticipation. He smiled, as if enjoying a private joke. "Will half a dozen be enough?" He dropped the white bag into her lap.

"Yes, oh, yes." Her hands tore at the paper. "Thank you."

"You're welcome." And he winked.

Hands crumpling the lips of the bag, she absorbed that wink like an electrical shock. Thank goodness the scent of sugar restored her senses. Then Ryder was gone, tromping up the ladder and whistling as he climbed. The bag of doughnuts released warm wonderfulness in her lap when Phoebe opened it. No time to be choosy. She grabbed the first thing her fingers found and crammed it into her mouth. Sweet blueberries exploded on her tongue, along with nutmeg and cinnamon. While she slowly chewed, she settled back. What a great morning. The lake breeze flowed over her skin, cool and damp.

Her contentment was restored.

As she enjoyed her stash, Phoebe wondered how Ryder's business was going. Hadn't he said he was expanding? How could he take off all this time? Well, his dad no doubt had that under control. After all, the first Branson Motors had been Stanley's. Ryder had grown up with grease under his fingernails.

One of the bad things about a divorce was that you not only lost the man, you lost the family. Phoebe took another bite. Ryder's mother had passed away when he was only thirteen, so Phoebe never knew her. But his dad? Stanley was a jewel. Just thinking about him brought a smile. Oh sure, he was all rough and tumble like Ryder. If he shaved three times a week, they were lucky. Stanley knew every raunchy joke in the book and loved to shock her.

Right, like that could happen. Oh, she'd blush but she laughed too. Stanley had a heart of gold and boy, could that man cook. After the divorce, Stanley had texted her, saying stop by any time. But she couldn't. If she dropped in at the shop, Ryder might be there. The hurt cut too deep, her feelings still too raw. The less she saw of her ex, the better.

But losing Stanley had left a hole hard to fill.

Fingers crusty with sweet glaze, she stared into the open bag. Maybe time for the frosted raspberry jelly puff? Perfect. Taking it out, she swiped off the chocolate glaze with her tongue. Man, oh man. Mandy Klavis had a great bakery. Next time they'd get the cheese braid.

Bluebirds scolded in the trees as she sat munching, licking off an extra dollop of raspberry filling now and then. Mandy always used a generous hand in filling her pastries. But after three doughnuts, Phoebe called a halt. After all, she liked to think she had some self-control. Up above, the nail gun pounded, strong and fierce.

Pump, pump, pump. She could feel that driving rhythm in her chest, or thereabouts. Hands sticky, Phoebe folded the top of the white bag and pushed it to the other side of the table. Time for some restraint, which wasn't her strong point.

She glanced at the clock. Not quite ten o'clock but it felt like noon. Heaving herself up from the table, she made it as far as the sofa, dragging her leg behind her. When was that dull ache going to stop? The pain pills made her groggy. Although she hated to admit it, Ryder was right. Dr. Swanson had told her to take them and she should. "Let your body heal without fighting the pain," he'd said. "Pain can leave you all knotted up."

Well, so could desire.

In fact, Phoebe felt like a pretzel.

Delete, delete. What was wrong with her?

Making herself comfortable on the sofa, she decided to rest for just a second. Then she'd get busy with lunch. The locusts sang high and thin in the trees. The thumping continued. In her sugar-crazed head, Ryder was there. His muscled body worked above hers while he whispered naughty stuff in her ear.

But she liked it. Oh, how she liked it.

Next thing she knew, she woke up. Drool dampened her cheek, now mashed into a flamingo pillow. And she was raging hungry. Again.

Giving her head a shake to clear it, she swung herself up so fast, dizziness nearly took her down. Squirrels scampered through the trees above, and the smaller branches dipped under their weight. Enjoying their effortless leaps from limb to limb, she felt the weight of her cast.

She was grounded this summer. Grounded and plagued by thoughts that had no business in her mind. Or her body.

Ryder was still working on the roof. He must be starving by

now. Crutch under her arm, Phoebe clomped into the kitchen. The clock said almost noon. The least she could do was fix lunch. After all, he'd gone to pick up doughnuts. Opening the refrigerator, she got out the ham and cheese and snagged the caraway rye bread from the counter. Where would she be without Clancy's delivery service?

Setting to work, she made the three-tiered sandwich just the way Ryder liked it and a simpler one for herself. Why, she could get all weepy thinking about the things she'd done for that man when they were together. Even though she hated raisin bran, she even bought his favorite breakfast food and cheerfully ate it. But once all the divorce stuff started, she tossed it out. Then she went through the house, pitching anything she could lay her hands on that meant something to Ryder. But you can't carve out pieces of your life without hurting yourself. Some of this they'd purchased together, like the light tower clock. The losses would cut too deep.

So she threw out what she could handle. Her peach clothes? Gone to Goodwill. Back then, she wore pale orange all the time just because he said she looked like a peach in them. Following the divorce, she switched to pink. Bright flamingo pink. And her soft caramel curls, the long hair where he loved to bury his face? Now short and sheathed in mauve. She wanted to be as badass as possible.

Sniffing, she figured if she kept up this trip down memory lane, the caraway rye bread could get soggy. The screen door slammed behind her. Ryder was a man of habit. If it was noon, then it was lunchtime. Turning, Phoebe felt like she'd been punched in the gut.

There he stood, all six foot two of sweaty man. His white T-shirt stuck to his chest, and her fingers tingled to trace that six pack all the way down to his belt line. The jeans had been washed a hundred times so they hugged his thighs. And those rugged work boots? The final touch. "Is that for me?"

Her head snapped back. *The sandwich, Phoebe. He's talking about the sandwich.* "Right. Sure is." She raked shaking hands through her short hair.

For a second their eyes locked and tangled. In five short seconds the things their eyes communicated made her break into a cold sweat. That eye language? Rough and tumble, down and dirty.

And all in her head. Phoebe dropped her eyes. Sometimes she could be such a dope, especially when it came to Ryder Branson.

Dwarfing the kitchen, he whisked off the bandana and blotted his forehead. "I've got to clean up first." Moving over to the sink, Ryder looked so comfortable, like he did this every day—because he had. Pouring blue detergent into his palms, he lathered his hands under a stream of warm water. For a guy with broad shoulders, he had the slimmest hips.

Picking up a knife, she sliced his sandwich in half and then hers. How amazing that she didn't cut off a finger, trying to keep him in sight while she wielded the knife. Phoebe had never been any good at multitasking. While some hairdressers balanced two clients at a time, letting color set while styling the hair of the next customer, she never did that. Her clients got her whole attention, and that was a good thing. Melissa Ryan had never forgiven her for that pink hair intended for Greta Gaines. You can't strip hair twice in a row or it might just break off. But then, Melissa had always been fussy. She looked good in pink.

The soapsuds bubbled up to his elbows, and Ryder hummed as he cleaned up. Back when they were married, he used the same technique with her in the shower. Start at the top and work down. Oh so carefully, she sliced her own sandwich into quarters. Heat hung in the air. She loved it when he went va, va, voom with his low bass. Ryder always told her she was his va-va-voom.

Well, men can say a lot of things.

In Michigan people waited for summer. Longed for warm weather the way you'd long for a man to come walking through the door, not that she thought about that much anymore. Now summer was here and the air was warming up along with the humidity.

Watching Ryder, she felt heat take her hostage. Quietly, she moved around the table so her back was to the sink. No way could she look at him another second and not want him.

The water was turned off, and Ryder came up behind her. How could soap smell so sensual? Maybe looking at him had been safer than smelling him, safer than feeling his warm body behind her. In more ways than one, her ex had always been a roaring furnace. *Stand up straight and concentrate, Phoebe.* Hadn't Miss Laus, her fourth grade teacher, taught her that? Oh yes, it would be way too easy to slump back against the muscled strength of his chest. Feel his firm body against her softness.

But she would. Not. Do. That. *No, no, no.*

Throwing some ruffled chips onto the plate, she managed to

send a few to the floor. "Want a pop?" Trying to look casual, she moved to the side but the incriminating crunch under her cast brought his eyes to hers.

If eyes could be sweaty and hot, then his were. "I can get it."

"No, I will." Teetering on her leg, she winced.

"Sweet Cheeks…" Ryder's voice dropped but his eyes didn't. "Why don't you just go sit on the porch. Stop being a stubborn girl. I'll bring everything out."

A stubborn girl once had been *my stubborn girl.*

Her chin came out along with her lower lip. Ryder was right. Yeah, she could be stubborn and he knew it. Well she'd show him stubborn. Ignoring his comment, she shuffled to the refrigerator, opened the freezer and slid out a tray. In a second he was next to her.

"Let me help with the ice. You never could handle that tray."

Her resistance growing, she hugged it to her chest. Cold seeped through her thin pink top. Grabbing the tray with both hands, she swiveled and thumped it on the edge of the sink.

Ryder's attention had shifted to the refrigerator. He laid a hand on the top of the harvest gold refrigerator like he wanted to push it over. "Stanley gave this to us, remember? It had been down at the shop."

"Of course I remember." Stanley had been so sweet about it. "If it lasts three years, Phoebe, I'll buy you another one," her frugal father-in-law had promised. The refrigerator had lasted longer than their marriage.

The weight of the cast dragged at her while she struggled with the ice tray, but the ice wouldn't come out. Finally she tossed the tray into the sink. "Do whatever you want."

But he didn't move away. Instead Ryder leaned into her face, so close she could watch a drop of sweat trail down his stubbled cheek. She closed her eyes against the gray glint igniting in his eyes. His scent did that to her. And it wasn't fair.

When he nudged her with a shoulder, her eyes flew open. "Phoebe, darlin'? If I did what I wanted right now, you know what that would be and how we'd do it."

Immersed in heat that felt more like August than June, she shuddered. "And that, Ryder Branson, is never going to happen."

How she wished those words hadn't been so hard to say.

Chapter 8

Then before Phoebe's very eyes, Ryder deflated like a balloon. A cool breeze blew in from somewhere. He was probably picturing what his girlfriend would do to him if he got cozy with Phoebe, not that she'd allow it.

She couldn't. She wouldn't.

As he opened that refrigerator and dipped his head into a cool blast of air, she had to remind herself. *Phoebe Hunicutt. Never again. Remember Trixie.* Crutch tight under her arm, she limped onto the side porch.

Remember Trixie. Thump, thump. Remember Trixie.

Fernando was giving her the eye. *You got that right, amiga mia.*

"I know, I know."

Ryder stuck his head out the door. "What did you just say?"

"Nothing."

Fernando kept his eyes straight ahead. But then, he always did.

While Phoebe got situated in a chair, Ryder made two trips to the kitchen for their lunch. Then he took the seat across from her. The heat was gone. He was all business. The only thing he seemed hungry for now was his ham and cheese sandwich.

Somewhere in the bushes, mourning doves crooned. How she loved that sound. They mated for life, a comforting thought. Why did she have to think of that right now?

His face shuttered, Ryder opened his can of pop. Coke shot all over him and some even landed on her. While she blotted her shirt with a napkin, she watched Ryder lick pop from his lips. This wasn't a man that used napkins, not for lunch. Never breaking eye contact, he bit into the mile-high sandwich.

Oh, her thoughts felt wicked. She wanted to be that sandwich. Feel his lips on hers again. But she couldn't. Phoebe would never be a quick hop in the hay just because he was fixing up her place. Well, okay. *Their* house. Those days were over. Picking up a potato chip she nearly poked it up her nose. Phoebe dropped her hand, the chip still held tight.

"If you don't want to eat those potato chips, I do," Ryder managed to say around a mouthful of ham. Glancing down, she realized she'd pulverized the chips in her tight fist. But who could blame her? Any girl would do the same thing confronted with massive masculinity. She crammed the crushed chip into her mouth. The slower she chewed, the faster he devoured that sandwich. Oh, baby. She knew just what he was thinking.

When you've been married to a man for two years, you know a lot about him. You know what's on his mind when he glances at your shirt. Ryder wasn't thinking that her T-shirt needed to be washed. No, he was picturing what was under that fabric.

A thought danced through her head. Maybe she would just make Ryder really uncomfortable for the next month or so. Isn't that what he'd done to her? After one of her customers mentioned that she'd seen Ryder in the Rusty Nail with his hand on Trixie's waist or thereabouts, the end to their marriage came fast. Phoebe had agonized about it, but there was only one course she could take.

At the time, she didn't know Trixie Tatum that well. But the word was, she was one skinny chick. To put it politely, Trixie didn't have Phoebe's assets. That much she knew. Lifting her napkin, Phoebe slowly dabbed the front of her shirt, paying attention to small details Ryder liked. When he sputtered and choked, she glanced up, all innocence. "You all right, Ryder?"

The way he convulsed, his mouth opening and closing like a fish? She felt a thrill of satisfaction. Her ploy was working. But maybe she better ease up. Giving him the Heimlich would definitely be dangerous for both of them. First off, she couldn't even hobble over to administer it.

While the fan whirred overhead, the fan that he himself had installed that first year, her thoughts spun along with the fan blades. Oh, yeah. Maybe this was what she was going to do all summer. Turning on Ryder, her fix-it man, only to shut him down fast would become her pet project. If he thought he was going to work on the place and then convince her to sell, she was not going to make that easy.

But she had to stay strong.

Cardinals twittered in the pine trees while Phoebe sat transfixed, watching Ryder lift his glass and drink, his Adam's apple working in that thickset throat. Rigid in the chair, she recalled taking her time with that neck. She'd coast her lips over the tendons and dip her tongue into the warm hollow while his breath caught. Feeling her body kick into gear, she had to change her focus. So she shifted her gaze to the black-eyed Susans growing crazy, interspersed with the hydrangeas and a mess of weeds. Drawing in the lake breeze, she savored it, so cool and inviting.

But her darn mind went right back to Ryder. When she pursed her lips, he gave a strangled cry. Her eyes lifted. "Everything okay, Ryder?"

He mumbled something that sounded like "Not really."

Pulling out her T-shirt a bit, she left the air cool her tummy. "Oh, my it's hot today."

"You're telling me," he muttered, taking another bite.

"Gosh, I miss the beach."

"I miss a lot of things."

"Me too." She ran a hand over her bare midriff. If she closed her eyes, she could picture Lake Michigan stretching to the horizon, a mass of blue and green waves undulating under the sun. The sound of the trashcan opening and closing in the kitchen made her jump. While she sat here daydreaming, he'd finished his lunch.

"Thanks for the sandwich, Phoebe." Oh, so they were back to Phoebe and not Sweet Cheeks. Disappointment threatened to upset her stomach. Maybe it was those pain pills. Yeah, she'd blame it on them.

"You're welcome."

Then he was gone. Out of sight, out of mind. But not really. Up on the roof, Ryder's nail gun went crazy. She picked up the phone and called Carolyn. Phoebe needed an intervention. Time to check in and see how things were going with Brody. What a relief when her friend picked up on the second ring.

"Hey, Phoebe. How's it going? I was just thinking about you."

So she filled Carolyn in on her broken leg and the accident.

"A wooden ladder? Are you kidding me? Aren't they dangerous? They can rot."

"Yeah, I found that out. I know it was foolish."

"So now you have your ex-husband working on your house?" She heard the laughter in Carolyn's voice.

"*Our* house and that's the rub. He's acting like he owns it even though it belongs to both of us."

"Sounds like a man with a method," she said slowly and then laughed. "Well, aren't they all?"

Sitting down on the futon, Phoebe propped her leg up on the coffee table. "How are things in Santa Fe?"

"Just fine." The lilt of Carolyn's voice suggested things were way more than fine. But Phoebe couldn't be jealous of her own friend.

"How's Mama V's wedding coming?" Carolyn's grandmother, a widow, was getting married in July.

"We're having tons of fun with that. She put me in charge of the flowers. I think we'll have bouquets of pink calla lilies. What do you think?"

"Bright pink," Phoebe murmured, her eyes finding Fernando. Ryder had taken the pretty metal structure from the back door and plunked it down near the screened porch so Phoebe could see it.

"Right, Mama V will like that. She wears a lot of lilac and pink."

"You still living with her?" The girls had a bet that Carolyn would move in with Brody by the end of June.

"Well, I didn't want to get underfoot while she was doing all that planning with Howard."

Yeah, right. Looked like Phoebe was going to win that bet with Kate, who'd insisted Carolyn would stay with her grandmother to help before the wedding. "So let me guess. You're at Brody's place?"

"He's helping me work on overcoming my fear of heights. Still lots to do in that area."

Phoebe snorted. "Carolyn, that is so lame. Your voice? Sounds like you're working on a lot more than that."

A sigh was her only answer. Her friend was in L-U-V. Not what Phoebe needed right now.

"What kind of work is Ryder doing?"

"So much needs work." By the time Phoebe finished listing everything that needed repairing, even she was tired.

"All that could take a long time," Carolyn said. "And he drives all the way down from St. Joe every day?"

"It's only forty minutes or so. Half an hour if he rides his motorcycle. He's been keeping most of his tools here."

"Ah, huh." Carolyn didn't sound convinced. "Still, that's a long ride."

"I wanted to hire someone," Phoebe continued. "But he's saving me, well us, a lot of money by doing it himself. Except I have a plan. My plan is to make things tough for Ryder. I'm enjoying teasing him a little bit." Well, she didn't mention he was doing the same to her, without even trying.

"You are so bad." Laughter bubbled in Carolyn's voice. "And that's why you are my friend."

"Right, but my plan has its down side too. Truth is, I'm making myself uncomfortable. I'll be the one tossing in my bed tonight, trying to get comfortable with this stupid cast on my leg." Her mind stuttered to a stop. Carolyn had given her an idea.

"Okay, what are you thinking? Earth to Phoebe. You've got something on your mind, Phoebe Hunicutt, or you wouldn't be so quiet."

"Hmm. I'm thinking that it would be way more fun if Ryder was really underfoot. And I really was driving him crazy."

"Let's talk about options." Her friend jumped right in. For a few crazy minutes, they plotted and planned together. Carolyn gave Phoebe some advice. But there might be some drawbacks to her plan, one of them being that Phoebe would have to be strong.

"Go for it," Carolyn said at the close.

"I...I can't."

"Oh, come on. Channel Chili. That girl would do anything to make Ignacio jealous. Go for the whole enchilada, as Chili would say."

With the nail gun picking up speed overhead, Phoebe laughed. "I'll let you know how it goes. Say hi to Brody for me. I'm looking forward to seeing that man again. When he stopped in at the end of the school year, he didn't stay long."

"I know. Business called, but he's talking about a longer visit. It's been a long time since he lived in Gull Harbor. I think he's curious."

"Ah, hah." There was something different in her voice. "Are you having second thoughts?"

"Oh, I don't know." Uncertainty slowed Carolyn's words. "I kind of miss the lake and everything."

"You could always come back for a vacation. Bring Brody with you."

"I'll think about it."

By the time they hung up, Phoebe's eyes felt heavy. Talking about men could tire you out. Stretching back on the futon, she scrunched a pillow beneath her head. She watched the blades of the fan circle slower and slower and...slower.

Next thing she knew, Ryder was standing over her, hands on his hips. A smile tipped the corners of his lips.

Maybe it was the nap, but for a second Phoebe just forgot. Forgot that this hunk of man wasn't her husband anymore. That he'd done the down and dirty with another woman. The look on his face told her he'd forgotten too.

"Ryder?" Reaching up, she opened her arms.

Before she knew it, he was on his knees next to her.

Her cast brought her to her senses. While she was getting warm and cozy, thank God that cast stayed stick straight.

"You look so pretty, sleepyhead." When he ran the back of one hand up her cheek, she swatted at it. His expression shifted, like suddenly she was the next-door neighbor.

Carolyn's words came rushing back, reminding Phoebe of the plan. The whole point was to turn up the pain, not the passion.

Struggling to sit up, Phoebe said, "So, you finished for the day?" She had no idea what time it was, but she had to get her head on straight.

When Ryder stood up, he swayed like he was off balance. So, she could still do that to him? "Yep, right." When he whipped off his sweaty bandana, his curls sprang up, a thick and luscious mess. Her fingers curled, remembering how they felt.

But in her mind, she could see Carolyn standing behind Ryder. She was shaking a finger. *We'll have none of that now, Phoebe. Stick to our plan.*

Yes, Ma'am. Phoebe stopped batting her eyelashes. Between Fernando and Carolyn, she had lots of support.

"Guess I'll hit the road." He backed away, his face impersonal and closed again. She struggled to her feet. Her conversation with Carolyn replayed in her mind. Following him into the cottage, Phoebe struggled to put the words together. The words that wouldn't suggest she was wimping out. The last thing she wanted was for him to suspect that she was a woman with a plan. Crutch under one arm, she followed him outside.

While she stood thinking, Ryder was getting on that Harley. "I'll see you first thing in the morning. I should be here by nine." All businesslike now, his eyes were hooded and detached.

Yep, Carolyn was right. He intended to stretch this out all summer. She was putting an end to that right now.

"Ryder, I've been thinking." Leaning on her crutch, she must make quite a picture. What woman can be sexy with a crutch? Maybe this plan wouldn't work at all. But she forged ahead.

"What is it?" Head tilting to one side, he looked cautious, like he was afraid she'd tell him to take his tools and go. But that was not her plan.

"Well, you know. It takes so long for you to get down here. We're losing all that working time." She twisted the bottom of her T-shirt in her fingers.

"Okay." The word came out long and slow. Sitting back on his long two-up seat, he waited. "And so?"

She fluttered one hand in the air. The left hand. The one without the wedding ring anymore. "After all I have—*we* have—" Heck, it killed her just to say it. She cleared her throat. "We have three bedrooms here."

Ryder sucked in a breath and held it. The man leaned into the pause, like he wanted to drag the words out of her and hoped they'd be the right ones. "Sorry, I'm not sure I know what you're talking about."

So she had to hold up cue cards? "I mean, if you wanted to stay here, this whole process might go a lot faster."

Was he even breathing? "Well now, that's real nice of you, Phoebe." Suddenly he was being so proper. She wanted to giggle. "And you're so right. It would make things easier. Faster. I mean, more convenient. Ah, faster."

Pressing a hand to her stomach, Phoebe fought a giggle.

Reaching behind him, he snagged his helmet and jammed it on. "If it's all right, I might just bring a few things down tomorrow. Stow them in the guest room."

If he expected a protest, she wasn't going to give him one. "That sounds fine, Ryder." He was playing right into her hands.

"See you tomorrow then."

"Bright and early," he said, new energy in his voice.

She waved goodbye as he roared out on his Harley, looking so badass it made the breath catch in her throat. She knew where that new energy came from and that was so not going to happen.

At least she didn't think so.

Chapter 9

Ryder shoved his boom box into the back of his pickup. *Almost packed.* Backing up, he viewed the boxes and bags. His gym equipment weighed a ton and had taken a while to load. The barbells and hand weights hadn't been bad. Disassembling the one-man gym had been a bitch.

That detached garage would make a great workout area. Would he have to talk Phoebe into leaving her car outside? At least she wouldn't be bashing the hell out of her Mini Cooper anymore. She'd never been good with that old, narrow garage.

Clothes bulged from a black trash bag, with some towels stuffed into another. No more of those prissy pink towels. Phoebe's were so fluffy, lint ended up all over when he dried his hands. He didn't even want to think how the rest of him would end up after a shower. His tools were already at the house.

He slammed the back closed.

At least he traveled light. Living over the garage this past year had been a good idea, even though his dad called it "squatting." Stanley took a dim view of his son's lifestyle. Since the divorce, nothing he did was right. Sprinting up the back steps to the apartment, Ryder didn't want to dwell on that. He was a grown man. If his mother were alive, she'd support him.

Would she? In his heart he knew that wasn't true. Ryder stumbled on the steps, tripped and bruised his shin. Phoebe would have found her way into his mother's heart. She would have given Ryder what-for about his "lapse of good judgment," as his father called it.

But not now. Time to do a final walk through of the apartment. With only three rooms, it didn't take long. Bathroom medicine chest was empty. Same for the bedside table drawer, not that he ever kept anything there. He'd made the bed with one of the old chenille spreads that had been his mother's. Looked kind of quaint but felt homey.

His bedroom. Had he wasted the past year? All he'd done was sleep in this room since the split and it looked like it. Truth was, after Phoebe kicked him to the curb, and for good reason as his father told any stranger who would listen, he'd settled down.

"A little late, wouldn't you say, son?" his father had said, voice heavy with sarcasm. Stanley was not the kind of father who cut a guy any slack. Now Ryder had a chance to set things right.

After fixing a cup of his Brazilian dark roast coffee, he emptied the Keurig and left it to drain. Phoebe already had one. But she hadn't said anything about kitchen privileges. The thought made him uneasy. Why hadn't he asked questions? He must have been in shock when he heard her suggestion.

Feeling unsettled, he started down to the shop. His father stood in the back doorway, studying the truck. "What in tarnation is going on here?"

Taking another sip of coffee, Ryder clapped a hand on his dad's shoulder. "I'm in, Dad. Phoebe's letting me move back."

His father lifted his bushy gray brows. "What you mean? That doesn't sound like her."

"She needs me, Dad. She can hardly move around with that cast. And I was driving to hell and back every day to fix her house, well, *our* house now."

His dad frowned. "A bit of exaggeration, maybe? It's only a thirty-minute drive. Do you mean, she's letting you stay like the hired hand?"

Ryder let that remark sink in. "Truth is, I'm not clear on the details." The thought stuck in his gut like a jar of nails.

"Son, I think it's time for you to step back."

Oh, oh. This was the tone Stanley had used when he told Ryder he couldn't play football and ice hockey in the same season. The drive to the Notre Dame ice rink three nights a week wouldn't leave enough time for Ryder's studies. "You know nothing about restraint, boy. That's always been your problem."

Oh crap. Here we go again. The look on his father's face fried him.

"Stanley, don't you think you could leave this decision to me?" The days were gone when he had to listen to his father all the time. "After all, I'm the one who's been hammering on that blasted roof all week."

"Right. And calling or texting me every hour," Stanley grumbled.

Head down, his father trudged back into the shop and began opening up, the way he did every day. If Ryder was smart, this would be a good time to leave. But he couldn't. Instead he followed behind his dad, travel mug in hand.

This place was what he knew. He and his dad had built Branson Motors together. Edging closer, he overheard his father mumbling something like, "Damn fool. Going to screw everything up again."

Irritation boiled behind his eyes. "I can't hear you when you mumble like that, Stanley." He set his travel mug on the counter so he wouldn't spill it.

Slamming the cash drawer shut, his dad faced him. His father's face was all scrunched up like a prune, like he'd sucked all the sorrow of the world inside and didn't like the way it tasted. This was the expression Ryder had seen after his mother's funeral. Stanley may have changed over the years but that look hadn't.

The morning sunlight caught the glint of his father's unshaven face. "Whatever it is you're doing over at Phoebe's you got one good chance, the way I see it. And you might just blow it." He brought a fist down hard on the glass counter and the mug jumped.

"Thanks for the vote of confidence, Dad." Throat thick and dry, Ryder ran a hand over the glass countertop. "Let's not go breaking stuff, okay?"

His father snorted. "You're talking to *me* about breaking stuff?"

He had a point. The spunk drained out of him, as if his father had just pulled the plug in the bathtub. Ryder was circling the drain. Slumping against the counter, he crossed one work boot over the other. "Maybe I'm afraid I will, Dad. I just got to get that woman back."

"*You* do? Do you know what it's like to sit across from your sullen face at Christmas? Who else loves my turkey stuffing like

Phoebe Hunicutt?"

"Phoebe *Branson*."

"Yeah, right." His dad snorted. "She *is* Phoebe Hunicutt. Didn't want to keep our name, did she? Now the way I see it, you got one chance, boy."

His father wagged a finger in his face. "One opportunity to make things right. I'm going to tell you, your chance at success is slim to none if you go down there with your truck piled high with all your worldly possessions." By that time, his father had wandered back outside. Arms folded across his chest, he eyed the black pickup like it was a hearse.

"You think I'm rushing things?" Had Ryder imagined that passionate spark in Phoebe's eyes when he handed her the doughnuts? Had he been mistaken when she'd opened her arms to him after that nap? "She needs me. Wants me. I think."

No one ever did a strawberry like his father. Ryder could never understand how his father could suck air from his gut and blow it through his lips like that. "Now you just unpack that truck," Stanley said when he was finished with the rude sounds. "Go light. Work your way in gradual so you don't make a mistake. Test the waters." Here he swirled his hands around and Ryder didn't dare laugh.

"Take your shaving kit and maybe some clean undies rolled into a ball. Drive down there light and casual like." By this time they were face-to-face, close enough so he could watch Stanley's nose hairs prickling. That's how worked up he was about this. "Let's remember, you are wooing that woman."

"Wooing?" He was taking his shaving kit from one of the boxes and stopped. He had to get his mind around this. "What the hell is that?"

"You know. Wooing." Here his dad used his hands again, like he was tossing a pizza crust.

"How the hell am I going to do that?" This was a humbling moment.

Stanley's jaw dropped. "How did you do it the first time?"

Ryder thought back. "I sweet-talked her, I guess. That's all I remember. We were singing karaoke..."

Another rude sound sputtered from his father. "You couldn't carry a tune in a bucket."

He had a point. "Yeah, well, anyway. She was singing and I stepped up..." Why she hadn't pushed him off that stage still puzzled him. They'd ended up out in the parking lot, making out like crazy in the pickup. To say they'd had chemistry would be an understatement. Just thinking about it got him so overheated, he'd need a shower.

"No, you don't. There'll be none of that." Maybe his dad could read his mind. His dad's hands became windshield wipers. This conversation was making Ryder dizzy. "You're going to rush things, son. This calls for thought. Take things slow."

Ryder recoiled from the insult that cut close to the bone.

Scratching his chin with one hand, Stanley was on a roll. "Remember back when you met Phoebe you were twenty-eight or so, a man of the world." And the way he used the term told Ryder just what he thought of that. "And Phoebe was only nineteen. She was such a sweet young thing. Look what you taught her."

Good thing he'd only had toast for breakfast. Disgust made his stomach heave. "I know. She trusted me." Thinking back to those early days of romancing her at the Rusty Nail made him sick over what he'd lost. She'd been like a dewy peach. So sweet, her eyes shining every time she glanced his way. Why, she hung on his every word. Batted her eyelashes as if she couldn't get enough of the sight of him. And she could have had any man. They all wanted to take care of Phoebe and probably still did. She was just that kind of woman, all soft curves and sweet sighs. Made him sick to think back.

But his father wasn't finished. "And you couldn't remember that you were a married man when that little dingbat made eyes at you at the Rusty Nail. You had a good woman at home and you pick up with trash like…"

This was one trip down memory lane Ryder did not want to take. The truth slammed into him like a semi, feeling extra bad since the words were coming from his own father. "I get it, Dad. Trust me, I damn well know what an idiot I was."

"Well, then." His father leaned back, lips drawn tight. "Enough said."

Ryder eyed the truck. "Okay I'd better hit the road. I don't want Phoebe trying to finish the roof for me."

"She wouldn't." His father hesitated.

"She would." They both spoke at the same time.

For the next twenty minutes Ryder hauled stuff off the truck and stacked it just inside the garage. "Man, you really did have high hopes," his father said when he saw the pieces of workout equipment.

Talk about feeling like a fool. "Just leave it all here," Ryder said rolling up the personal items his father had mentioned. "I'll deal with it later."

His dad chuckled. "Suits me. Remember, be casual. Take the Harley but leave the truck." That swimming motion with his hands came again. Of course, he adored Phoebe. "Don't rush it. You'll scare the poor girl."

His father whipped out his phone. "And I will be right here, like always. Just a call away." Then he stared at the phone like he'd never seen it before. "Is it really nine o'clock?"

"Okay, gotta run." This had gone beyond embarrassing. All the way down Red Arrow Highway, Ryder cussed himself out. He hated the fact that his dad was right. His feelings seesawed from frustrated to grateful. After all, he might need some emergency calls, just to touch base.

Winning a woman? Hell, he could do that. Winning a woman *back*? Now that was uncharted territory. Stomach churning, he tucked into a turn.

Uneasiness slowed his speed. Maybe Phoebe needed a guy like his dad, a man who was rock steady and slow to act. That sure as hell wasn't Ryder, although he wanted to be like that. What was stopping him? Hadn't he changed over the past two years? He sure hoped so. Hell, he could do this. Gunning it, he roared past a truck that was taking its sweet time.

To make things right, he might have to channel his dad. Crazy but he might have to ask himself, now what would Stanley do? He'd been the perfect husband just like his mom had been the perfect wife.

When he got to the road leading to the cottage, the past unfolded in his mind. How many times had he taken this road knowing Phoebe was there waiting for him? He let memories wash over him like a beach breeze. The softness in the air with just a hint of honeysuckle helped hope bloom inside. Maybe his dad was right. Maybe this was his one chance to get her back.

And he wanted more than just the sex. He wanted her sweet laughter. Her updates on *Days of Our Lives*. He even wanted her poor housekeeping and her crummy frozen meals. The only thing he could stomach was her meatloaf, and that was Stanley's recipe.

But how could he make her see he'd changed? He would make one stop on the way.

~.~

While Phoebe waited for Ryder that morning, memories came flooding back. Seeing him every day made her realize how much she missed him. Having him move in had been a dangerous idea. Maybe Carolyn could handle a situation like this. But Phoebe didn't know if she could. Sitting out on the porch watching two mourning doves canoodle in the grass, she felt sad and alone.

But of course she always had her therapist.

"I feel so lonely, Fernando."

But you always have me.

"Yeah, but you're just a metal bird. You can't wrap your arms around me like Ryder."

There are limitations, chica.

"I know."

Que lastima.

"Yeah, it really is sad."

The roar of his Harley tore her from that pity party. She tried to jump up. Right. That worked out well. Grabbing the edge of the chipped wooden table, she steadied herself. Wouldn't that have been pretty? Ryder would have to save her. Again. Being rescued by that man annoyed her no end. She'd learned to live without him, and she wanted to keep it that way.

At least she thought she did.

Getting cleaned up and dressed that morning had taken over an hour. Her conversation with Carolyn was still on her mind as she studied her closet. The weather was turning warmer. Her green bikini lay stretched out on her bed. But no way could she manage to get into that bottom. In the end she struck a compromise. After slipping into the bikini top, she zipped up the denim skirt. Grabbing a soft white sweater her mother had sent her last Christmas, she knotted the sleeves over her shoulders.

Nursing her coffee on the porch, she couldn't help but think back. The rumble of the Harley stoked a forbidden excitement. She'd been so happy to see Ryder at the end of each day. Usually she got home from the salon before he left the garage. She'd have dinner waiting. Well, something that was close to dinner, like boxed macaroni and cheese with a boiled bologna ring.

If she had time, she might fix meatloaf, one of Ryder's

favorites. Thank goodness Stanley had shared his recipe after she promised not to leak the secret ingredients. No one could ever replace Stanley. She'd always think of him as her father-in-law. How she wished she'd known Ryder's mother. From what he'd told her, his folks had the perfect marriage.

"Phoebe?" Ryder's voice came from the kitchen.

"Out here!" She whisked her fingers through her up do. These mauve gelled spikes hadn't won Ryder's approval. He used to love playing with her soft curls.

"Have you had your breakfast?" In his hand was a carton of eggs, which were probably scrambled from being on the Harley.

"You sure they're not cracked?"

She almost giggled watching his mouth drop open.

Ryder's Adam's apple bobbed in his throat, and his hand gripped tighter. Yep, she was sure she heard a couple of those eggs crack.

"I thought I'd cook up some eggs. Good for us, right? Protein or something?" Lordy he was having trouble making sense. Yes indeed this is going to be a very interesting summer.

"Sounds good. All I had was cinnamon raisin toast."

His tongue tipped out to swipe his lips. Ryder love toasted cinnamon raisin bread. "Did you make it with the cinnamon butter?"

"Sure did." Trying not to laugh, Phoebe nodded. "Yessir. You used to like it that way, didn't you?"

"Yeah. I still like it that way." But his eyes were rolling over the hills and valleys of her green bikini top. Cinnamon butter was probably not what the man had in mind.

"Well, I sure do appreciate it."

"What?" Leaning against the table as if he were woozy, he blinked.

She giggled. "The eggs, Ryder. And cinnamon toast? Sure I'd like some."

His tongue licked his lower lip like he'd just come in from the Sahara and she was a deep well. "This will just take me a minute."

Now, she should've just ordered him onto the roof. Have the man get busy. But the truth was, working in that kitchen was a bear. It was the bending part that got to her. Sure she could move around okay and sitting wasn't a problem, but bending over? She just about fell on her bum. Why not let Ryder do the hard work?

Glancing up, she watched the sun rise higher through the trees. This was that peaceful time of the morning when she used to take a walk along the shore before heading off to work, especially after the divorce. That summer she'd needed to be put together with super glue. Her book of meditations in her hand, she walked until she'd collapse in the dune grass. Then she'd open the book and read. The hopeful meditations calmed her mind. Got her ready to face another day without Ryder.

At first, getting out of bed to face another day hadn't been easy. Thank goodness she had her salon to keep her busy every day. Jen and Carly helped field her calls. She blocked Ryder's number on her cell. It was easy to delete texts and emails. Somehow she'd gotten over him and all that pain. At least, she thought she had. Having him around like this? Made her seriously wonder.

Maybe she was playing with fire. Before long, she smelled the sizzling butter and the cinnamon toast. "You want me to butter the toast, Ryder?" she called out.

"If you would." Sure sounded like he was having a time of it. Chairs were sliding, plates were clapping together and the air carried a burnt smell, almost like the leaves in fall.

Bumping along slowly to the door, she stood there. The straps of her bikini top felt tight, and she took her time adjusting them.

Casting a glance her way, Ryder burned himself. "Ouch. Man!"

Phoebe bit back a giggle. "Cold water." She motioned toward the sink.

"What?" He nearly dropped the pan trying to slide the eggs onto the plates.

Taking baby steps to the sink, she turned on the cold water and let it flow over her fingers. "Put your hand under the cold water. You've got work to do. Can't have you injuring yourself." She kept her voice clipped, and he shot her a look.

"Thank you for your concern."

"Don't mention it." No way was he getting any pity from her. While he stuck his big paw under the cold water, she sat down at the kitchen table to slather the toast with the cinnamon butter that he loved. The delivery boy from Clancy's had come yesterday, and he even helped her put the groceries away. Eggs had been part of that order but she wasn't going to mention that now.

Drying his hands, Ryder slanted her a look. "Want to sit on the porch?"

Well, of course she did. But not this time.

"No need. Let's just eat quick so you can get to work."

"Slave driver."

As they sat there sipping coffee and eating the eggs, Ryder begged for compliments. "Almost tastes better than Rosie's, right?"

Sometimes the little boy came out in him, all shy uncertainty. "Delicious. You did a great job, Ryder. Really. I appreciate it." And she did.

Satisfaction softened his jaw and crinkled the corners of his gray eyes. He'd showered and shaved. She let the cinnamon butter melt in her mouth. There's something about a man who'll cook for you.

"Just leave those dishes in the sink," he told her when they were finished.

"Oh, I will." But after he left, she managed to clean up. To her amazement, she still loved doing things for him. And that was a problem.

Chapter 10

Phoebe would sure be glad when Ryder finished with the roof.
That nail gun was getting to her. Or maybe it was the heat, which
had taken Gull Harbor hostage. By noon, it was eighty degrees, not
the usual June weather. When lunchtime came, she hustled into the
kitchen to make ham sandwiches. She slathered the caraway rye
bread with mayonnaise and mustard, just the way he liked it. And
although it took her forever, she somehow managed to make
cucumber dip. Chopping up the cucumber would be good for her
upper arm tone. At least, that's what she told herself. Then she
attacked the onions. But she'd forgotten to add dill to her Clancy's
shopping list, so they wouldn't have that.

Cucumber dip or nachos? She could handle those. But the main
meal? Not her thing, even though a big guy like Ryder needed
hearty food and plenty of it. She may have let him down in that
area. But in other wifely duties? No need for a guilt trip there.

Phoebe set up lunch on the porch. High in the sky, the sun beat
down with summer ferocity. Families were headed to the beach.
She could hear the rumble of the wagons loaded with beach toys
pass by on the road. Happy voices lifted with excitement.

Before long, Ryder burst through the door, washed his hands
and sat down. Eating across from Ryder Branson was a treat—

almost enough to make her forget he was off-limits. Her ex ate the way he approached everything else, with lusty enjoyment. No nibbling for Ryder. Well, at least not when it came to lunch. He took big bites, chewing with obvious enjoyment. She wondered if Trixie was a good cook.

"This dip is great, Phoebe." His eyes sparkled across the table while he dug chip after chip into the thick mixture.

"Glad you like it, Ryder. It's one of my favorites." Time for some fun. Taking the biggest chip in the bowl, she edged it under large chunks of cucumber. "Moderation in all things," she said softly. Savoring that one bite, she let it roll over her tongue, enjoying the onions along with the black crushed pepper.

Ryder's facial muscles went slack while she chewed slowly. Eyes glazed, he fumbled for the bowl of chips and then jabbed one into the mixture. The chip cracked. He kept going.

"Pretty good, isn't it?" he muttered between bites.

"Perfect, right?" Pouting her lips, she did that air kiss thing that used to drive him wild when she was complimenting him.

His dazed features made her swallow a giggle. While the fan worked to cool the room, his forehead beaded with perspiration.

"Haven't had this for a while," she whispered. "Tastes good, doesn't it?"

"No, I haven't had it in....a long time. Tastes *great*," he said, fumbling for another chip. "You did a great job. With the dip, I mean."

By that time, who knew what they were talking about?

"Well now, thank you, Ryder."

Being complimented by her ex felt good. Until it didn't. After a while her tummy felt stuffed. But the real problem? Oh, he hadn't even started to satisfy her need. The need she didn't realize she had until she spent time with Ryder again.

By the end of lunch, they were both gasping for air. It was the first time in her life she'd ever served a meal that was X-rated. Phoebe felt a food coma coming on as she tried to push up from her chair. Had she made a terrible exhibition of herself? Did she care? Just watching his confusion had been worth it.

Phoebe liked to think she still had that power. That effect on a man.

Especially this man.

"Leave the dishes in the sink, Phoebe. I'll clean these up tonight."

"Okay. Thanks, Ryder." Tonight. He was going to be here tonight. Hormones raging, she didn't know if she could stand it.

"You look tired." Ryder peered down into her eyes. "How about a nap?" Coming around the table, he looked like he wanted to touch her but didn't know how, not with that bikini top.

She pushed back her damp hair. "Maybe." With a sigh she glanced over at the crutch that had rubbed her skin raw.

Following her eyes, Ryder scooped her into his arms. His chest was broad and firm. She flattened one hand over the beat of his heart. Even the rumble of his chest could get her aroused.

"I'll take you to your room." His eyes swept her bare chest. "The porch might be too cool."

"Sure. Okay. My head feels so heavy."

Cupping one hand over her head, he brought it to his chest. "Rest now, Sweet Cheeks." The last words were added in a husky whisper. He'd always made her feel like a sweet little thing. She curled her hand tight on his chest so she wouldn't whisk it over his chin, feel the stubble tease her palm.

There will be none of that, Phoebe Hunicutt.

No matter what, she was sticking to her plan. Boots scuffing on the cracked linoleum, he carried her to the bedroom. Feeling so content she could purr, Phoebe felt herself drifting off to sleep. They were almost there. But he stopped sharp in the doorway. "What happened in here?"

"What?" She blinked her eyes open. A soft breeze blew through the white dimity curtains. The darkened room felt comfortably cool. Her white frame bed stood against the pink wall, with the green and peach quilt that her mother had made for her. She longed to slide under that quilt. "Why are you stopping, Ryder?"

"The damn room's pink. That's why. Pink?" He deposited her on the queen-size bed she'd bought after kicking him out.

Pushing herself up on an elbow, she looked at the walls with satisfaction. "I thought it would be good if they matched the house. But I only got to two walls. I still have work to do."

His head was swiveling like a bobble doll. "No man will ever sleep in this room."

Suddenly, she was wide awake. And she could not stop laughing. "Not an issue, is it? Close the door on the way out, okay, Ryder?"

~.~

Something smelled spicy and delicious. Brown sugar beans. Phoebe's stomach growled as she rolled toward the window. A cool breeze blew softly over her face, and she blinked her eyes open. What time was it? Felt like she'd been asleep for hours. Whenever she took a nap, she always woke up feeling cozy and wanting company. The kind of company only a man can bring and Ryder knew that. She squirmed a bit on the bed. Somewhere Ryder was whistling, off tune of course.

Then she remembered. Cold reality straightened her out fast. Ryder wasn't her husband. He wouldn't come through the door with that hungry look in his eye. *I want him gone.* But the words rang hollow in her heart. Especially after that shameful display eating lunch. What was wrong with her? What had happened to her self-control?

Stretching, she remembered she was wearing her tiny little bikini top and smiled. Flipping onto her stomach, she rolled out of bed and pushed herself up onto her feet. She was getting pretty good at this maneuver. The air felt too cool for a bikini top and goosebumps rose on her skin. After rummaging through her drawers, she pulled on a blue T-shirt that said *Saugatuck* in white script.

Full of renewed purpose, she stopped in the bathroom. The shaving kit on the counter pulled her up short. Darn it. She turned as limp as Ryder's damp towel hung over the shower door. There was a time when she hated to find his toothbrush on the counter. The stubble in the sink made her cringe. Now just looking at that worn leather kit turned her to mush.

Think messy sink, not gray suede eyes.

Crutch tucked under her arm, she thumped down the hall. When she got to the kitchen, she paused, took a deep breath and smiled. "What is that delicious smell?"

When Ryder turned, his eyes went straight to her chest. "Saugatuck?"

Meeting his gaze, she saw their memories there. "Yeah. Remember?"

"How could I forget?" He swallowed hard.

Not too long after they got married, they spent the weekend at a bed and breakfast in Saugatuck, a Michigan tourist destination with a capital T. Later they laughed about the fact that they hardly got to see the town. Crazy for each other, they even stayed in their room for meals. Saugatuck became a synonym for what-the-heck. Their room sat right on the channel. Boats slowly chugged past as they sat on their veranda, sipping Bloody Mary's in the morning and cold beers at night. Ryder would run out for takeout, and they'd have fried chicken or burgers on their little table.

Shoulders slumping, Ryder had turned back to the stove. His curls wet from the shower were darned appealing. Of course he had the flame under the beans up way too high. Her ex-husband knew less about cooking than she did.

The yummy smell of brown sugar beans was turning into a burn. Phoebe's stomach growled. A side-glance told her the plates were set on the table. Her hunger turned a little squishy inside. What would they talk about? Her nervousness made her regret what she'd thought was a bright idea, him staying here. "You need to turn down the heat, Ryder," she blurted out.

"But I'm not…?" Then he looked at the spatula in his hand. "Oh, that."

Now what in Sam Hill did he think she was talking about? Okay, he was one fine looking man. That fresh T-shirt stretched across broad shoulders. His biceps moved enticingly while he worked. And then there was that slim waist. When he reached up for the salt, she saw enough skin below that shirt to make her hungry and not for beans. She wanted to tunnel up under that cotton with her fingers. Drink in his fresh scent and lift her face for a kiss. Instead, she grabbed the back of a kitchen chair and hung on like a passenger on the Titanic.

"Sorry I slept so long. I wasted the whole afternoon."

"Guess you needed the sleep." He gave her a lopsided smile. "Not a problem. I got a lot done today. I'm about finished with the roof, and then I can start painting."

So he was in a hurry to finish the job. Disappointment seeped through her. "Can I help with anything? Supper, I mean?" All she could smell was the beans.

"No." He hitched a shoulder toward the porch. "Why don't you sit down. I'll have dinner ready in a minute." Confident words but the confusion in his eyes told a different story.

So he felt uncertain about their situation. Well, she knew how that felt. Wobbling out to the porch she took a seat and drank in the cool night air.

The cottage was hidden in the woods about half a block from the beach. When they bought it, they'd liked the privacy of the property. The sounds of restless waves drifted up from the beach. How many times had she wandered that beach at dusk or dawn, wondering where she'd gone wrong with Ryder? What made him turn to another woman?

The lake didn't have any answers.

And neither did the therapist who'd about emptied out Phoebe's bank account. That's when she bought Fernando at an art fair.

Maneuvering into a chair, she thrummed her nails on the scratched table. Having Ryder around was like ripping off the bandage and discovering you hadn't healed. The wound was still red and raw.

Now, Phoebe. Patience, patience. Carolyn stepped into her head, wagging a finger at her from Santa Fe. A night chill descended and Phoebe brushed her hands up her arms. They'd declared a truce this summer and for a good reason. Mentally she ticked them off. The repairs would be made. She could make her ex-husband crazy. She might get to see Stanley. That rational approach adjusted her attitude. Somehow she had to make peace with her decision.

"Here's the coleslaw." Ryder bustled out, looking so domestic.

"Thought you didn't like pink." She pointed to the apron he wore.

With his face the color of the flamingo on the apron, he plunked down a bowl of fries and another one of coleslaw. "I didn't want to get messed up." He looked down. "Okay, the bird is kind of girly."

"Don't worry about it." He just didn't know how girly this

summer was going to get. He hadn't even started with the pink paint yet. When he came back with a bowl of beans, she couldn't help but notice they were clumped together. Burned canned beans——pretty hard to pull off but somehow he'd managed. She put a paper napkin on her lap. "Looks delicious."

Sitting across from her, Ryder wiped the back of one hand across a beaded brow. "You think so?"

Well, he was never going to rival Martha Stewart. "Absolutely." Hey it was food and she was starving. "Anything to drink?"

"Oh, yeah. Sorry." Opening the refrigerator, he returned with a frosty beer in each hand. She hadn't had any pain pills that day, and a beer tasted delicious on a summer evening. Minutes later they were eating. Chipmunks chased each other around the yard. How she envied them their mindless scampering. She'd be tethered to this chair all summer.

And to Ryder. A chill passed through her.

Beyond the hedges, families were coming up from the beach, trundling wagons full of beach toys behind them. If they spoke at all, it was in hushed tones. The sun and fresh air could do that to you. Settle you down so you slept real good. Picking up her fork, Phoebe played with the beans. Sitting here with Ryder just felt so homey that it brought tears to her eyes.

Just then Ryder happened to glance up. He set his beer down. "Hey, what's wrong? I know the beans are a mess but..."

Trying to hide her sniffles, she shook her head. "Yeah, I think you went a little heavy on the pepper."

"I'll do better next time." He looked like summer, the white shirt setting off the deep tan from working on the roof. Whatever this was, he was trying and he was trying for her. If the roof was almost done, maybe the painting would go just as fast. Then he could hightail it out of here and get back to his life. She'd still have the house. Wasn't that what she wanted?

Phoebe liked Clancy's coleslaw so she dug into it. Ryder studied the ceiling as if he was having a conversation with it. "At least we don't have to worry about leaks anymore. I sure didn't want that ceiling getting ruined."

The tongue in groove ceiling had been his pride. "I appreciate everything you're doing, Ryder, I really do." Sometimes the cozy cottage felt like too much work for her, not that she'd admit it.

"How's Dad doing?" The word slipped out so easily. She bit her lip. Even Ryder looked surprised.

"Fine. Stanley's fine. Crusty old guy. He'll take care of the business while I take care..." Ryder shifted a shoulder. "Help you out."

Her father-in-law had always been dependable. "That's good."

Eyes swerving to the yard where weeds abounded, Ryder chewed thoughtfully. "Stanley misses you, Phoebe."

The coleslaw felt like cotton going down. "I told him I'd meet him for lunch anytime."

Ryder shifted in the chair. "You know what I mean. He misses you being part of the family."

Looking down at her beans, her vision blurred. "I miss him too. A lot."

They ate the rest of the dinner in silence.

When they finished, Ryder jumped up and began to clear the table. He'd probably crack half the plates by the time he was finished, stacking them like that.

"I'll run these later," he said, as if he could feel her eyes on his back. Then he turned. "I've got a surprise for you."

"You do?" The man was full of mystery.

Reaching to the top of the refrigerator, he took down a white bakery box. Looking at Ryder, box in hand and a pleased expression on his face, her mouth watered. While he pulled down two smaller plates and grabbed forks, she loved the way his body moved. The man was all muscles and power as he prepared the delicate cannolis. Who cared about dinner when you could have dessert? Watching him, Phoebe knew just what she'd been missing and it wasn't cannolis.

When he caught her staring, he smiled.

"Why don't you...go out and sit down?" Ryder tilted his head to one side.

"Right. Sure." She did as she was told. After all, the man had bought cannolis.

He set a lime green plate in front of her. "Oh, Ryder." The pastry was dusted with powdered sugar. Puffs of rich ricotta spilled from the ends of each cannoli, and she could see slivers of pistachios.

"I haven't had dessert in a long time." What was she saying? Heat burned her cheeks. She poked a fork down at the pastry. "I mean not *this* sweet, rich thing."

"Me neither." His eyes held hers and he cleared his throat.

Ryder made a circling motion with his fork. "I mean, you know, not *this* dessert."

"Right. A cannoli. I love it. I miss it....them." Her hold tightened on the fork until it bit into her hand.

Heat banked in his eyes. Had they both stopped breathing?

You are an idiot, Phoebe Hunicutt. Dropping her eyes, she inhaled the sweet scent. The crust of the pastry cracked when she nudged a fork into it. Right now? She felt hungry, starving. When she looked up, Ryder's eyes were on her. They seemed to glow fiery red. She'd better chew or she'd choke when she tried to swallow.

When they were finished, Ryder cleared the table. Getting up, she tried to help. "Look, Sweet Ch..." Oh, that nickname came so easily. And her body roared to life just hearing a suggestion of those words. But Ryder cut them off with a guttural groan. "You can't bend over, and it's probably not good for your leg to even try."

"Well, all right, Ryder," she said softly, feeling like she was walking on the dry edge of a sand pit that might crumble without warning. Although it was agony hearing the clatter of her precious plates, she left Ryder with the dishes and settled into one of the big rattan chairs. The birds were singing their sweet nighttime songs as the shadows deepened under the trees. Usually people drifted back down to the beach after dinner to watch the sunset. Grounded up here for the summer, she'd really miss those peaceful moments.

Another crash of dishes as Ryder pushed the lower tray into the dishwasher. "You can turn the TV on, Ryder. That won't bother me." How many nights had she sat out here, while he listened to sports on the TV inside?

He filled the doorway. "If you don't mind company, I'd like to sit here with you."

"Of course I don't mind." She happened to glance over at Fernando.

Fine with me. But be careful.

Ryder always left his work boots at the door. Inside, he wore a pair of soft leather moccasins she'd always loved. He called them his at-home shoes and she smiled, remembering. After he took the seat across from her, he folded his hands on his stomach and stretched his feet onto the hassock until their toes nearly touched. As darkness fell, fireflies danced out from the trees, leaving glittery trails along the grass, their tiny lights blinking on and off. Before she knew it, Ryder's head bobbed and he began to snore, just a little bit.

So they sat there, together but not together. Conflicted feelings had a heyday in her head while she watched him doze, loving every exhausted dip of his head.

She'd always pictured little boys with Ryder's reddish brown head of curls. They'd have his gray eyes too. Mischief makers. There was a time when she loved to think of her husband that way. Ryder had that adventurous air about him. But all that changed. Her dreams of a family with him burned away fast. He seemed so different now. A lot of the quick, snappy comebacks had been replaced by moments when he seemed to turn things over in his mind. That pause? Totally new. New and nice.

A slight smile tilted his lips. What was he dreaming about?

Or *who?* Her muscles tightened painfully. More than once she'd see him come out of the garage with his phone. But she wasn't asking any questions, of course. She had no right.

Well, time to get some shut eye. Hating to wake him up, she hesitated. Then Phoebe grabbed an afghan from the back of the sofa and spread it gently over his sprawled frame. After turning off the lights, she just stood there for a second, watching him breathe. This wouldn't be the first time he'd fallen asleep exhausted on that porch.

The back porch light glanced off Fernando's metallic head. "You take good care of him now, you hear?"

Slipping back to her own room, she got ready for bed. The mini-skirt was easy to zip off and it wasn't hard to slip out of the bikini top. That light in Ryder's eyes when he caught sight of it?

She had enjoyed seeing that again. Way too much.

Girl, you are a glutton for punishment.

Chapter 11

When she woke up the next day, coffee hung in the air and no hammering was going on overhead. What time was it? Phoebe eased one eye open. Nine? Really? Jolted awake, she scrambled from bed. No bikini top today. Rifling through her closet, she found a gauzy green sundress that flowed over the top of her cast. A quick dab of lipstick and she was ready.

After a quick call to the salon, she was almost disappointed at how composed Jen sounded. "Everything's under control," Jen told her. "How are you doing?"

My life's out of control. "Fine," Phoebe told her employee. "I'm good."

Silence hummed at the other end. Finally, she heard Jen take a deep breath. "Okay, then. Let me know if I can help with anything." Jen didn't believe her. She knew how stubborn Phoebe could be and that she'd never ask for help, even if she needed it.

After the call ended, Phoebe filled a bowl with cereal and ate it in gulps, standing up. All that sitting and standing took a lot out of her. Taking her crutch, she walked onto the porch. The faint smell of paint hung in the air, and she heard the rhythmic slide of a brush. True to his word, Ryder was working on the siding today. Excitement quivered in her stomach. She would finally get the full effect of an entire wall of pink.

"What do you think of that, Fernando? Are we looking good or what?" Her metal sculpture seemed to approve.

The summer breeze teased her. What a great day to walk to the beach. Why not? Tying a hoodie around her shoulders, she jammed a sun visor on her head. Crutch tucked under one arm, she walked to the driveway, edged past the Harley and continued to the road. Sun filtered through the trees and too late, she realized she hadn't put on sunblock. Another couple steps and the road turned to quicksand.

Although the sand had been compressed by the traffic, her crutch sank right through it. *Just take it slow.* She was going to see that beach if it killed her. It had rained last night. The air felt moist. That meant there would be a haze over the lake. She loved it when it looked misty like a watercolor.

One step at a time. Crutch, swing leg. Bring other foot up. Perspiration formed on her upper lip. Her left leg protested from taking most of her weight.

This began to feel like a bad idea.

"What are you doing?" The words sliced into the quiet morning.

Looking back, she cringed. Ryder marched toward her, disapproval wrinkling his brow.

"Walking to the beach." But glancing down the road that once took ten minutes, Phoebe knew she'd never make it. The crutch had rubbed her raw and her shoulder ached.

So close now, almost too close, Ryder bent his head. Tipping her chin up, he forced her to meet his eyes. "So you want to go to the beach?"

"Ah, huh." She tore her eyes away, embarrassed by the feelings rippling through her. The beach? Right now she wanted more than sand and water.

"Tonight, okay?"

"Tonight? Really?" Hope surged.

"Yeah, tonight I'll take you down there."

"Oh, right. The beach." Mentally she beat back thoughts that had no business in her head.

"That's what you wanted, right? To go to the beach?" Now it was his turn to look confused.

"Absolutely." *Not.*

His head swung back toward the house. "Right now I'm..."

"That's all right, Ryder. I'm fine."

He dropped his hand. Goosebumps still chased up her arms. Must be the cool morning air. "No, you're not, Sweet Cheeks. We'll go tonight. I promise."

The concern in his eyes flowed over her like molasses. Phoebe never knew she liked molasses this much.

"But I'll be taking you from your work." The faster he finished the projects, the sooner she'd be free of him. Right? Her eyes traveled from that badass bandana down to the work boots, taking a few detours in between. She needed him gone. The man was dangerous.

Putting his hands on his hips, Ryder looked toward the sound of the waves. Were they getting to him too? "Our evenings are free, as far as I can see."

Our? There he went again. All this *us* stuff was making her nervous, like he was encroaching on her territory. But who was she to fight this? Her aching arm told her to cool it. Caution flattened her excitement. If his evenings were free, then what were all the calls about? Every time she turned around he was on the phone.

Maybe he was calling the garage. But the therapist she'd visited during her divorce had told her not to make excuses for someone else. "Get the facts," Dr. McCabe had advised.

Phoebe wasn't real good at that, and now she had no right to ask Ryder anything. And why did she care if he was calling some other woman? "Okay."

Slowly, they made their way back. Phoebe felt grateful that he'd stopped her. She never would have made it. With every step, the crutch sank deeper into the loamy sand. She pictured herself collapsed in one of the ditches, now filled with brilliant orange tiger lilies. What a picture that would make.

Finally they reached the gravel driveway. The going got easier although Ryder's touch on her elbow gave her an erratic heartbeat.

"The yard looks terrible," she said when they reached the back door. "Will you just look at those poor daisies and hollyhocks?"

Ryder shrugged. "Looks fine to me." He'd never been much of a flower man.

Her eyes swept the scene. Drop cloths and paint supplies littered the grass, which hadn't been mowed in a while. "Pretty soon it'll be the Fourth of July."

"You got that right." Ryder eyed the house, as if he wondered if he could finish this up before then. The thought made her surprisingly sad.

After the Fourth, Clancy's would be crowded with carts. The wait time for restaurants would skyrocket as summer got into full swing. Usually by the time a few freckles had bloomed on her cheeks, she was taking daily trips to the beach. This year?

This year all she had was her broken leg and Ryder. And she didn't know which one was worse. Having him around often felt like a pebble in her sandals. But then again, she was a girl who collected rocks. Strewed them across her dresser until her mother coaxed her into pouring them into a pot. Phoebe loved them, each one so unique.

Oh, her ex-husband was unique all right.

Ryder went back to the ladder. Peering up at the roof, she saw the neat edges and the orderly pattern of the roofing tiles. "You did a great job, Ryder."

He stood back, obviously proud. "Thanks, honey." The word slipped out so easily. Ducking, Ryder sucked in a breath through set teeth. "Sorry. I meant, 'Thanks, Phoebe.' "

Stepping into the cottage, she pretended she didn't hear him. *Honey.* She wanted to hug that word to her chest and wasn't that silly? But she'd been his honey. And she'd liked that security. Until it changed.

Inside, she pulsed with newfound energy. Putting eggs on to boil for egg salad, she tried to straighten up the cottage. Crutch tight under her arm, she folded quilts and afghans, arranged magazines on the coffee table. Taking a sponge, she wiped down the shelves in the refrigerator, carefully balancing on her cast.

What had gotten into her? Making the egg salad, she grated more of her fingers than she did of the eggs. But she fixed it just the way he liked it. Lots of brown mustard and pickle relish. Then she took a loaf of olive bread from the freezer. She may not be a great cook, but she knew how to buy the right stuff and pop it in the freezer.

When she took out the potato chips, she noticed some games stacked in the pantry. She remembered when she'd bought the checker game, but they never had time to play. Taking it down, she carried the flat box out to the porch.

When Ryder came in for lunch, the table was set outside. After washing his hands, he sat opposite her, staring down at his plate.

"Olive bread." He lifted one of the toasted pieces of bread heaped with egg salad as if it were the key to his next Harley. Taking a bite, he munched on it, eyes closed. Watching him was killing her. The open face sandwich was pretty good, and she nibbled on her own. But watching him eat was way more fun.

"More?" She started to push up from the table after he finished his second piece.

But he jumped up before she could move. "Stay right where you are. I'm fine. I don't want to put on weight." Then Ryder grinned. This had always been one of their private jokes. He'd make comments about his weight so she didn't have to. Phoebe was the one always worrying about the extra pounds. But Ryder insisted that he liked her curves.

Her mouth dried. The last bite of egg salad was hard to force down. On his way back into the kitchen, he spotted the checker box on the table next to the futon. "What's this?"

"Just something that was tucked away."

"Guess we never had time to play." And then he stopped. They both knew how they'd spent their weekends and evenings.

"Except at Cracker Barrel. Remember how we sat at that huge checker table in front of the fire?" She could almost feel the heat from that crackling fire.

"Yeah, we used to go up there a lot in winter." His eyes softened. "That was fun."

"Maybe we could play some night." Phoebe was getting a little nervous about how they'd fill their evenings. "I'll whip your hide."

"You're on." Wearing a grin, Ryder went back to work. Phoebe put their glasses into the dishwasher. Having a plan made her feel better. This felt almost like a date. But wasn't that silly?

After lunch she was ready for a nap. The cast wore her out, and she was glad she wasn't going into the salon. Then she heard the car coming up the driveway. Peeking out, she watched Diana step from her yellow VW.

"Hey, girl. You're back." Phoebe called from the open door.

"Thought I'd check up on you." Diana walked toward her, blonde hair ruffling in the breeze.

It wasn't easy to hold out her arms and keep the crutch in line but Phoebe tried.

"I am back and just in time." Stepping back from a cautious embrace, Diana gave her a critical eye. "What happened to you?"

"I decided to paint the house."

With a crooked smile, Diana glanced up to the roof. "Looks like you found a handyman."

"Temporary help," Phoebe muttered, leading the way back to the cottage. "Come on. Let's catch up over some lemonade."

Comfortable on the porch with frosted glasses in hand, Phoebe began the interrogation. "So, how did it go?" No way was she asking Diana about the mosquito bites on her face and arms. Her gorgeous friend was very aware of her looks. That moon-shaped scar on her face shone white against her honey-colored skin

But Phoebe didn't have to mention the bites. Running a hand across her cheek, Diana said, "Will you just look at my face? Upper Michigan has so many mosquitoes. They could export them to other countries."

Phoebe smiled. "Did you forget I grew up there? Those deep woods breed armies of mosquitoes."

Diana blushed. "No insult intended."

"Don't worry about it. Did you enjoy camping?" Although her dad had tried to turn Phoebe into a wild woman who liked to sleep under the stars, it never worked. But for Will's sake, Diana had thrown herself into her outdoor honeymoon with enthusiasm.

Her friend's stormy expression almost made Phoebe laugh. "Camping lasted exactly three nights. Do you know you have to share a bathroom with other people at those campsites? There were a bunch of guys in a camper next to us who partied all night. Don't get me wrong. I like Willie Nelson but not at three in the morning."

The mental picture made Phoebe explode with laughter. "Did

you cook Will's breakfast over one of those cute little campfires in the morning?" Diana definitely wasn't a campfire person.

Her friend's jaw dropped. "Did you just meet me? Do you know how hard it is to find a fast food place in the wilderness? Finally, Will took pity on me. We found a room at a resort with ten little rental cabins near Mackinaw. The owner played the accordion around a campfire in the evening. That was our entertainment." By this time they were both chuckling. "Some people go to Vegas for their honeymoon and big stage shows. Me? I have Michigan."

"And Will," Phoebe reminded Diana.

"And Will." The way she said her new husband's name was so darn cute.

"Newsflash, Diana. Honeymoons are not about entertainment. At least, not that I recall." Now it was Phoebe's turn to blush.

"Probably right." Flipping her blonde hair behind her shoulder, Diana leaned closer. "So what's with the guy on the roof? From what I can see, he's hot."

How to explain this? "That's, er, my ex-husband. He's helping me out with some projects." Although Phoebe tried to be casual, Diana's gasp told her she'd failed.

"*That's* your ex? You never told me." Her brows drew together as if she were trying to make sense of the tidbits Phoebe was tossing out. Where to start? Diana was a good friend. Phoebe purposely had never said much about Ryder at book club. It had been a year, and she still couldn't talk about her divorce.

"The situation's awkward, Diana. We own this cottage together, but it's falling apart. I love this little place and had big plans to work on it this summer. Ryder offered to help after I broke my leg."

Diana's lips formed a perfect oval. "Wow, Phoebe. I go out of town for a week. You break your leg and enlist the help of a Greek god, who just happens to be your ex." She shook her head. "No one could write a story as crazy as this."

Might as well come clean. "That's only part of it. I'm still pretty mad at him. Carolyn and I figured I could have some fun by showing him just what he's missing." Looking down at her cast, she shook her head. "What was I thinking? I offered to let him stay in the guest room upstairs. He was doing so much driving back and forth."

"Ah, huh. How interesting." A Cheshire cat smile tilted Diana's lips. "How's that working out for you?"

"He's only been here a couple nights, and I can hardly stand it."

"I can see the problem. Geez." Diana tossed her curls.

Phoebe drummed her fingernails against the glass. "Carolyn and I cooked up this scheme. I'd drive Ryder crazy in my bikini top."

"Really? Is it working?"

"No. The tables turned. Ryder in a white T-shirt? Sexy as all get out."

"I can see your point."

"Yeah, well. I should feel grateful. After all, he rescued me when the darn ladder broke."

"I'm so sorry I wasn't here."

"That's all right. This arrangement is weird but it makes sense. After all, we do both own the house, so we're both responsible for it." She wouldn't mention the check she'd torn up. Diana owned Hippy Chick, a shop along the main street. They were both businesswomen who worked hard for their money. Diana might think she'd been crazy.

"So, has he remarried?"

"I don't know what his situation is right now. He lives up past Stevensville, so I hardly ever saw him until this summer." She leaned closer. After all, they were on the porch and Ryder was painting just around the corner. "I'm wondering if he wants to fix up the place so he can get me to sell it."

Diana's eyes darted to the corner and back. "Would he do that?"

This lemonade needed more sugar. "I don't know but it's a possibility."

Looking out at the peaceful setting, Phoebe thought about last night. How familiar it had all felt. "The truth is, Diana, having him around is making me crazy." But she didn't want to go into simple things like olive bread or cannolis and how they felt right shared with Ryder.

"Give it some time," Diana said. "We all have our own crosses to bear. Will's niece is working at Hippy Chick this summer. Maisy is a handful. She gave Rachel a hard time while I was gone."

"But she thinks the world of you, Diana."

Her friend lifted a shoulder. "She likes us just fine, but she also likes to have her own way. Will's parents rented a place in Gull Harbor to be with Maisy this summer. They're delighted to spend time with her. Get to know her better. But she's a teenager with growing pains."

"And a neglectful mother, as I recall. Remember last Christmas when you brought her into the salon? Not a peep out of her until I suggested the green streak in her hair. I wish I could work with her again, but Jen will do a great job. She's managed the shop just fine without me."

"Of course she has. You have a competent staff." Setting down her empty glass, Diana squeezed her hand. "Well, time to hit the road. I have to go grocery shopping. Doesn't that sound domestic? Kind of like, gotta feed my man."

Thinking back on the dinner of cole slaw and beans, Phoebe giggled. "Sounds good to me. I'm ordering from Clancy's almost every day, or Ryder drives down to Whistle Stop or the Roadhouse for takeout."

The visit had worn Phoebe out. She just didn't have the same stamina since she broke her leg. Waving goodbye to the happy bride, she fought a twinge of jealousy. She remembered those post honeymoon days. Having Ryder around had brought back that special time with an uncomfortable rush.

But the itchiness that plagued her under the darn cast got her attention. Grabbing her ballpoint from the side table, Phoebe tried to ease it under the tight white tube. But the pen didn't extend far enough. She could not scratch that itch.

Chapter 12

Ryder was wielding a paintbrush in the hot afternoon sun when he heard the sound of his own pickup truck. *What the hell?* Setting the brush on the edge of the tray, he turned. Sure enough, his black pickup turned into the drive, Stanley slouched at the wheel. Ryder's shoulders tightened. *Now what?* His dad looked "growly," as his mother used to say.

Swatting at mosquitoes, he trudged toward the driveway. If this heat was June, he didn't even want to see July. Would he still be here then? That all depended on Phoebe. He had to find more projects after he finished the painting.

His dad pulled up behind Ryder's Harley and got out. He was the last person Ryder wanted to see right now. Was Stanley checking up on him? Hitching up his jeans, his dad looking more like a Mafia hit man than a nosy father.

"Hey, Dad. What are you doing here?" Stanley gave the back door a furtive glance. Oh sure. He was hoping Phoebe would rescue him. Ryder didn't want his ex-wife to know that this was a full-out, father-son assault. His dad was going to blow it.

"So how's it going?" Not about to be blocked by a moody son, Stanley edged around Ryder to squint at the back door again. Yep, he definitely wanted to see Phoebe.

"Fine. So who's watching the shop?

His father worked on his spearmint chewing gum. Stanley was trying to quit smoking. Again.

"Mick. You making any progress here?" His dad's eyes swept the yard as if he expected to find snipers in the bushes.

Taking his father's elbow, Ryder eased him out of earshot. Since her accident, Phoebe had started taking a nap in the afternoon. The last thing he needed was the two of them ganging up on him. "If you mean am I getting the painting done, it's going slow."

"That's a good thing right?" His father's eyes brightened.

Ryder wiped the back of one hand across his brow. "Not in my book. It's hot as a bitch out here, and the mosquitoes are having me for lunch."

His father's eyes narrowed. "Let's remember. You're a man with a mission. Missions take time. Endurance." Widening his stance, Stanley hunkered down.

"I'm well aware of that, Dad."

A smile tickling his lips, his father scrutinized the cottage. "Pink, huh?"

"Incredible, right? She insisted."

"And you followed orders?" Stanley looked pleased. "I'm starting to enjoy this."

"Well, I'm not. Look at me." He stared down at his jeans and shirts, splattered with pink paint. "I'm going to have to throw this stuff out. Her bedroom's half pink too."

"You've been in the bedroom?" Hope sparked in his father's eyes.

"Not really." The words cost him. "Only to well, tuck her in."

"Tuck her in?" Head swiveling to face him, Stanley repeated the words as if they were sacred. Or foreign.

"She's tired, Dad. It's the cast, I think. Anyway, I'm getting nowhere fast, at least with Phoebe. I'm about ready to throw in the towel. Hire a professional to paint the place."

"Now, son. Buck up. No one said wooing was easy." More furious chewing.

He almost laughed when his father used that word. *Wooing? Really?* Ryder struggled with a sense of failure. "I had no idea it was going to be this hard. She's sashaying around in her bikini top and a short skirt that barely covers her privates, as you would say. It's enough to make a grown man cry."

Damn. He cleared his throat. Must be exhaustion. Phoebe Hunicutt was wearing him out. This wasn't the way he liked to get exhausted with Phoebe.

Crossing his arms over the chest Ryder had inherited, his father frowned. "Ryder, you never did have any patience. If your mother mentioned popsicles, you wanted one now, not after dinner."

Stroking his chin, Ryder smiled. "Haven't had any in a long time. Banana popsicles, I mean. Well, that and things I like better than a banana popsicle." Longing twisted in his gut. Phoebe was killing him with her flimsy summer outfits.

His dad burst out laughing, which didn't help anything. Holding a finger to his own lips Ryder shushed him. "Stop it! You'll get her out here."

Stanley's eyes bulged. Ryder was afraid he might choke on his gum. "Sorry, son. I never thought I'd see you in this predicament."

"*You?* What about me? I'm spending my summer slaving away. All I get are sweet smiles at dinner right before she sends me off to brush my teeth and go to bed."

Well, that got his dad laughing again. This time Ryder chuckled along with him. Laughing was better than crying and he felt damn close.

"So what's your game plan? How are you going about this?" Oh yeah. His father would dig for details.

"Going about it?" Ryder swept a hand down his paint-stained shirt and jeans. "I'm painting."

His father nodded. "And what else? You can't just be outside every day. This has to be an inside job." Suddenly his father had switched from military man to bank robber.

Casting another glance at the back door and screen porch, Ryder gave a brief rundown. "We get up and I make the coffee."

"Yeah. Right. Go on."

"We eat…whatever. Sometimes I go out and get doughnuts." He smiled. Phoebe had really liked that.

"Good, son. That's real good. Bringing a woman sweet stuff never hurts."

"Then I get to work and Phoebe does whatever she's doing. She makes me lunch. We eat on opposite sides of the table. In the kitchen or on the porch, we're across from each other." Crap. He was using his hands just like his dad.

"Across from each other?" The hand movements continued when his dad sketched a bridge in the air.

"Do I need to draw a map?" Ryder exploded. "Look, it's better than me eating out here alone under a tree with the mosquitos."

"Ryder, you have to *engage* that girl." More frantic hand movements. "Can't you sit next to her?"

His father didn't understand. "You think I have a choice? Frankly, I think she's getting bored. Phoebe says she doesn't want to go into her salon. And I sure don't want her there all day. That would not be in my favor to have her laughing it up with the girls."

The grin fading, his dad got serious fast. "A group of women in a hairstyle salon. Now that's trouble." More chewing of the gum.

"Tell me about it. After lunch, it's back to work for me and she takes a nap." He rolled his eyes. That part killed him. He remembered all too well how cuddly Phoebe could be when she woke up from a nap. "Alone."

Hand to his chin, Stanley considered that. "Poor girl. A cast is a heavy thing to lug around."

"So are blue balls," Ryder mumbled.

Cupping a hand to his ear, Stanley said, "What was that?"

"Nothing." His mother had been gone a long time. How had his father coped after her death? Ryder had been thirteen when his mom died. He didn't remember his father ever dating, even though a lot of casseroles had come through the door. But his folks had the perfect marriage. His father probably figured no one could top that.

"What about dinner? You're not letting her cook or anything like that?"

He gave his dad a stern look. "Did you just meet me today?

Phoebe never liked to cook, remember? It's not her thing. Usually I grab something from Whistle Stop or the Roadhouse."

That pursing of the lips usually meant his father's wheels were turning. "What about fixing a romantic dinner? Candlelight. A little wine, a little music."

"Isn't that going overboard, Dad?"

The comment won Ryder a sharp poke to his chest. "That's one of your problems. You can never see past your nose. Women like to be romanced. Don't forget, you're..."

"Wooing her. Right." Ryder glanced at his watch. "I should get back to work."

His father wasn't leaving. "Wooing. That is your mission. And don't forget it."

"Oh, Dad. Get real. I'm tired." He slapped another mosquito.

"You're spoiled," his father shot back. "That's your problem. Your mother and those two sisters of yours spoiled you."

"That's not true." But it was. His dad threw an eye lock that felt more like a headlock.

"Don't give me that. You know that's the way it was. Your mother was always picking up those smelly football jerseys you left all over the house. When she got sick, Stephanie cleaned up your room on the sly. And when it was your turn to do the dishes, Lisa subbed for you. You always used football practice to get out of work."

By this time spittle was flying from his dad's lips. Ryder stepped back. "It was a goddamned conspiracy. That's what," his father said.

Yep. Ryder would have to shower.

"Okay, they were my older sisters and they helped out." He threw out the words as if they were nothing, but that's not how it was. His big sisters had pampered him after his mother passed away. They felt sorry for him so they filled in.

His father's disgust met Ryder's despair. The two clashed like Fourth of July fireworks before fading away. Ryder was about to give up.

"You need help, son," his dad said in that matter-of-fact tone.

"You don't get it. She's treating me like a brother." His father had probably never been to one of those "girlie shows," as he called them. But if he ever did, he'd probably analyze the girls' dancing capabilities. That's how much he missed the point.

"That's because you're not wooing her." His father's frustration stretched through the summer air like taffy being pulled. "I got a plan."

The words struck fear into Ryder's heart. But man, he needed something. Anything. Listening to his dad outline the stupidest idea he'd ever heard, Ryder decided maybe his dad knew what he was doing after all. Ryder never would have thought of this. Maybe he'd been too busy on the roof.

Plans were finalized. "The end of the driveway? Around five? What if she sees you?"

But as he listened for Stanley's answer, the screen door slammed. "Stanley! Papa, I thought I heard your voice. What are you doing here?" Crutch tucked under her arm, Phoebe hopped toward them through the tall grass. Stepping out from behind the truck, Ryder tried to look as if they weren't hiding.

Of course his father melted at Phoebe's pet name for him. *Papa.* Looking at the two of them together, Ryder felt so guilty. Before the divorce, Stanley would sometimes fix Sunday dinner for them in the little house up in Bridgman, where he'd grown up. Stanley and Phoebe had been tight. Ryder rarely saw Stanley Branson get gushy. But Phoebe had made a different man of his father.

The two hugged. "Just checking to make sure Ryder's taking care of you," his dad said.

Batting her eyelashes, Phoebe purred, "He most certainly is. I got me some real good help here."

And she smiled at him over her shoulder. The distance in that smile sucker-punched him. That's about how she was treating him. To Phoebe, he was a hired hand and it was killing him. Stanley's smile froze on his face.

Taking his dad's hand, Phoebe batted her lashes at *Papa.* "Why don't you come visit me more often?"

His father shifted. "Well I always mean to, but I figure you're real busy with your hair place and all." They weren't comfortable with each other anymore. And that was all Ryder's fault.

"Guess I better get back to work now. Boss lady might get mad at me." Ryder backed away from pain he couldn't heal. He left the two of them with their heads together. Not long after that he heard the pickup truck leave.

After he'd dipped his brush in the putrid pink paint, as he called it, Ryder's mind moved right along with the brush. Of course he knew how to be romantic. Hadn't he been romantic with Phoebe for two years? Maybe not. The brush moved faster. Maybe his dad was right. Doubt bombarded him. The brush got heavy and his arm moved slower. Maybe once they got married, Ryder just fell back into his bachelor ways.

His way hadn't worked. Maybe his dad's would.

Chapter 13

"Sure was nice seeing your dad today," Phoebe said as they sat down to eat that night. She was wearing that Saugatuck cutoff shirt again. He remembered buying her blue moon ice cream that day. They took turns licking the cone, knowing damn well what they were going to do once they got back to the bed and breakfast.

"Ryder? You hear me?"

He faced her over the burgers he'd picked up at the Roadhouse. "Why don't you let me fix you a nice dinner tomorrow?"

Her face flushed. "You mean something you cook yourself? No frozen meal, not that there's anything wrong with that."

"Yeah, that's what I mean." *Sort of.*

"So, you've taken up cooking?" Phoebe batted those long lashes at him.

"I've been honing my skills as a single man." *Horse pucky,* as his dad would say.

"Hmm." She was probably thinking back to the coleslaw and beans. Her lips were pursed, plump and shiny with that stuff she used. He could hardly stand it. His tongue swiped out, imagining how her lips would taste. In the summer she used to wear lip gloss that tasted like watermelon.

"You'd do that for me?"

Head and hormones pumping, he exploded. "I'd do anything for you..."

Distrust darkened her eyes. He'd gone too far.

"I mean, of course I would," he said softly. Ryder hardly recognized himself anymore.

They stared at each other for what felt like forever. He saw the shift from total disbelief to uneasy acceptance. "That sounds real nice."

Picking up a french fry, she dangled it in front of him before swirling it through the ketchup on her plate. When had she taken up playing with her food? He wished she'd cut it out. This wasn't eating. This was food sex.

And she didn't stop. He had to endure this for the entire dinner. One french fry after another. Dipping, munching. While he gulped his burger in huge bites so he could end this disgusting show that was turning him on, she nibbled her bun. Nipped at the burger, the way she once nipped at his neck. He groaned.

She looked over, all innocence. "You feeling okay, Ryder?"

Hell no. But he nodded. "Sure thing."

"Oh, good." Phoebe went back to her nibbling. He dug in and tried to concentrate on anything but her sighs of satisfaction. He'd heard those pleased whimpers before. And they hadn't been at the kitchen table.

Well, okay. There had been that one time.

Sure. Right. And that memory took him right back where he started. This could take all night. When he finally finished eating, she wasn't even halfway through. Time to move things along.

"How about that trip to the beach tonight?"

~.~

Her full stomach brought contentment as Ryder carried Phoebe down to the beach. At least, she told herself it was the food and not his strong arms around her. Not the steady thud of his heart that she could feel in her own chest. She didn't even care if the neighbors saw them. Most of them were renters anyway. They wouldn't know this hunk was the man she'd kicked out. No hurtful gossip would circulate through Gull Harbor, and there had been plenty when they split up.

A beach blanket folded on her lap, Phoebe had her arms around his neck. No crutch tonight, which was just fine with her. She wound her arms tighter. This was just for tonight.

Just a trip to the beach.

An act of kindness, nothing more.

"Are you sure I'm not too heavy?"

"Yes, I'm sure." Ryder was so darn close. She could smell the onion from his burger. And Phoebe didn't even think she liked onions. Sucking in a deep breath, she grinned like the fool that she was.

"What are you smiling about?" Ryder fixed her with a penetrating gray gaze.

"Oh, nothing."

But he smiled too.

When they reached the top of the stairs, the sight of the beach blew her away. "Oh, Ryder, isn't this just the most beautiful thing you've ever seen?" He set her down on the wooden bench. They both took in the broad expanse of sand and the lake that stretched to Chicago.

"It is pretty, isn't it?" He almost sounded surprised. "Living over the garage, I don't get to see the beach much."

"You mean, you don't go to Silver Beach at St. Joe, or up to Saugatuck?" Okay, she was fishing and he probably knew it.

"Nope." And he swept her up again. End of conversation. The stairs were steep but Ryder negotiated them with ease. For a big guy, he was graceful. When they reached the bottom, he managed to kick off his moccasins, leaving them in the dune grass.

The beach looked deserted. A red bucket sat in the sand next to a green shovel, ready for the next day. So simple, so perfect—the scene took her breath away. Sometimes you don't realize how beautiful things are until you can't have them anymore. If not for Ryder, this could have been the summer without a beach. The man had his good points.

Hands linked, a couple strolled along the shore. They looked so comfortable together, two silhouettes merging into one against an orange sun. When the pair stopped for a lingering kiss, she had to look away.

As it fell toward the water, the sun set fire to strings of clouds. Setting her down for a second, Ryder shook out the blanket and settled it over the sand. With his help, she managed to sit down, although the cast complicated things. To get comfortable, she leaned back on her elbows. Her gauzy green dress lifted and fell with the lake breeze, and she was glad she'd brought her white cardigan. Once the sun went down, the beach got chilly fast.

As she watched the waves tumbling into shore, she realized Ryder wasn't looking at the lake. He was staring at her.

Flustered, she said, "It's so beautiful down here, right?"

"Yes, yes. You are."

"The lake, silly." She jabbed a finger toward the water.

"Oh. Right." Turning back to the horizon, he faced the spectacular sunset. His profile was caught in the ruddy glow of the setting sun. At that moment Ryder did look like a Greek god. She ran a hand over the sand. "Feel how warm the sand is from the sun." When she turned with a handful, he held out his palms. Smiling, she poured the sand into them and he held it like a present.

After letting it trickle slowly back to the beach, he dusted off his hands. "It was hot today. This sand isn't going to cool off for a while."

Concern prickled her conscience. "Is it too hot, Ryder? To be painting and all that?"

"Nope. Not at all." Breaking off a piece of dune grass, he bit down on it. Only Ryder could look rugged but playful, a piece of dune grass between his teeth.

"You're being so sweet, Ryder." And she meant it. He was.

"Aw, come on. It's nothing."

Was he blushing? "Helping me with the house isn't 'nothing.'" Maybe this was the time to weasel the truth from him. Find out what his intentions really were.

But the evening felt so peaceful. She didn't want to ruin it.

Sometimes the truth hurt. Maybe she didn't want to hear his answer. For tonight? He was a nice guy who'd brought her down to watch the sunset. No way would she ruin these moments with suspicion.

Right now? She wanted to be here. With *him*. The realization rocked her.

"What is it?" Rolling toward her, he stretched out and leaned his head on one hand.

"Huh?" She'd lost track of the conversation. What was dreamier? The sunset or this man?

Right now, nature was losing.

"You jumped," he said, still working that strand of beach grass. "You know, the way you do. Like you remembered you left the stove on or something."

They both laughed. One Easter, they were headed up to her folks' place in Escanaba for the holiday. They were almost to Petoskey when Phoebe insisted she'd left the oven on. The whole thing was crazy. She hardly ever used the oven. But the night before she'd cooked pot pies, and she couldn't remember turning it off. They headed back. Of course, the oven wasn't on. The loop back added about eight hours to the trip but they'd laughed it off.

When had Ryder become so observant? Twisting onto her side to face him wasn't easy, but she managed. Over the slope of his shoulder, Phoebe still faced the sun. Nothing would make her miss the moment when the day slipped away. "Gosh I've missed this. Thank you."

Ryder shrugged. "It's nothing. I should have thought of this myself. We never used to sit up at the house all the time."

"No we didn't. We came down here."

"That's why we bought the place, remember?" Eyes lazy, he swept the tender skin under her chin with the grass. "You loved the beach."

"And you didn't?" She swatted at the grass. "Hey, that tickles."

So he stopped. Now in the past, Ryder might have kept up the teasing. But not now. He was keeping his distance. She should feel relieved. Instead, his detachment sometimes made her crazy. Lifting a shoulder, he said, "I liked what you liked. Wanted to make you happy."

"But..." She couldn't say it. He'd made her sad. So very sad.

His silence told her he realized that. Suddenly, he pulled in like a startled turtle and stared off into the distance. Up above, gulls screeched, diving for bread an older couple had brought down. The two looked so happy. Sometimes Phoebe and Ryder had carried leftover bread down with them. His eyes followed the cute pair down the beach. Was he remembering those times together? Then his attention swung back and Ryder gave a deep sigh.

"I'm sorry, Phoebe. So damn sorry."

When had Ryder Branson ever said he was sorry about anything?

"There's no excuse for what I did, for how I hurt you. We were both so busy back then. You were opening your salon."

"I was half crazy. Got that building for next to nothing."

"And it looked like it. You had work to do."

"I was gone a lot."

"Nothing seemed right."

Thinking back, she remembered nights when she'd come home so tired. And he was exhausted too, working long hours before they hired Mick. "Guess a marriage doesn't work right when you're both too tired to talk to each other."

"Right." Truth was, after a while they were too tired to do a lot of things. Tears brimmed in her eyes. Trying to turn away so he wouldn't see, she only made it partway. This darn cast. "Only a few more minutes now," she said, brushing at her tears.

He leaned closer. "Hey, Pheebs, are you crying?"

She wanted to dig a hole and crawl into it. "No."

His hand squeezed her shoulder. "Look at me. Please."

Something in his voice made her turn. Ryder was always in control, and she'd never heard that pleading before. He edged closer and she shrank, grateful for the fading light. Phoebe didn't want him to see her like this. Didn't want him to know how badly he'd hurt her. After all, she had her pride. No one could take that away. With a thumb, he whisked away the tear.

"If I could turn back time," he said, sounding so sad. Then he stopped. "Hey, wasn't that a song?"

She punched him. "It was and you know it was." He couldn't even be original. But that was Ryder. He wasn't polished. He wasn't perfect. Never had been. Like his dad, he was rough around the edges. Heck, rough like her own dad, if she were honest.

"Aw, Pheebs." His palm cupped her face. She sank into that warmth, as if she were coming home. Her body came alive. *More. More.* But she spotted a horrified Carolyn hovering just beyond

Ryder's shoulder. *Watch it, Phoebe. Don't you weaken.*

How could this be bad? Squeezing her eyes tight, Phoebe imagined how that hand would feel on her skin and, okay, the spots lower than her chin.

Closer, closer. But the cast pinned her in place. Her body failed to yield like warm taffy, the way it always had. No matter, Ryder kept coming. But the poor man was cautious about it, as if he were afraid she'd push him away.

How could she? She longed to touch him. Reaching out, Phoebe traced his profile with one finger. "I always liked your nose."

Somehow he managed to kiss the finger skating over his face. "That nose has been broken plenty." He closed his eyes, as if he really enjoyed her touch. "Not my best feature, I'm afraid."

"Yeah, I can understand how it got broken." But she was kidding. Football was the cause, not some bar brawl. Phoebe knew that. She'd heard the whole story of the game that left him bleeding in the locker room. Stanley had insisted that the crooked nose added character. "No matter, it's your best feature. Well, one of them, I mean."

His body heat warmed her. Ryder had always been a walking furnace. When he exhaled, she breathed him in. Let his scent fill her until her heart pounded so fast, so loud. She could swear his heartbeat quickened into the same rhythm. Flattening her hand on his chest, she checked. Yep.

He cupped one hand over hers. "What's another one of my best features?"

"Your eyes," she said, searching their gray depths. "That's easy."

He wrinkled his nose. "They're just eyes."

"They're gray suede. I want to…well, I *used* to want to wrap myself in your eyes."

"But you can't do that."

"No. No I can't." What was she saying? What were they doing? She slipped her hand out from under his.

"My mother's eyes," he said.

"You never told me that."

"Stanley's eyes are blue. I don't remember a lot of details about my mom. I hate that." The sadness in his face made her want to hug him. She fought the urge. "But I remember her eyes. They were gray."

"I'll bet she was pretty."

"Beautiful. At least, I thought so. My sisters kind of look like her."

She couldn't imagine how it would feel to grow up without a mother. "You must have missed her a lot."

"Yeah, well. Sure." Now she'd embarrassed him.

"Your eyes are great, but don't tell Stanley I said that." She socked him playfully to shake him from the dark mood she'd caused.

"What'll you give me if I keep that secret?" Leaning closer, he nuzzled her neck.

Phoebe's breath caught in her throat. The sun had set. Darkness cloaked the beach. Even the gulls had gathered in clusters for the night.

When Ryder kissed her, his lips felt familiar, yet new.

And God help her, she kissed him back. Just took leave of her senses. With a groan, she kissed him hard and wide and wet. Their tongues explored, reckless and hungry. Finally she drew back, just to breathe. "Ryder, I..." Her chest was heaving.

Ryder held her chin in the palm of his hand. May as well have been her heart. "Don't. Please. Just a kiss. Please."

So she didn't say no. Not no to the kiss. Not no when his hands wandered from her face. It felt so long since she'd been kissed or touched as if she were some precious thing.

"Watermelon," Ryder said, after a while.

"What?" she blinked up at him.

"You still wear watermelon lip stuff. I've thought about that a lot."

"You have?" The comment turned her to mush.

But when she tried to move closer, her cast brought her to her senses. And she could swear she saw Carolyn frowning at her over Ryder's shoulder. Her finger ticked at Phoebe, like *no, no, no.*

She pulled her cardigan tighter. "We should go up."

The whites of his eyes widened. "You mean…" Hope flickered.

"No, that's not what I mean, Ryder." Had she let this go too far? Carolyn was nodding in agreement. *Too far, Phoebe. Good girl. Put a stop to this now.*

"Yep, time to go back up." He got the message. Jumping up, he helped her stand.

Silly fools, they both smiled all the way back up to the cottage.

"Want to play checkers?" she asked when they reached the back door.

"Sure." And tonight? This time they actually played.

159

Chapter 14

All night the beach replayed in Phoebe's dreams. She woke up exhausted. Every time she'd tried to get comfortable, gritty sand greeted her in the sheets. Apparently she'd brought the beach back with her.

Outside Ryder was hard at work. The thump, thump of his brush on the siding shook the house. And he was singing. Something about a night shift. Phoebe smiled, picturing hip thrusts and gyrations. Ryder couldn't sing but the man sure could dance.

When she pushed a hand through her hair, her fingers came away coated with sand. That did it. Throwing back the covers, she limped down the hall to grab a black garbage bag and a roll of duct tape from the kitchen.

Back in the bathroom, she maneuvered her leg into the bag and then taped it to her thigh. Duct tape was a wonderful invention. Reaching into the shower, she turned on the water. When they were first married, Ryder had a friend install the shower over her protests. They couldn't afford it. Now she sure appreciated it.

Knowing that Ryder probably wouldn't approve, she stepped in quickly to move things along. "Yikes!" Freezing water hit her. Teeth chattering, she worked the knobs until the spray began to feel so darn good. How she'd miss a hot shower. But when the soap slid from her fingers, she groaned. "Now what?"

No way could she bend over to find it. Besides, the black bag was slipping. Maybe she'd just work on her hair. Massaging the shampoo into her scalp, she let the warm water stream over her. Cocking on eye open, she spotted Ryder's Irish Spring. He wouldn't mind, would he?

The curved green bar felt forbidden in her hands. After lathering up, she soaped the upper part of her body while her imagination went into overdrive. Oh yeah, his soap was enough to do that to her. The smell took her back to the days when they'd shower together. Just when her small bathroom began smelling orgasmic, Ryder yelled through the closed door. "What are you doing in there, Phoebe?"

Cripes. "Nothing." She slid his soap back onto the holder.

The door to the bathroom banged open and cool air chilled her. "This sure doesn't look like nothing. What if you fell?" The shower curtain was yanked back with a metallic screech. Trying to turn away, Phoebe slipped.

He caught her. "You're going to kill yourself." But Ryder didn't sound mad. Amazed, amused but not mad. Water cascaded over both of them.

Reaching behind her, Ryder twisted until the water stopped. "You sh-shouldn't be in here, Phoebe."

"Neither should you."

"I know." He helped her out until they both stood dripping on the bathmat.

"You're soaked," she told him, laughing. His wet T-shirt was molded to his body. Wet curls framed his devilish gray eyes.

"So are you."

"Don't look."

"I'm trying not to." His arms tightened around her.

"The sand was making me crazy."

"You're making me crazy." Lowering his head, he nuzzled her left ear. "You still ticklish here?"

"Yes. Is that a good thing?"

"Could be. It all depends." Eyes averted, Ryder yanked a towel from the bar so hard that the rack came off.

"Cripes, Ryder. I'm going to need a handyman."

"You already have one." He wrapped the towel around her.

"I do?" she squeaked.

"Yep. Me. And this is probably the hardest thing I've ever had to do. It's way above my pay grade. Or maybe it's below it."

Phoebe started to giggle again. "You sound confused."

"I am." His eyes went on a rampage, from her hair on down until they rested on her leg. "Duct tape?"

"Right." She felt pretty proud. "Even stays tight in water."

"So how were you going to get it off?"

Phoebe worked her bottom lip with her teeth. "I hadn't gotten that far."

"Guess it's up to me." Flipping the top down on the toilet, he said, "Sit right here while I look for something to take off that adhesive. You have very sensitive skin."

"I know." Ripping it off didn't seem like a good option.

He sniffed and smiled. "Hey, did you use my soap?"

"Yes, are you mad?"

"I'm flattered. It always turned me on when you used my soap."

"You never told me."

"Sweet Cheeks, I never told you a lot of things." His gray eyes found hers and there it was. Everything she wanted to see. *I want you. I need you. I love you.*

Of course he didn't say any of that.

Wait until she told Fernando about this.

Opening the medicine chest, Ryder studied the bottles and tubes. "What's this pink stuff?"

"Nail polish remover."

"Might just work." He grabbed some cotton balls. Ten minutes later the black bag was in the wastebasket.

She stared down at her white cast, rimmed with pink skin. "That wasn't so hard."

"It sure as hell was." It was kind of cute how he tried not to look at her.

"You're panting."

"I'm leaving."

Back in her own room, her imagination went into overdrive. The beach, the shower. Didn't matter where they were or what they were doing, she was still wildly attracted to her ex-husband. Pulling on her denim mini skirt and a Silver Beach T-shirt, she stumbled into the kitchen and slotted a mug into the coffee machine.

Grabbing her coffee, she took a sip. "Ouch!"

Her lower lip pulsed. What was that saying about being twice burned? Panicked, she looked around. Her stomach was churning so she definitely didn't want food. But energy pulsed in her body. Maybe she'd organize her kitchen. Isn't that what her mother used to do when she got stressed out?

Throwing open the cabinet doors, she started pulling glasses and plates from the shelves. How she loved her Fiesta crockery in blues and greens, plus lime. Then she turned to the spices, which she never used. This would keep her busy for a while.

When Ryder walked in for lunch around noon, he stared at the crowded counters. "What's all this?"

"I'm organizing." She pushed back a wave of hair. "This is one thing I can do standing up."

"Yeah, but you never organize stuff." Hands on those trim hips, he glanced around.

"That's the old me. The new me? Organized."

His shoulders sank. "But I liked the old you, Pheebs."

That comment got her right in the stomach and twisted.

Coming closer, he had a cautious look in his eye. "You know, the *you* from last night."

She backed up until the counter etched a ridge in her back. "Last night was a surprise. I don't think we should..."

When he put a hand gently over her mouth, she could taste the paint. It wasn't bad. "Don't, okay?" He dropped the hand.

She licked her lips. "All right, but I'm turning over a new leaf. A woman should know where to go for anything in her kitchen."

"Really?" Ryder didn't look convinced. After all, her kitchen was more a scavenger hunt than a Martha Stewart makeover.

Quietly, he set about making sandwiches, including one for her. While they ate, she planned on one of her yellow notebook pads. What did her mother used to say? The plates and glasses should always be close to the dishwasher? Or maybe that was the garbage.

After they finished lunch, she kept working, putting her piles together below each cabinet. By three o'clock she still hadn't gotten anywhere and it was naptime. But she couldn't sleep.

Lying there on the bed that afternoon and watching the fan circling lazily above didn't bring answers. Instead it brought arousing dreams that made her wish she were back on the beach. When Phoebe woke up, her face burned from what she'd been doing in her dream. And she'd enjoyed it. Patting the empty pillow next to hers, she was disappointed to find she was alone in bed. Ryder was supposed to be there with her.

Phoebe, Phoebe. Carolyn's image perched on the edge of the bed, and she was shaking her head with sad disapproval. *You have to organize more than your kitchen, girlfriend.* Okay, Carolyn was right. What Phoebe had now was a roaring relapse.

But a wonderful smell drifted down the hallway from the kitchen. A quick glance at the clock told her it was time for supper. Well, all right then. Time to freshen up. The evenings turned chilly so instead of a sundress, she pulled a extra-large T-shirt over her head. This one said Silver Beach. St. Joe, Michigan. Together, Phoebe and Ryder had visited just about every town along the Lake Michigan shore. Silver Beach in St. Joe held special memories. After dabbing mascara on her lashes, she swiped watermelon pink gloss over her lips. Then she zipped her denim miniskirt up the side. Where would she be without it?

Well, she couldn't go there. Because she knew where she'd be. Back in bed with Ryder and she couldn't let that happen. *What you need, girl, is a chastity belt.* Carolyn wouldn't let up. Maybe that's what friends are for. Metal chastity belt?

Ouch. She'd rather work at being good.

When she reached the kitchen, she came to a halt. Only Ryder Branson could look this cute in a full-length, pink polka dot apron with lime green trim.

"I had no choice, okay?" With that he lowered the top part of the apron. His pristine white T-shirt was speckled with some kind of brown sauce.

"Your efforts are appreciated," she said between giggles.

The afternoon had brought rain so Ryder had set the kitchen table, instead of the table on the porch. The man had even thought of candles and it didn't matter that they were Christmas red. Teal green cloth napkins matched the placemats.

"Wine?" He held up an empty glass.

"Sounds good. I'm not on my pain medication anymore so there won't be any problems."

"How do you feel?" He poured a ruby merlot for each of them.

"Better every day." *More confused by the minute.*

After handing her the wine, he raised his glass. Looking at that handsome face being so serious, something turned inside of her. He was trying so hard. "To you," he said but his eyes held so much more. "The prettiest girl of...all."

"To our project." And she clinked her glass to his. A shadow passed over his face as he sipped.

Now what was that about? "Should I light the candles?"

"Sure." He handed her the lighter. One flick and the candles cast an intimate glow in the small cottage. Sometimes they used to eat like this, just two of them. It could be broasted chicken from the Roadhouse or a shrimp salad from Whistle Stop, they'd take it slow, knowing where the whole evening was going to end.

She missed that. She missed him.

Thumping over to the pot, she picked up the lid and peered inside. "My, this looks and smells delicious. What is it?" She knew very well what it was.

Concentration tightened Ryder's features. "Chicken something or other." He blanked out.

"Looks and smells like chicken cacciatore to me." This had been one of Stanley's Sunday specials. Time to poke the bear. "Where did you get the recipe?"

He glanced around. "The newspaper."

"Last Sunday's newspaper?" She didn't get the daily paper, just the weekend version.

Ryder gave a nod. His nose should be a foot long by now.

Stanley was helping his son out, and his fatherly concern touched her heart. She just hoped Ryder appreciated the effort.

"Delicious," she said halfway through the meal. You can never miss with Italian food.

"Yep, it sure is." Then Ryder remembered that he'd cooked it. "Thank you."

"To...d-dinner," he said, lifting his glass for the second time.

Phoebe suspected that he'd almost said Dad.

Suppressing a giggle, she joined the toast. "To dinner." She wasn't going to grill him and spoil his efforts.

After dinner, they sat on the porch. She always loved this time of day. Everything got so still down on the beach. The children had all been put to bed, leaving a faint hush and only the sound of the waves lapping the shoreline.

"I kind of miss the bowls set around to catch the rain," she said.

"You do?" Ryder sat next to her, close enough that she could see his surprise in the gathering shadows.

"I'm teasing. Of course I'm glad you fixed the roof."

"You're always teasing me."

"No, I'm not."

"Then what was last night?" But Ryder didn't look mad. His lips tipped into a lazy grin, and she gulped. Leaning his head on one hand, he gazed at her. "I'm really tired."

"All that painting."

"All that thinking." Heaving a sigh, he ran his fingers up through those crazy curls.

"And the cooking," she added.

"Right. That too. Maybe you should go to bed."

A light flicked on in his eyes. "Are you, ah, going to bed now?"

"No, not yet." This might call for more self-restraint than she could muster. After all, she didn't want to end up at the bathroom double sink with him. "I think I'll just watch the fireflies."

His face sagged with disappointment. "Then I will too."

What? He needed sleep. "Oh, Ryder, you must be exhausted. All that painting and cooking."

Did she hear him add *wooing* to that list under his breath?

"Sure, but I'll just keep you company." The poor guy only lasted ten minutes before he was nodding off, his head bobbing while his eyes fluttered open and shut. "Ryder, go to bed," she finally whispered in his ear.

With a reluctant grin, he heaved himself up. Oh, my. She got a good glimpse of his full-bodied Greek godness. "You really are a tease. You know that, Phoebe Branson?"

"Hunicutt."

"Uh huh. Right." Bending, he brushed a kiss across her forehead. The sweetness of the gesture jolted her. He smelled of the kitchen, and for some reason that was a turn-on. She had to fight the urge to pull him down again.

But she didn't. She was being so good. This time.

That night she took her time cleaning up the kitchen. Amid the mess, she found a note scrawled in Stanley's handwriting. "350 degrees for one hour." Crumpling it up, she smiled and tossed it in the trash.

~.~

The next week passed slowly. Every day Ryder was out there painting. Because of the heat, he'd gone from jeans to shorts. The sight of his muscled legs wore on Phoebe. In the past she'd had a lot of use for them. But that wasn't happening. After that evening on the sand, he felt distant. Oh, he kept taking her down to the beach every night for the sunset, and sure, she was grateful. They sat there together, a sand pail away from each other.

No kisses. No cuddling.

Although Phoebe tried to convince herself she liked it this way, the strain wore on her. She'd be glad when this fix-up process was behind them and he was gone. But when she thought of Ryder taking off with his toolbox, she felt a whole new sense of hollow open up inside where her heart beat.

"The siding needs a second coat," he told her, coming in one day. "I'm headed over to Melvin's."

"Can I come?" She was bored silly. Her efforts to reorganize her kitchen had failed. In the end, she just jammed everything back into the cupboards.

"Of course. Okay if we use your car?" His father still had his truck, and Phoebe was glad. With the grass and weeds so long, it was starting to look like a junk yard. If she didn't watch it, the neighbors might complain.

But when they got inside the Mini Cooper and buckled up, she started to laugh.

"What?" They were backing down the driveway and he put his foot on the brake. "What's so damn funny?"

"You crammed into this car."

Looking highly offended, he took his foot off the brake, and they continued down the lane. "You thought this car was cute when I bought it for you."

That sobered her up fast. "Was one of the sweetest things you ever did for me." Sometimes she hated using the past tense with him.

The muscle jumped in his cheek, and he turned his attention to the road.

Getting out felt great. Melvin's was only a mile down the road, and they reached the paint store in no time. When they swung through the door, Melvin and Louella were the only ones in the place. Melvin looked up from a calculator and waved. "Hey, look who's come to visit, Louella."

Turning from her project, his wife smiled. Then her greeting turned to concern. "Goodness me. Whatever happened to you, Phoebe?"

"I fell off the ladder. Do you believe it?"

Louella exchanged a glance with her husband. "Well, you shouldn't have been up there anyway." Obviously curious, her attention swung to Ryder. "Haven't seen you in a while."

She'd always had a soft spot for Ryder. Maybe every woman in town did.

By that time the four of them were clustered at the register. "So what are you two up to?" Melvin asked, although Phoebe thought she saw Louella give him a poke.

"Just getting more paint for the house," Ryder said in a matter-of-fact voice. She was proud of him.

While Ryder dealt with Melvin, Phoebe made her way over to Louella's work area. "What are you working on?"

"A table. I've always thought our supper table needed a little oomph, if you know what I mean. It never had much character."

"Louella, this looks beautiful." The table had been painted a pale blue base. Green tendrils decorated the edges with brilliant deep blue morning glories blooming among the vines and down the legs. "I love it. Wish my table could look like this."

She'd found the table for the porch at Harbert's Antiques. The only stylish thing about it were the legs that arched gently to the floor.

"You seem like a creative girl, Phoebe. Why don't you paint the table?"

"Well, maybe. After all I did start the painting project, well, before I broke my leg. Might be nice to have something to do while Ryder works outside. I've been bored but I don't want to go into the shop." No way could she endure the frank curiosity of her employees and customers. Everyone in the darn town probably knew Ryder was working at the cottage. There would be no end to their ribbing, especially if they found out he was staying with her too.

"Easy peasy. Ryder could just set you up with a stool. First you put down the base." As Louella took her through the steps, Phoebe's confidence grew. She'd taken art class in high school and had done well. By the time Ryder was lugging four more gallons of paint to the car, Louella had talked Phoebe into sky blue paint, along with some pints of green and sand beige. She was going to do the lakeshore. Picture all the places she loved.

"And I want some red paint too," she told Melvin. "Just a small can for red buckets."

"Let me help you," Ryder said, taking the brushes from her. "You look like a woman with a plan."

"Wait until you see."

Ryder's phone pinged. Another blasted text message, and she turned away. Ryder tapped on his phone screen while she stood there silently, feeling something die inside. So what happened with him on the beach that night didn't mean anything? He hustled her into the car. She was quiet all the way home.

"You feeling okay?" Ryder asked when they reached Lake Shore Drive. "You're being mighty quiet."

"Oh, I'm fine. Just tired, that's all."

"Maybe you shouldn't be taking on this project."

Now he was giving her advice? "I guess I'll be the judge of that."

They didn't speak the rest of the day and she felt miserable.

The next day Phoebe spread newspapers all over the porch. In two shakes Ryder had the paint can open and had taken sandpaper to the table. Overnight, the tension between them had eased. So silly. Working together felt a little uncomfortable at times but right.

Chapter 15

The brightest spot on Phoebe's calendar was the Fourth of July parade. Even though Ryder had taken her to visit the salon a couple of times, people asked too many questions. One look at him and they didn't want to know how she was. They wanted to know what she was doing with Ryder. Especially Jen, since her assistant had been the one who saw Ryder with Trixie Tatum that night.

The Fourth of July dawned sunny and warm, without being too hot. Phoebe slipped into the flag-striped top that bared her middle and the mini skirt that had become the main staple of her wardrobe. Her sparkling star earrings were the final touch, as was the glittery star glued to her right cheek.

"Don't you look nice," Ryder said when she made it out to the kitchen area. But his eyes said way more than nice. They navigated her body like a GPS, and she flushed right to her toes—not easy considering the cast. "So, you don't have the other half of that shirt?"

"Gee thanks, Ryder." Scooping the car keys off the hook next to the door, she tossed them to him. He was still scowling. "Let's hit the road."

Clutching the keys, he gave up. She could see it in his face. "Your earrings look cute."

"Got them online. One twist and they blink." She demonstrated.

He rolled his eyes. "Terrific. Like you need those to call attention to yourself."

This was getting ridiculous. "Look, you're not my father, Ryder. And you're not my husband. But you're sounding like both."

The air felt strained so tight, she could have bounced a quarter off it. A dark red stain worked its way up Ryder's neck. For a second he looked at a loss. "You're right." His shoulders dropped. "Sorry."

Apologies came hard for Ryder. His words on the beach that one night had surprised her. Still, she was drawing a line. "You look nice too," she offered. Kind of a consolation prize. The pale blue polo accented his tan and gave his eyes a dusky blue cast.

"Thanks, Pheebs." He gave her a half smile.

Okay, they were back to sounding like a couple. Time to get out of here. "Are we ready?" she asked, eager to hit the road.

Next thing she knew, she was sitting in the Mini Cooper, with Ryder sandwiched into the driver's seat—a picture that still made her giggle. Ryder had adjusted the seat to accommodate his height. The position definitely didn't look comfortable. "That's it. I'm having my truck driven down here next week."

"Probably a good idea."

More of his stuff around. But she didn't want to make a fuss. Phoebe was getting used to having Ryder and his belongings around, and it felt way too good.

When they reached town, Ryder found a parking spot on a side street near the library. "You think you can walk this far?"

"Sure, no problem." No way was she letting this cast get her down. Although she told herself that every day, the weight and clumsiness took a toll. By nighttime she could hardly drag herself to bed. Then she'd lie awake, listening for Ryder in the bedroom above her. Every foot fall sent a different message. Was he tired? Did he regret coming? Ridiculous how much she read into that creaking above her head.

Sliding out of the Mini Cooper, Ryder came around to open her door. "Phoebe?"

When she jerked, her earrings danced against her neck. "Sorry. Daydreaming, I guess." Helping her from the car, he handed her the crutch. The doctor said that soon she'd be in a walking cast and she couldn't wait.

Physically, she felt a whole lot better and had to admit those afternoon naps had helped. Since she started on her table, she hated to take naps. The painting kept her excited, not that her project was turning out that great. Sometimes she wished she'd never started it. Phoebe was still working on getting the base coat smooth. Ryder had found a stool for her that was just the right height.

The way he fussed about her touched her heart. Still the texts kept pinging. He was being very secretive and that made her suspicious.

People were lined up along Whitaker Street. Once they saw her crutch, folks stepped aside.

"Look, Ryder. There's Kate!" Phoebe waved so hard, she

almost lost her crutch. Being with other people would be such a relief.

Cole steered Kate through the crowd as if he had precious cargo onboard. His daughter Natalie came close behind with Priscilla, the Great Dane, holding up the rear. The huge dog's tail whipped back and forth, clearing the area.

"Guess you have your own parade," Phoebe said as Kate drew closer and bent to give her a hug. The guys exchanged a quick handshake. She wondered what Kate had told Cole about their situation. "You look as if you might deliver any second now," Phoebe said.

"Nope. Still have a ways to go." Kate pressed a hand into her back. "All I want to do is sit on the beach. How are you feeling?"

"Fine, just fine."

Behind them, the two men got into a conversation about the future of Gull Harbor. That was a main focus of Kate's new husband, since he was the city planner.

"Natalie, did you bring a bag for your candy?" Phoebe asked. The wrapped candy was a parade tradition. Everyone on the floats tossed candy to the crowd while the children scrambled to pick it up.

"Sure did. But dad says I can only have two pieces a day." Natalie rolled her eyes. "Do you believe it?"

Phoebe exchanged a look with Kate. "He's only trying to protect your teeth, Natalie. You don't want to end up with cavities like me. Not unless you like going to the dentist."

When Natalie made a face, Kate gave Phoebe a thumbs up.

Seeing Cole and Ryder deep in conversation, Phoebe felt a wave of contentment. Wouldn't it be nice if this was her life? Being part of the community with a man at her side? Idle dreams and she jerked herself back to the excited crowd dressed in red, white and blue.

Just as the band began to play, Diana and Will showed up with Maisy and Will's parents trailing behind. Dressed in black with that green streak in her hair, Maisy was a stark contrast to the rest of the townspeople today. Poor Diana, trying to cope with the rebellious teen. But if her step-niece bothered her, Diana never showed it. Eyes sparkling, she greeted everyone, introducing Maisy and Will's parents. Of course she looked gorgeous in a long flowing skirt, the kind she sold in Hippy Chick. Will's parents looked thrilled to be there, taking everything in.

Raising her brows, Diana glanced over at Ryder and then circled back to give Phoebe a questioning glance. But Phoebe gave her a slight shake of the head. No way did she want her friends to think that anything was going on. The questions would be unbearable.

Besides, nothing was happening. Ryder had become distant, well, except for the checker games. They both liked to win, so the games became heated. And that's when they were fun.

The blare of brass instruments halted her wandering mind. The high school band led the parade, their glittering hats sparkling in the sun. As they marched, they swung their shiny instruments in time to the music. If only Carolyn could see this. Taking her phone from her shoulder bag, she snapped some pictures. Last summer Phoebe had come to the parade with Carolyn. An English teacher, she knew the students in the band and shouted encouragement as the kids strutted past. Clearly they adored her.

But this summer? Carolyn was in Santa Fe. And Phoebe couldn't wait to hear more about it. Of course, Carolyn would want a report about Phoebe's own situation, and she didn't have one. Sunglasses in place, Ryder watched the parade. But he must have felt her eyes on him and he bent his head. "Everything good?"

"Fine, just fine."

"Here, lean on me. You shouldn't be standing like this." And he pulled her gently against his body. At first she stiffened but why not? Phoebe let her weight sag onto Ryder. Once she got close to his warmth, she had to sling one arm around his waist. Just for support of course.

Her loneliness gradually was banished by the sunny day and the circle of friends.

As the first float from the Gull Harbor Community Services came past, the crowd erupted into cheers. Kate waved to her sister Mercedes, perched on the float in all her blonde beauty. She tossed candy from a big blue basket, her smile brilliant. "Thank goodness, I'm pregnant," Kate told Phoebe. "Otherwise it would be me up on that float." The two sisters worked together in the Gull Harbor public relations department.

Just about every business in town took part in the parade. Crepe paper streamers floated in the breeze while the people on the floats waved and tossed candy.

"Butterscotch balls," she cried, spying her favorites. "Oh, I wish I could have some."

"Stay here." With that Ryder dove into the crowd, returning

with three cellophane wrapped balls.

Balancing on her one leg, she took them. "You are so sweet."

Pulling her against him, Ryder smiled. "And you are such a little girl sometimes."

Candy bulging in one cheek, she pouted. "Am not."

"Hey, I mean that in a good way." He tousled her hair. "That's why I love—"

"What?" Lifting her head, she barely had breath for that one word. But his smile faded, and she was left with hard candy. For now, that would have to do.

Ryder Branson had never been a guy to toss the L word around. Oh, he was great at flirting. Generous with compliments. But *I love you*? That took work.

And thought. And feeling.

Besides, in their situation right now, she'd never believe him. No, that comment had come from some deep place in their past.

Still, she didn't peel away from Ryder's body. "The candy okay?" he asked a couple seconds later. A nod was all she could manage.

Across the street Sarah stood along the curb next to her mother. The two women kept a tight eye on Nathan and Justin as they snatched up the candy. This day must be sad for Sarah, now a young widow.

Ryder squeezed her shoulder. "Hey, you doing all right?"

"Sure. I'm fine."

"Good." He tugged her closer.

She knew every hollow and ridge of this man's body. And

despite their weird situation, she wanted him in the worst way. Phoebe moved restlessly.

"Anything wrong?" Ryder asked.

"Nothing. Everything's good."

"Glad to hear it." He kissed the top of her head.

Just like that. The way he had in the past.

Kate caught the gesture and raised her brows. Phoebe turned her attention back to the parade while her heart galloped inside.

After the restaurants came the politicians from the towns along Red Arrow Highway. More candy spiraled through the air. Parents watched carefully to make sure the children didn't get too close to the floats.

Parents and kids. Sun hot on her shoulders, Phoebe felt an icy hand squeeze her heart. When she married Ryder, they'd agreed to wait to have a family. Sometimes she regretted that. Would it have made any difference? They both wanted children, just not then. Phoebe had been an only child, and she'd enjoyed being the total focus of her parents' lives. Maybe she felt the same about Ryder back then. She wanted to enjoy their time together, and he was in no hurry either.

Comfortable resting against his strong body, she felt like warm taffy. If only their lives could just twine together, the way they were before. If only Trixie hadn't happened. But it had. *She* had.

Did Ryder still want a boisterous family? She had no clue. Once upon a time, they'd talked about having a slew of kids. Ryder seemed to expect that.

Just not now. Then not now became never.

~.~

Ryder studied Phoebe while she watched the parade. The sun was shining and it felt so good to have her tucked under his arm. But she was in a funny mood today. Smiling one minute and then giving him a hard time the next. Right now? She'd fallen into a funk. Watching her expression darken, he gave her a little squeeze. "What is it?"

"Nothing." She ran a hand down her cute little flag shirt. Drove him crazy—the shirt and the woman. "Just having fun looking at all the kids."

"Right. Wait until their family gets those dental bills."

"Spoilsport." Phoebe sounded pissed off. Was she tired of having him around? Maybe Stanley's wooing idea wasn't going to work. Damn.

Ryder could hardly look at Phoebe in that outfit without wanting her. More than one guy had given her the eye. Ryder fixed them with his icy stare, the kind of look that made his dad laugh. The guys backed off.

At least Cole had been decent to him, talking about the development of Gull Harbor. How much did her friends know, and what did they think of him? Ryder wasn't one to care about other people's opinions. But when it came to Phoebe? Yes, he wanted to be seen as a man who kept promises. He wanted to say, "Hey, look. I made a terrible mistake. Before then, I was a normal, good man like you."

But that was crazy. He could almost hear his dad in his head.

Buck up, boy. Ryder straightened his shoulders.

The little kids running into the street made him nervous. Children. The past washed over him, bringing back the discussions they'd had about a family. *Their* family. When they got married, Phoebe wanted to go right into parenthood. Said she was feeling like a "fertile turtle." He smiled, remembering.

But he'd held back. "Let's just put that on the back burner, okay?" Back then he had called most of the shots, and it embarrassed him now to think about it. What the heck had he been waiting for? He was twenty-eight at the time and not ready.

Back then, he felt too young. Now he felt ancient. Thirty-one with no wife or children on the horizon. He only wanted one woman, and apparently no matter how hard Ryder or his dad tried, he couldn't have her.

Ryder felt majorly messed up. Like he was playing a role but didn't know the script.

The parade passed by. The band faded into the distance, and the whole town took a deep breath. Another Fourth of July. Where would he be this time next year? He didn't even want to think about it. Uncertainty churned in his stomach. People began to wander off, some filtering into the shops and restaurants.

Phoebe waved to Sarah and her mother. "Sarah! Sarah, over here."

Seeing Sarah with two small kids and her mother was almost painful. What happened to Jamie shouldn't happen to any family. No family should be without their father. And Jamie had been one of the best. Although Ryder had grown up in Bridgman, their team played Gull Harbor in football. Jamie had been one heck of a running back. If it weren't for that land mine in Afghanistan, he'd be standing here, mustered out this summer.

The crowd had thinned and Sarah crossed the street. "Wasn't that terrific?" She always wore a smile. Both her kids clutched a bag of hard candy. But underneath those smiles, Ryder thought he saw confused sorrow. In a way, he knew how that felt. Sometimes life could get all screwed up. Suddenly you looked around and didn't know why things had turned out so badly.

Phoebe pushed away from him, and Ryder felt the loss of her sweet body.

"I'm feeling sticky," she said, pulling her top away from her curves. "You are a walking furnace."

"Trust me, only where you're concerned."

She swatted at him but looked pleased.

"Can we go to the Swirly Top for ice cream?" Natalie asked, stretching her neck to see the big cone marking the stand on the corner.

Kate's eyes circled the group. "I'm for that. Phoebe?"

"You bet." Bouncing on her crutch, Phoebe started to move into the empty street.

Hustling up behind her, Ryder took her elbow. "Someone could run into you."

Swinging forward, she tossed her head. "I'm fine."

Diana linked her arm through Phoebe's. "Besides she's got big fat mama here"—Diana pointed to Kate—"and me." So with pregnant Kate leading the way, they all headed to the Swirly Top.

Seeing the women with their heads together made his gut clench. Was it paranoid to think they were talking about him? Probably yes. Trying to relax, he fell back with the guys.

When they reached the Swirly Top, the group squeezed around two picnic tables. Prissy stretched out beneath one of them while the guys took the food orders and went inside. Then it was back into the sun for fifteen minutes of watching Phoebe lick her cone. He polished his off in three chomps. But he'd ordered a small vanilla cone. Phoebe had the full twirl of chocolate and vanilla.

"So what are you doing this summer?" Phoebe asked Maisy. Now this teenager was going to be trouble. Ryder felt that in his gut.

The girl shrugged. "Nothing."

"Oh, Maisy. That's not true. You're helping me with the store." Diana seemed upset and Ryder couldn't blame her. His eyes went to Will, who was studying the two women and looking helpless.

"Right. Folding stuff all day long."

"Hey, I need someone to weed," Phoebe said. "Volunteers welcome."

To Ryder's surprise the girl seemed to perk up. "If I come over, can I go to the beach?"

Glancing over at Ryder, Phoebe lifted her brows. He shrugged. "Your call. Not my decision."

But he didn't miss the satisfied look that swept her face. Had he just given the cottage away? Didn't matter. What did he care about that house? He cared about the woman who lived there. "Sure, we can go to the beach," he said. "Why not?"

Phoebe's smile was his reward. The conversations moved along. These were women who talked over each other, and no one seemed to finish a sentence. They were all in a book group, as he recalled. But finally Phoebe wound down.

"You feeling okay?" She was starting to look a little tired.

"Yeah, I'm fine." She brushed a wisp of hair from her face. That crazy mauve color didn't bother him anymore. But the hair was only one sign that Phoebe had changed.

She wasn't the carefree, naive girl he'd run into at the Rusty Nail one summer night three years ago. That girl had been crazy about him. Now Phoebe had her life together. She had a circle of friends here in Gull Harbor. Oh, he might have been the drawing card when she moved down here. But today he could clearly see that she'd made a life for herself. She might not have any use for him.

The thought terrified him.

Chapter 16

Ryder was quiet on the way back to the cottage. After the commotion of the parade and friendly conversation, the silence bothered Phoebe. In fact, it made her downright twitchy. "Did you have fun today?"

"Sure. Of course." But the words came reluctantly. "You have a great group of friends."

"Yep, I do." The book group meant everything to her. Then it hit her. "But you don't know most of them, do you? Diana, Kate, Mercedes. They're all new here."

Suddenly that one-year gap felt like the Grand Canyon between them.

"You're right. I don't know them. But they seem like good people. Nice husbands too. Cole's got a good head on his shoulders." He chewed his lower lip.

"So what's wrong?" That lip biting thing? She recognized it. Ryder had looked like this the time Stanley got the flu and couldn't shake it. Something was wrong.

Ryder tightened his hands on the steering wheel. "They seemed so settled. The other couples, I mean. Not that we're a couple." The last words came out twisted and fast.

Phoebe saw his point. Was Ryder feeling the same way she did?

That the whole world was moving along, except for her? Them?

But there was no "them." She had to keep reminding herself. "I guess they are settled. Diana and Will just got back from their honeymoon. Kate and Cole are going to have a baby." Her voice softened on the word.

"Do you ever think about that, Phoebe?" He caught her eyes in the rearview mirror.

The wonder in his voice? She'd never heard that before. "What? Do I ever think about having a baby?"

"Right. Babies." His eyes went back to the road but not before she saw the cloudy gray.

"Sure. We used to talk about it, remember? A family." For her, that's what it was. Any woman could have a baby. But a family? With all members present and accounted for? Not so easy, as she'd found out. "Of course I want a family one day. But back then, we made that decision...

"The wrong decision."

Had she heard right? "What did you just say?"

Ryder cleared his throat. "I said, I made the wrong decision. Seems like I was doing a lot of that back then. Calling the shots. Not knowing what I was doing or how it might affect you."

Who was this man? "Gee, Ryder. I never thought I'd hear you say that."

His broad shoulders shifted. "We should have talked about it more. Thought it over and looked ahead."

Maybe Phoebe should stop right here. This sure felt like unexplored territory. Did she really want to go there?

Oh, what the heck. Why not. "But then there was Trixie." She had to mention it, not knowing how long Trixie had been on the scene. Had he seen her at the Rusty Nail early in their marriage? Could that be possible? She'd never asked but now she had to know.

Ryder turned off the highway. Familiar white cottages came up along Lake Shore Road. Almost home but Phoebe didn't want this conversation to end.

"Look, I know you might not believe this," Ryder said, his jaw tight. "Trixie was never anything to me."

Was? "But she was to me. She ruined my marriage."

Hunching over the wheel, Ryder radiated pain. A sick satisfaction swept through her. And then she felt terrible. Sure, there'd been so many times she wanted to hurt Ryder. Wanted him to feel the ache that had kept her awake nights. But that was stupid. Ryder had so many good qualities. *No one is either bad or good.* Her father had taught her that. And at the end of the day, she still loved Ryder.

She loved him.

Her whole body sagged and she clutched the edge of the seat. If Phoebe still loved Ryder, she was in big trouble.

By this time they were on Lake Shore Drive. Families with arms full of inner tubes and water toys were headed for the beach, full of holiday excitement. Cutting his speed, Ryder edged around them. Then his phone rang. Glancing at the console where he always left his cell, Ryder said, "It's Stanley, Phoebe. Can you get it?"

"Sure." Snatching the phone, she put the call on speaker. "Hey

Papa, what's up?"

"Phoebe? You surprised me, girl." But Stanley sounded delighted. "I figured Ryder's voice was changing again."

Papa always loved to kid. "Nope. Your son's driving. We were at the parade." Ryder pulled into the driveway, cut the motor and reached for the phone.

"Gotta go, Stanley," Phoebe said, handing the phone over. "Here's your son."

The smile Ryder wore looked forced. "Hey, Dad. Happy Fourth." He clicked the call off speaker.

Ryder had always been careful to include his father in any holiday plans. That had been a given. The Christmases when they drove back to Escanaba? If Stanley wasn't visiting his daughters, he came with them. Today was a holiday, and Phoebe had been so busy, she hadn't even thought of Stanley. Phoebe tugged on Ryder's shirt and mouthed, "Ask him to come for supper."

Now, that did bring a smile, a real smile that reached Ryder's eyes. "Hey, Dad. We're grilling brats today. Want to come over?" Bratwurst was one thing Ryder knew how to cook. Oh, he hadn't fooled her at all with the romantic dinners. That chicken last night? Had Stanley written all over it. Who else cooked a chicken with a beer can inside?

"Of course I'm going to cook," Ryder told his father. "Don't I always?"

Yeah, sure. Phoebe smiled as Ryder chortled. Whatever Stanley was telling his son, it made him cup the phone closer. Sliding from the Mini Cooper, Ryder came round and swung her door open. He raised his brows. "Can Stanley bring anything?"

"Potato salad?"

"Phoebe says potato salad," he told his dad. "Of course you've already got it made. New potatoes and bacon, right?" *What time*, he mouthed to Phoebe, extending a hand to help her out.

"Six," she said softly as he pulled her up. Phoebe loved this interaction between son and father. She'd missed it.

"Great," he told his dad. "See you around six."

Once she had her footing, Phoebe let go of his hand. But it felt imprinted on her palm. And she liked that.

Walking slowly to the house, Phoebe got a clear view of the pink siding. She circled the cottage. Ryder had finished three of the four sides. "Things are shaping up, Ryder."

"Is that what you'd call this? Shaping up?" He wasn't looking happy about all the work he'd done.

"What? You don't like it?"

Shaking his head, he unlocked the back door. "I'm not a pink person, I guess." He pushed it open.

The cottage isn't for you. The words almost sprang from her lips.

But the truth was, after having Ryder around for awhile, it felt like theirs again. Their private place in the woods. After the trim was painted, the new flooring was laid and the leaks were all fixed, she'd be left with a house that had Ryder's stamp on it. As he tossed the key on the table, Phoebe stood there wondering. Uncertainty hung in the air, a huge question mark. Since the night on the beach, they'd treated each other with care. Avoiding all physical contact. She missed it.

"Hungry?" Ryder asked, swinging the refrigerator open.

"Starving."

Pulling out lunch meat, he began to make her a sandwich.

The homey action thickened her throat. Her accident had brought him back, a changed man. Phoebe saw that more every day. He wasn't the guy with the slight swagger in his walk. Oh, he still exuded confidence. No change there. But in the past, Ryder sometimes took that over the top. Voice a little louder. Gestures almost grand. Not anymore.

He pushed the plate with a perfect ham sandwich toward her. "What's up, Phoebe? You look dazed. Feeling all right?"

"Huh? Well, I..." Words swirled in her mind. She wanted to be careful. "You've been real sweet to me, Ryder. Don't know what I would have done without you. You know, my leg and everything."

Reaching for the mustard, he gave her a look of disbelief. "I was glad to do it, Phoebe. You know that. Thank God I stopped by that day."

"No, I don't know that. Just like I don't know why you aren't with some other woman today." There the question was out.

Setting the knife down, he scowled. "I don't have a girlfriend, Phoebe."

Could she believe him? "You don't? What about Trixie?" She searched his gray eyes. All she saw was pain.

"She was history before we even got the divorce. I told you that." Impatience frayed his words.

"Did you?" She thought back. He'd called, emailed and texted. She hadn't read or listened to any of it. Like a lot of their relationship, there hadn't been much talking. After Jen told her she'd seen Ryder at the Rusty Nail with Trixie being very cozy, Phoebe kicked him out.

With a rude snort, he squirted mustard onto the rye bread. Then it was time for the mayo. "You weren't listening to anything back then. And I don't blame you." His aim shifted and a stream of mayo splashed onto the table.

"Oh, Ryder."

"*Oh, Ryder.* What? Yes, I took the flirting further with Trixie than I should have. I won't deny that. Maybe I was just trying to prove something to myself. But it didn't take me long to realize I'd made a huge mistake." Turning, he flung his arms open. Pain etched his face. Ryder Branson looked helpless.

Coasting her hands up his arms, she rested them on his shoulders. The warmth of his body drew her closer. "I'm sorry. I just couldn't handle it back then. And I was so confused. So hurt. I didn't know what was the truth and what wasn't."

His arms went around her. "Phoebe, I own that failure. I let you down big time, idiot that I was."

"Yes, but I didn't want to talk about it."

Ryder lifted a brow. "You sure didn't. And that was a first."

"Oh, Ryder." But her pat became a caress. She couldn't help it. Suddenly her hand had a mind of its own.

"What?" He tipped his head.

"Maybe I was an idiot, after you were an idiot." How amazing that she could laugh about it.

"Look, you were right to get angry. I never blamed you for

that."

"I wouldn't talk to you." Her voice trembled just remembering those days. "I was too hurt."

"Oh, Pheebs." Lips twisting, Ryder rocked her in his arms. "I hate the fact that I hurt you. You should have shot me."

"You know I don't know how to use a weapon," she murmured.

He gave an earthy chuckle. "Oh, yes you do." Turning her palm up, he kissed the pulse point of her wrist. Heat surged through her body. *I'm going to fall.* But when her body tipped forward, he was there. Steady. Strong.

"Look at me, Phoebe." Heat rolled off Ryder in waves. His eyes were glowing coals. "Now do you believe me?"

Scorched by his eyes, she said, "Yes."

The word sealed it. His lips claimed her. Overhead the fan slowly circled while one kiss turned into another. They needed a higher speed. The blades weren't even touching the rising temperature in the room.

"Baby, baby," she whispered, tamping down any doubts in her mind. "How I want to believe you."

"Let me prove it."

Their kisses soothed and stoked her at the same time. Fingers snarled in his curls, she cupped his head in both hands. "Oh, Ryder, I've missed you so."

"Sweet Cheeks, you don't even know." His lips burned through doubts like tissue.

They healed a painful past with scorching kisses and warm

caresses. They both wanted to forget and forgive. Of course she forgave him. Nothing else was possible. Not for her. When he peeled off her top, she offered no coy resistance. Why pretend? Stumbling back to the bedroom, she swallowed each moan with a kiss. Hard to tell whose. Her cast scraped the wall and she winced.

"Sorry, babe." Ryder hoisted her in his arms.

He could make her feel weightless. Help her forget the cast and any discomfort. None of that mattered. Lunch was forgotten. She wanted something far more satisfying than food.

When they reached her white metal bed in the half-pink room, he hesitated. Her heart clutched. "What, Ryder? What is it?"

His chest heaved under hers. "Phoebe, are you sure?"

"Don't stop," she begged him. "Please don't stop now."

So he didn't. The rasp of her skirt zipper promised release. The air cooled her skin but heated her heart. Outside the open window, crickets sang their mating song. *Missed you. Missed you. Missed you.* Her heart matched the rhythm.

"I love you, Phoebe. You know that, right?"

"I, I think so."

The look he leveled at Phoebe pierced her soul. "No, 'I think so,' Pheebs. Not now."

Indecision burned away. But she wasn't ready to say the words she never could take back. The simple phrase that might make her feel like a fool. "I want this."

Ryder's jaw shifted. He didn't look happy. "That's good enough...for now."

By the time they tumbled onto the bed, they'd reached an

unspoken arrangement. They wouldn't think about it. But while her body sent one message, her mind held a question. "I thought you wanted to sell my house," she whispered just when they were getting to the good part.

"*Our* house," he whispered, while he let her know he meant business. No hesitation at all about what he was doing. Ryder had always been thorough.

"Our house?" She hesitated.

"Not now. Please? Not now."

"Okay." When she fumbled with his T-shirt, he ripped it off. God he was gorgeous. All muscle. All man.

While Ryder tapped into all her secret places, Phoebe's thoughts flowed into the endless length of pleasure only he could bring. A beach without end, undulating under bare feet, just waiting for their footprints. "Oh, Ryder, please."

"Yes, sweetheart. Am I going too fast?"

"Faster." He was healing their past and opening the way to a future. In the process he made her feel precious.

Maybe I watch too many movies.

She'd have to bring that question up with Fernando.

~.~

"Pink." Ryder stared over at the damn wall. What did he care? Shifting to one side, he smiled. The half-finished room was so Phoebe. That was all that counted.

"Too girly for you?" With a cute smile, she ran a fingertip down his chest. Every nerve in his body perked up.

"Trust me. You could never be too girly."

"I've gained weight." Even her petulant pout turned him on.

"In all the right places. I like you just the way you are." He skimmed her soft shoulder, followed the line over her ribs before swirling back to cup her curves. "Your leg feeling okay?"

"Don't worry about it. This has been great pain relief." She ran a palm down his cheek stubble with such a light hand, it tickled.

"I won't argue that." Ryder grinned. "So you're feeling fine?"

"Want me to prove it?" she whispered.

"Absolutely. Let's put it to the test."

Chapter 17

Easing up from the bed so he wouldn't bother Phoebe, Ryder pulled on his jeans. She lay curled up like a kitten. Her cast looked uncomfortable but they'd managed. What an afternoon. Did it mean anything at all? He wouldn't overthink this. The light touched her body just so, and the fan feathered a strand of hair across her cheek. When he brushed it aside, she fumbled for his hand. "Ryder?"

"Right here, babe."

Opening her eyes, she smiled and stretched invitingly.

Then he saw the clock. "Whoa, it's almost five, Pheebs."

"What?" She struggled to sit up. "When will your dad be here?"

"Not for a while. I'm going to take a shower." He hated to tear himself away but one more kiss and he did. While he soaped up under the hot shower, Ryder tried to quiet his mind. The stuff Phoebe said had gotten him riled again. Trixie was in the past. How could Phoebe think she was still in the picture? That floored him. But he'd hardly seen his ex-wife over the past year. How would she know that he spent evenings at the Rusty Nail playing darts with the guys in the back room?

Bending his head under the hot stream of water, he closed his eyes while the afternoon rolled over him. No woman could match

Phoebe. Not for sweetness. Not for passion. But they didn't have time for that kind of thinking. Turning off the water, he stepped out. As he dried himself with one of her pink towels, he smiled. Ryder Branson with a pink towel. He liked it. Rubbing a circle in the steamed up mirror, he ran one hand over his chin and grabbed his razor. But Phoebe liked the scruff, just as he liked her soft palm on his chin. Ryder tucked the razor back in his kit.

One peek into the bedroom reassured him. Phoebe had fallen back to sleep. A contented smile lifted her lips. One glance at her body brought a quick reaction from his own. Time to think of Lake Michigan in the winter.

Ice floes. He had to picture ice floes as he headed back to the kitchen. The mess they'd left made him smile. All the sandwich making stuff was on the table. Nibbling on a slice of turkey, he cleaned up. Then he pulled out the brats for the barbecue.

"Looks like you've been busy." Her voice came soft from behind him, and he turned.

One arm up and curled around her head, Phoebe leaned into the door frame. The only thing covering her curves was his discarded shirt. And it wasn't very long. The cast was a weird turn-on. She could make a burlap bag look sexy.

"My dad will be here soon, Pheebs." The words came out scratchy and dry.

"Good thing. Can't wait to see him." She looked so pleased with herself, her crazy hair upended and her eyes green pools of pleasure.

"Don't be naughty now, please." He'd never been good at self-control. Not when it came to her. "We don't have time…"

"…to be naughty?" Her lips curved over the words.

He was a goner. Sliding the pack of brats onto the counter, he gripped a chair with both hands and hung on.

But she backed away with a laugh and a wave. "I'm getting dressed. Don't worry. I won't embarrass you."

Whew. With a sigh of relief, he grabbed some plates and silverware and took them out to the porch. He sure hoped his dad didn't stay long tonight.

~.~

By the time Stanley rang the bell, Phoebe was back in her red, white and blue top and that mini skirt. This afternoon had left her mellow but achy in a good way. Ryder. How could she ever think she'd gotten over him? "I'll get the door."

There stood Stanley, freshly scrubbed with a big bowl in his hands. Leaning toward him, she kissed his cheek. "You taste like Brylcream. I'd take that potato salad, but I'm still learning to balance on this darn cast. Can you put that in the frig?"

"Not a problem." Easing around her, Stanley headed for the refrigerator and tucked the bowl inside. "Be right back. I've got one more thing back in the truck."

Taking her glass of lemonade outside to join Ryder at the grill, she watched Stanley haul in what looked like guacamole. Leave it to her former father-in-law to come prepared. "One of my favorites," she called out. "Can you put it on the screened porch? I have chips."

"Sure thing." Hoisting the bowl, he scurried inside.

"Your dad is something." Her eyes followed Stanley into the house. That man never changed, and it felt good to have him here today. Right. It felt right.

When Ryder came up behind her, she felt the nudge of his shoulder. A wave of heat washed over her. His lips tickled her neck. "Guess I better take care of business." He went back to the grill. Phoebe rubbed her tingling neck.

Stanley reappeared and circled the cottage, studying the paint job. Phoebe ambled over. Ryder followed, and she could feel his tension. "So what do you think, Dad?"

Lifting a brow, Stanley turned to look at her and then his son. "Interesting."

Now when Papa used that word, he didn't want to say what he really thought. Phoebe knew that much.

"Okay, *I* wanted the pink." She didn't want Stanley to think this had been Ryder's choice.

Clapping one hand over his mouth, Stanley tried to hide a grin. His attention swung to Ryder. "Two-coat job, right?"

"At least."

Phoebe bristled. "Well, it's not my fault that the stupid house was brown in the first place. It needed some perking up. Do you like the roof? Ryder did that himself."

Stanley nodded his approval. "Looks fine, crisp and clean. The color...?" His voice lifted and hung.

Phoebe could hear Ryder suck in a breath. "...is unusual." He finished his father's thought and Phoebe chuckled.

"How about a beer, Dad?" As if he wanted to leave the scene of the crime, Ryder headed into the house. Phoebe followed along behind. Truth was, she was feeling a little sleepy. Content but sleepy. She'd forgotten how much energy making love could take. Heck, she'd probably worked off a couple pounds this afternoon. Once inside, she tried to get a bowl off a top shelf for the chips.

"Let me do that, sweetheart." Ryder's comment nearly toppled her.

Her back to Stanley, she couldn't see his shocked smile. But she sure felt it. Phoebe gave Ryder a little shake of her head. What did the afternoon mean? She needed to know the answer to that before they started telling the world.

Can you trust him again?

The question rippled through her stomach in a sickening wave. She had no answer. What about the next girl that caught Ryder's eye? And the one after that? And even if he wasn't the one looking, the man was eye candy. She'd seen the women checking him out at the parade. Would he respond when women hit on him?

When she glanced up, Stanley had taken his beer out onto the porch, and Ryder was studying her. "What's wrong?"

"Nothing. Why would you say that?" Taking the bowl from him, she set it on the table and struggled to open the bag of taco chips.

"Here. I'll do that." Whisking the bag from her arms, he never dropped his gaze.

"It's just that we don't know where this is going and I..."

The bag split in his hands. Chips flew everywhere. Ryder didn't even seem to notice. "Maybe you don't know where this is going. But I sure as hell do. Go with your gut feelings, Phoebe. Aren't we good together?"

"Yes, yes we are." They'd caught Stanley's attention. "Not now, okay?" she said in a small voice. "Let's clean up this mess."

Stooping, he scooped up some chips. "Do you have another bag of these?"

"No. Wish I did." When was the last time she'd cleaned that floor?

"No problem. We'll never notice." Frowning, he kept heaping them into the basket.

Out on the porch Stanley had started humming, looking out at the trees. As if he hadn't heard them. As if this little scene didn't bother him.

Pivoting on her cast she thumped out onto the porch. Ryder followed with the bowl and then went back inside for the beer. "I'm going to get busy with the grill," he said, avoiding her eyes.

"Fine, son. I'll keep Phoebe busy."

"I'll just bet." But Ryder smiled, as if he liked seeing them together. Then he left. Watching him go, Phoebe knew they still had so much to settle.

"How was the parade?" Stanley asked.

"Fun. We saw a lot of our...my friends." Scooping up some guacamole, she wanted to confide in Stanley. She really did. Her head was spinning from that kitchen conversation with Ryder, and a sip of beer didn't help a bit.

"Beautiful day, isn't it?" She flopped into the chair so hard her tailbone ached. That was all she needed. A broken leg and a broken tailbone.

"If you say so." Papa reached for the dip.

Birds flitted through the trees. Laughter drifted up from the beach below. This was a perfect day. Leaning over as far as she could, she took a big scoop of guacamole and just stared at it. No way could she eat anything, so she laid the chip on a napkin.

"Have you talked to Lisa or Stephanie today?" Usually Ryder's sisters always called on holidays.

"Oh, sure. Lisa's having Cal's family over for a barbecue and Stephanie's working. Can you believe how much time that girl spends at her job?"

"From what I hear, PR is a twenty-four seven career."

"And she's good at it," Stanley said with pride. When he put his feet up on the hassock, it felt like old times. The smell of burning charcoal filled the air.

Ryder stuck his head into the porch. "I'll be right back. Can you believe I forgot to get buns?"

"I'll run into town, son." Stanley started to get up.

But Ryder held up hand "No, you visit with Phoebe. Keep her out of trouble." Ryder and Phoebe shared a look that made her blush. And it wasn't lost on her former father-in-law.

After the truck had roared off, Stanley and Phoebe sat and sipped. Off in the distance some fireworks went off. The neighborhood dogs started barking. "Darn kids," Stanley said with a shake of disapproval. "Can't be satisfied with the public fireworks. Every idiot has to go out and buy his own. Drives the dogs crazy."

"I guess." When Ryder was with her, everything felt fine. But when he left? Doubts poked her with hot fingers. How could she live like this, getting nervous every time he was out of sight?

"You're sure looking serious, Phoebe. Anything wrong?" Leave it to Stanley to get right down to business.

"I don't know, Papa." She circled the lip of her beer bottle with a finger.

"Looks like you and Ryder are getting along just fine." Hope shone in Stanley's eyes.

"We are. And that's the problem." She could never hide anything from her father-in-law.

Things got quiet. "Why is getting along good a problem, Phoebe?"

"Because I don't know if I can trust him, t-that's why." The words tumbled out. Tears brimmed and dribbled down her cheeks. She couldn't help it and tried to brush them away. But she couldn't ignore the worry eating at her stomach. "Papa, I still love Ryder like crazy."

His pleased smile was something to see.

"But how can I trust him again?"

Stanley set his beer aside. The smile disappeared. When had he developed all those lines in his cheeks? "I think he's learned his lesson, Phoebe."

"Lesson?" Phoebe threw up her hands. "Is life school, Papa? He's a grown man."

"The man hasn't been the same since he lost you," Stanley said quietly. "Hate to say this, girl, but he wasn't grown up when you two got married. And it pains me to admit that. In his late twenties and Ryder still had some learning to do. But there you have it."

"What are you talking about, Papa?"

Hands folded on his stomach, Stanley took a breath. She couldn't recall ever seeing him this serious. "Ryder was about as spoiled as anybody could be. His mama spoiled him and after she passed, well, his sisters took over. The sun rose and set on that boy."

"I'll bet he was cute growing up." She couldn't help but smile.

"He was a royal pain. I worried about that boy constantly, especially after his mother passed away. What a relief when he came into the business with me. Gradually, he was taking it over. Sure, he partied on the weekends but he never got serious with anyone, as far as I knew. Then you came along."

Phoebe cast a quick eye on the driveway. She sure hoped Ryder didn't return soon. But Clancy's was probably crowded.

Stanley continued the story that Phoebe really wanted to hear, without Ryder. "He changed. I could see it. But he couldn't quite leave the past. When a man becomes an adult, he should leave childish things behind." He grinned. "Doesn't it say that in the Bible? Just means he should recognize his responsibilities. Live up to them."

"He sure seemed like an adult to me." Phoebe smiled, remembering how confident Ryder was when he came onto her at the Rusty Nail.

Stanley made one of his weird sounds. "Right. Seemed like it because you were so young." Killed her when Stanley's smile got all trembly like it was now. "So sweet."

"Fresh from Escanaba," she murmured. "Rosie and I were traveling down the east coast of the lake that summer. Having a great time. Oh, we were wild in the Upper Peninsula. But nobody was like Ryder. Not in my neck of the woods."

"Exactly. He should have been more careful. Realized what he had with you." The way Papa said those words, Phoebe knew he'd said all this to his son, maybe more than once.

"But he was so charming. Ryder was really sweet with me, Stanley." Sickened Phoebe that she jumped to Ryder's defense. "He took care of me. Just like he's doing now."

"Yeah, but you were busy with your shop. And Ryder was spoiled. Used to having all the attention."

Was Papa saying that Phoebe's Place had helped ruin her marriage? The thought sent a chill through her heart. "But Ryder loved me having my own business. He told me so. The salon made it possible for me to move down here."

Tilting his head back, Stanley studied the tongue and groove ceiling. "You two were about as close as any couple I've seen, but stuff happens. And you got married so fast. I always wondered about that."

"Four months isn't a very long time. But I felt I'd met the man of my dreams." Her eyes blurred, remembering.

"Ryder felt the same. I know he did. But a couple has to know each other before tying the knot. And the man has to get the beans out of his shorts."

"Papa." She giggled.

"No, I mean it, Phoebe. He has to realize what he's committing to and why."

Her laughter died. "My own parents felt that way. My dad had a fit. But Ryder and I wouldn't listen."

"No, you didn't. Marriage needs preparation and tending. Sometimes we forget that." Stanley looked so sad. Their divorce had hurt him real bad. Collateral damage, wasn't that what he'd called it? Another military term.

"But I did." She was trying not to cry. "I did try to pay attention to our marriage. But I was working a lot then and so was Ryder."

When Stanley's gaze swung to her, his blue eyes had turned watery. "I'm not talking about your marriage, girl. I'm talking about my own."

She gasped. "You mean you had an affair?" Looking at Stanley, she couldn't believe he had that in him.

But Stanley shook his head. "Not me. Marietta."

The world stopped turning. "Papa? No. Ryder never told me." And that fact made her feel she had never really known her husband.

Stanley fixed her with a level stare. "Because he doesn't know. And you have to promise you'll never mention it. Right now, I don't know what's down the road for you two. I'm only telling you this because I think you need to hear it."

"It's hard to believe, Papa. Ryder always said you two had a perfect marriage."

"I thought so too. Ryder was a baby and Marietta just lost it.

Postpartum something-or-other. It's a female thing. With each baby it got harder to shake. I was busy at the garage, working long hours. Too proud to hire help and doing everything myself. Marietta needed me and I wasn't there, I guess. She lost her hope in us." His voice broke on the last word.

"For how long?" Not that it mattered.

"Until I realized what was going on between her and one of my friends."

"Some friend," she spouted.

"Yeah, Earl was a TV repairman, if you can believe it. I sent him over to the house. The set broke a lot. She told me the TV was all that she had."

Phoebe didn't know what to say. "But you had the perfect marriage," she repeated, mind in a daze.

"That's just what I'm saying, Phoebe." And with that Stanley thumped a fist on the rattan arm. "No marriage is perfect. It's like a plant." Here he waved a hand toward her pathetic wild tiger lilies growing like crazy out in the ditch. "Earl's wife Mary came to me. I closed up the shop real quick after that conversation, let me tell you. Drove home like a maniac. Threw open that door, asking her to tell me it wasn't true. Begging her."

"What did she say?"

Phoebe was ashamed of probing for details. From his painful expressions, Stanley was reliving that terrible scene. "She cried, Phoebe. Just broke down. Those tears broke my heart. We cried together and we promised each other we would always tend to our marriage. I hired Fred Myer to help me in the garage. That worked out so well from the start that I hired a couple other guys so I could keep normal hours. Have a weekend now and then to take Marietta and the kids to Silver Beach. Funny thing was, that's when my business took off. Started to grow." His grin was back. Phoebe exhaled.

"But how could you trust her after that?" she whispered.

Silence ballooned on the porch, sucking all the air from her chest until Stanley finally said, "It takes time, Phoebe. I thought I knew Marietta. Knew the woman I'd married. But I'd made some promises to her too. And I don't think I kept 'em. No siree. I took her for granted, and she had her hands full with our family and all."

Turning Papa's words over in her mind, Phoebe wondered if she had that kind of hope, that trust. And if not, could she build it somehow? How she wanted to trust Ryder again.

"Give him time. You have to feel your way," Papa said. "I had to leave that house every morning, trusting she was the woman I'd married. I had to picture our marriage being strong. And it was, after that. In fact, it was stronger than before. We both said that. Sure, I could have kicked her out. No one would have blamed me. But I had to own up to my piece of what had happened."

The respect she'd always held for Stanley just grew by a mile. "You must have loved her a lot."

"Oh, I loved Marietta to the moon and back. And I knew she felt that way about me. But how can you keep that alive when the person you love is gone all the time? Marriage is about love, but it's also about forgiving," he said, as if he was still learning that.

Sitting there, Phoebe felt the whole world change. "Papa, this would devastate Ryder."

"Which is why he can never know." Stanley pinned her with his needle-eyed glance.

But she waved his concern away. "I'd never tell him."

"I don't want him to think less of his mama, that's all. Life isn't perfect, Phoebe, and that goes for marriage too. Sometimes you have to fight for what you want. That takes growing up. That's what I see in my son these days. For the past two years I've watched him struggle. That was not easy. And I'm telling you that just because..."

"Yes," she said, back in her teasing mode.

"Because I'd like to quit cooking these meals every night, girl." They both laughed. Phoebe didn't have to tell him that she'd known all along that Ryder sure as heck didn't cook those suppers that magically appeared.

"I was glad to have them," she finally said, wiping her eyes.

Reaching into a pocket, Stanley pulled out a clean handkerchief and handed it over. "You're probably the only man I know who still uses one of these," Phoebe said, blotting her eyes.

"Damn shame." And he reached for his beer.

Chapter 18

This felt wrong but it sure was fun. And it tickled. "So, where did you get the blue rope?" Phoebe shifted on the bed.

Ryder shrugged. "Stanley finally brought my truck down. Mick picked him up. What's a man without his pickup?" Brow wrinkled, he got back to work. A guy painting her toes. What could be sexier? Since the Fourth, she'd had a lot to think about. Stanley's words ran on a loop in her head. But tonight? No thinking allowed. They were just a couple having some fun.

"Guys' trucks carry everything."

"Right. Kind of like your trunk but bigger." He glanced up. Understanding sparked between them and didn't that feel awesome? Her trunk was a total mess and they both knew it. When she reached in for the hair spray she might come up with sun block. Just no telling. She'd seen Ryder's. Everything had its place.

Then Ryder bent his head. The frown grew deeper. His big hands wielding that delicate brush? Phoebe tried to hold her breath so she didn't ruin this moment with giggles. No luck.

His head reared up. "What?"

"Nothing. It's just that you look real cute." Phoebe exhaled and tried to look all innocent.

Brush in midair, Ryder gave her a wicked look. The kind of

wicked she liked. "Stop looking at me like that," he said. "I won't be able to finish."

"Don't blame me. Hey, watch it! You're getting nail polish on your jeans and the sheets!" The ropes pulled on her wrists when she tried to wave a warning, so she slipped her hands free.

Ryder gave her a disgusted look. "Didn't we agree on this?"

"We did. Sorry." She tried to jam her hand back into the loop and missed, so Ryder helped her.

But his peeved look didn't change. "I thought you wanted to do this instead of checkers tonight."

"I did. I do. I'm sorry, okay?" He just had no clue how cute he looked.

"I mean, this was your idea, acting out scenes from movies. I can't believe I'm doing this." He stabbed the brush in her direction and drops flew. "And don't you dare tell anyone."

"I won't." But it was tempting. The sight of him bent over her feet with a brush turned her on. But then, watching him think about his next move in checkers also caused a rush of heat.

"Damn." Looking totally panicked, he jammed the brush back into the bottle and grabbed a tissue. Of course, the spots of bright green didn't blot up from the sheets. Guys just didn't realize that.

Ryder kept scrubbing. She'd been so surprised when he'd come up with this idea after Papa left an hour ago. They'd had a special day together. She'd been complaining about her nails, and Ryder picked up on it.

Was this the new, improved Ryder? Caution waved a warning finger in her mind. As usual, she ignored it. She needed more time in the yard with Fernando.

"You could have another career as a nail tech," she teased softly after he went back to work. "Set up shop in my salon. Boy, wouldn't the women love that?"

"No way. I'm too busy painting your house."

"*Our* house." The words came so naturally.

His head jerked up and so did his hand. Droplets flew again. Face red, he grabbed another tissue. "Sorry. How did Kevin Costner ever do this in that movie?"

She snuggled down into her bed. "Oh, they probably filmed this scene twenty times."

"Is that it? Does it take a do-over to get things right?" Suddenly they weren't talking about polishing her nails. No, they'd waded into stickier issues. "Phoebe?"

Oh, how she wanted to say yes. But that yellow caution light in her head? It was blinking. "It takes practice to apply nail polish," she finally said. How lame was that?

"Sorry." He dabbed at another spot.

"Don't worry, Ryder. I can fix that later." She could buy new sheets. Ryder? There were no replacements for him. She knew that now. Deep in her heart, so deep that it practically poked through to her backbone, she realized there'd never be another man for her. While she let that truth soak in, he kept dabbing.

"You could have made this easier by using one color," he grumbled, reaching for the second bottle. "You had to have both pink and green?"

"*Flamingo* pink and *neon* green." Phoebe wiggled the toes of her right foot—not easy with the cast. "I couldn't decide."

"Your wish is my command." Another crooked grin.

"Yeah, right." But his playful tone? It played her body like a twelve-string guitar. Trying to get comfortable, she hoped she didn't end up with rope burn. What would people think—not that she saw many people nowadays. They used drapery tassels in the movie but Phoebe didn't have anything that fancy.

"Hey, are you okay, Pheebs?" He gave her a worried glance.

She settled back on the pillows. "Perfectly fine."

But he wasn't convinced. "No, really. Are you getting any cramps from lying so still?"

"Trust me. I'm having fun." And that was the truth. This Fourth of July was turning out to be the perfect day. Family, friends and naughty fun.

Ryder went back to the task at hand, and she returned to studying him. Her ex-husband was one fine looking man. In addition to hair that just wouldn't quit, his muscles were honed through hard work. Thick lashes shaded eyes that could be warm suede one minute and winter ice the next.

Phoebe was a warm gray fan herself.

After giving the bottle of Flamingo Pink a good shake, he twisted it open. Wasn't this just the silliest thing ever? But he was so darn serious. And they were having fun. "Maybe we weren't creative enough, you know, when we were married."

"What do you mean?"

How she loved that square jaw when he cocked his head a certain way. Phoebe made a circling motion with her head. "This.

Why didn't we do stuff like this before?"

His eyes drifted over her lips. Then he leaned forward to kiss her. First just a brush of the lips, then a sweet settling. Her breath came in quick gasps when he pulled away. "Maybe we took our marriage too seriously, Phoebe."

"Is that possible?" She let her tongue salve her throbbing lips.

He sat back. "I don't have any answers." Picking up the nail polish, he gave it another shake. "Sorry, but this job demands my full attention."

"Don't you think you've done enough?"

"You're always bossing me around." Grinning, he shook the bottle with authority before opening it.

"I told your dad he could stop cooking all those meals," she said after he'd finished two toes.

"What?" His lips parted and his face flushed. "You mean, you knew?"

"Come on, Ryder. When were you ever able to fix a brisket in the slow cooker? And my favorite sugar-burned carrots would have filled the house with a yummy smell if you really cooked them here. Fess up."

Ryder looked like a little boy who'd been caught with his hand in the cookie jar. "Okay. But still, couldn't we keep that good grub going?"

Now that really got her laughing and he joined in. "Right, but I think we can handle it."

His lips pursed. "I'm almost finished with painting the house."

"You said that before. Two coats?"

He looked offended. "Of course. You know, the big toe nails take a heck of lot more polish."

"I'm talking about the house, Ryder." She brought his attention back to what mattered.

"Right. Of course I gave it two coats. Now I start on the trim, right?"

"Make it smooth now." She said teasingly.

"Do you mean the trim or your toenails?"

"Right now? My nails."

The brush held too much polish, which ended up dripping onto the sheet. Again. Now the spots were both green and pink. She didn't care if the spots didn't wash out. They'd remind her of how much fun she'd had with Ryder today.

Heaving a sigh, he looked hopeless. "You'd never know that I'm supposed to be the one in charge."

"Well you are."

"No, I'm not, Sweet Cheeks." He leveled a serious look at her. "And you know it. "

But she couldn't deal with that right now. And she was getting a knot in her calf. "Use that bottle of clear stuff." She nodded her head toward the side bureau. "That'll harden the polish so it doesn't smear when I get active."

Setting the bottle of pink polish on the side table, he smiled and leaned over her. "Just how active are we going to get?"

"Wait and see."

She was still wearing her little flag top that left her arms bare. His eyes liquid, Ryder ran his fingertips down her arms.

She shivered and then winced as pain came out of nowhere in her good leg.

"What is it?" He drew back.

"I have a cramp in my left calf. Have to work it out."

Taking her leg in his hands, he started to knead it slowly. "I didn't think were going to get active, as you call it."

The heat of his hands fixed her leg real fast. "What if this is turning me on?"

His hands stilled. "It is?"

She nodded slowly. Yeah, this was weird, but when Ryder wielded that tiny brush, she could almost feel that light touch on other parts of her body. Massaging her calf? Just the cherry on the sundae.

Bending his head to the task, he unscrewed the topcoat bottle and got to work. She loved watching the late sunlight play over his curls. Loved his lips pursed in concentration.

But her conversation with Stanley that afternoon still played in her mind. How hard that must have been for Stanley and for Marietta too. And yet they'd kept their marriage together. She'd never thought that would be possible. Now she wondered.

She wondered and she hoped.

"All done." Setting the bottle aside, he smiled.

"What about my finger nails?" She fluttered them in his direction.

The box springs squeaked as he crawled toward her on the bed. The look in his eyes? Nothing but trouble. Slipping her wrists from the loops of blue rope, she crooked her fingers. "Come here,

Ryder. You did such a good job, baby. You deserve a reward."

~.~

Ryder's life felt like he'd opened a new can of motor oil, pure and fresh. Whatever was going on with Phoebe, he wanted it forever. He knew that deep in his gut, just like he knew his name was Ryder Branson. But did Phoebe feel that way too? Sometimes it hurt to look up and find her watching him, a question in her eyes, like she wasn't sure. So he'd wait it out. He was lucky he'd gotten this far with her. Ryder had to be more than her summer fling. He wanted forever. And he was willing to wait.

Painting the trim, he took his time. The brush was smaller—at least that's what he told Phoebe. But right now, he wanted to take it slow. Their lunches together felt special and the dinners too. At first his dad had looked relieved that he didn't have to cook their meals every day. Ryder had him scouting new locations for other sites for Branson Motors farther north, toward Mackinaw. When he came home, they sat out in the yard and talked about the possibilities. But Ryder wasn't eager to make an offer. After all, he'd have all winter to build out the garage. "I'm taking things slow," he explained to his dad.

"Hm. That sounds promising," his father said, scratching the underside of his chin. "You seen anymore of those pink walls? You know. The ones in the bedroom?"

Ryder laughed so hard, he was afraid Phoebe would peek around the back screen door. "You are a sly dog," he said, bringing his voice down. "But you might be right."

"I thought so." His father's eyes lit up.

"I'd like to think that enthusiasm is for me," he said.

Hitching up his jeans, Stanley said, "Just get the job done, boy."

And right then Ryder understood. "Geesh, Dad. You love Phoebe almost as much as I do, don't you?"

Damn if his dad's eyes didn't get misty. "You bet, son. Want her back in the family. Being around Phoebe feels like old times and..." Here his voice cracked. Ryder started to sweat. He thought he would lose it right there.

"Doing the best I can," he said, meaning every word. If his father only knew how bad he wanted that to happen.

Chapter 19

As July moved along, summer evened out like a peaceful lake at sunset. Everything felt perfect. Soft lake breezes teased her hair while Phoebe worked on her table on the porch. Because of her project, they'd started having dinner at the kitchen table. Ryder had moved it in front of the open french doors. "Are you getting all creative on me?" Ryder had teased, as he spread more newspapers under her project.

"Hey, wasn't I creative before?"

Kissing the tip of her nose, he said, "Absolutely."

Glancing up into those gray eyes, Phoebe felt her knees weaken. This man could make mush of her. Just when she was trying so hard to keep her wits about her.

This was so darn hard.

She loved having Ryder around. Sure, he was doing the work but it was more than that. When she painted hearts on the legs of the table, Ryder hummed along to the radio outside. Never did the man realize he was totally off tune. He sounded happy, and that made *her* happy. She wasn't about to tell him that he couldn't carry a song in a bucket. She'd known that when she first met him at the Rusty Nail on karaoke night.

No use having him sleeping upstairs anymore. Oh, she'd held

out on that one. But it was silly although Ryder didn't try to hurry her decision. She appreciated that. No, the man just waited for her to come around. When had he learned to do that?

The days passed, each one sweeter than the day before. Even though they'd told Stanley he didn't need to stop by with food anymore, he still did. Those pots of chili that came through the door suited Phoebe just fine. What did she care if it was eighty degrees outside? This was one more meal she didn't have to cook, and neither did Ryder. She'd never be a Rachel Ray, that's for sure. Stanley might stay for a beer and then he'd scuttle off, as if Ryder and Phoebe were a good color job waiting to set, and he didn't want it to do anything to mess it up.

A few days after the Fourth, Diana called.

"Phoebe? Am I interrupting something?" A teasing lilt lifted Diana's voice. Diana, Carolyn and the rest of the girls wanted to know more about Ryder living here this summer. Phoebe wasn't sharing details.

"Nope. Are you ready to have Maisy spend some time with us?"

"I sure am." Her friend's voice had a strange echo. Diana had probably stepped into her storeroom. This must be serious. "So, what's Maisy doing?"

"She's trying on all the clothes and leaving makeup on them."

"Tell her to clean up her act." Easy for Phoebe to say.

"Oh, I can't do that. Will is turning inside out for her. Says his sister Delinda hasn't disciplined her, and he's just an uncle. Doesn't feel it's his place."

"What about Will's parents? I thought that was the program for the summer, to spend time with them."

"So did I. But Maisy doesn't want to and she's very vocal about it. Nothing shy about this girl." Diana's voice dropped even further. "She uses the word *boring* a lot when she talks about her grandmother."

"I hope Will's mother doesn't take that personally. Didn't you tell me she's thirteen?"

"Yep, going into her freshman year."

Phoebe snorted. "Oh lordy, remember those first years of high school? We were all brats."

"Maybe so. I can't remember. Right now my mind is a blur."

"You don't need this right now. After all, you're supposed to be a blissful newlywed." Phoebe felt terrible that Diana had to cope with an angry teen she'd inherited through Will. "Bring her over. She can weed."

"Really?"

"Of course. Maisy seemed open to it on the Fourth. Heaven knows, this place is a mess." Queen Anne's lace hung in tufts among the black-eyed Susans. Hollyhocks drooped along the garage. Phoebe's yard was totally out of control, like her life.

"Will tomorrow be too soon?"

Phoebe turned her attention back to the conversation. "Of course not. Can you drop her off in the morning on your way to the shop? I'd come get her but..."

"No need. No need." Diana sounded downright dithery. Man, she really was in trouble. "I'll have her there at nine forty-five tomorrow. You're a good friend, Phoebe."

"Aw. Now you're getting all syrupy sweet with me."

"Okay, enough. Have you read the book for book club next week?"

"No. Have you?"

"Not yet, and I'm having the meeting here. Maybe I can spend all my time in the kitchen that night."

"Maybe I'll be right there with you," Phoebe giggled. "We all know the book club is just an excuse to get together."

"You got that right. See you tomorrow."

When Ryder came in a few minutes later, Phoebe was fixing lunch. Clancy's had sent over a bunch of cold cuts, and Phoebe was slapping them onto the bread. Her breathing got ragged when Ryder came up behind her, turned her around and made her forget all about food. Was she imagining that the kiss held an edge of desperation? Curving into his warmth, she felt them melt together. What they had right now felt almost too comfortable. She couldn't trust it. But pulling back from the edge was so hard.

That night Ryder took her to Oink's for ice cream. Armed with double-dip strawberry and pistachio cones, they drove two blocks to the beach and found a picnic table where they could watch the boats trail into their moorings for the night. The air felt rich with summer. Every day the temperature rose higher. Phoebe could hardly lick her cone fast enough before it melted.

"So what's up?" Ryder asked when they'd finished. Facing the lake, he was leaning back on the table, elbows braced on the picnic table. "You're not saying much."

"What do you mean?" Phoebe put her sunglasses in place.

Turning, Ryder gently took them off. There was no hiding with this man. His steely gaze held her in place.

"Us. What about us?"

"What about us?"

"Hey, Sweet Cheeks," Ryder said softly, tracing a finger down her cheek. "What's next? I'm almost finished with the trim."

"It looks wonderful. You're doing...you did a great job." How could she even think? His finger awakened all kinds of sensations. But his eyes stayed so serious.

~.~

She was stalling. Ryder knew it and it made him crazy. But the commitment he wanted so desperately had to come from her. "Do you want me to..."

"Work on the kitchen linoleum," she supplied, blinking real fast. He could almost feel those lashes on his chest, the way they'd prickled last night.

Swiveling, he swung one leg over the bench of the table and faced her full on. His heart squeezed tight when she turned to study the horizon. "Phoebe, where are we going?"

A muscle jumped in her neck, that neck that drove him crazy. She'd slapped those damn glasses back in place, and he wanted to see her eyes. But maybe he didn't need to. Just then a tear dribbled from below the lower rim of her glasses and rolled down her cheek. Her chest started to heave.

"Phoebe, are you crying?" This was tearing him apart.

Wiping her cheeks quickly with the flat of one hand, she

sniffled.

"You are crying. Now don't deny it." He pulled her into his arms. "Oh, babe. Pheebs, you are everything to me. I love you. More than anything or anyone else in the world, I love you." Then he stopped. The more he said, the less it seemed to mean.

"Ryder, I love you too." Great, now she was bawling openly. A middle-aged couple passing by threw them a horrified look. Ryder wanted to become the invisible man. But he also wanted an answer first.

"So you love me...but." His finger tilted her head toward him. "So what's the but?"

She shook her head. "Just but. We should be careful."

"I thought you said you were on the pill."

"I am. That's not what I mean."

"Then what is it?" Sometimes he felt so confused.

But she wouldn't say anything.

So he'd say it for her, even though it cut like a knife. "Can you trust me again? That's the problem, isn't it?"

"Yeeeeeees." Phoebe's wail caught him by surprise. He might have clapped one hand over her mouth, but then people would think he was really messing with her.

"Phoebe, I wouldn't hurt you. I love you." But he saw the problem. Once someone has let you down, how can you believe in him again?

He was screwed. Getting back with Phoebe might never happen.

Walking back to the car, his own eyes felt damp. He was glad it was dark. Men didn't cry, not in his family at least.

~.~

Thank goodness Maisy was coming the next day. No way did Phoebe want to be alone with Ryder. She had so much to sort through. Heck, she couldn't even straighten out her cupboards. How could she ever make order out of her feelings for Ryder?

Could they start over with open hearts? Neither one of them seemed to have the answer. The reassurance she wanted? Maybe Ryder would never be able to give her that. The thought sent her into free fall.

The night of their serious talk, Phoebe could not sleep. Early the next morning, she crept out to Fernando with a cup of coffee. The lawn chair she pulled up beside him was dewy. She sat down anyway. "You got to help me."

That's what I'm here for .

"I'm all confused."

Pobrecita. Join the rest of the world.

Coffee cup in both hands, Phoebe shivered. "No, this is serious. I love this man like crazy."

That's not a problem. That's a gift.

"You think?" she turned so quickly, coffee spilled on her nightie. "Oh, darn it!" She tugged her hoodie tighter.

Life happens. Does it ever turn out like you planned? Look at me. I'm a lawn ornament.

She tried to get her mind around the first part. "So you mean, I should just go with it?"

Got it. How are you going to feel if he gives up? Goes home?

"Oh, no. Terrible." The bottom dropped out of her world. No more checkers at night. No more other fun and games. No more "Sweet Cheeks," said the way only Ryder could say it. The early morning gray shadows disappeared, and the birds began to chirp.

Hear that?

"Yeah. The birds?"

They sing every day and they don't know why.

Phoebe sat real still. "So I should sing?"

Lord no. It's enough that he tries to sing. But enjoy life. Take some chances.

Getting up, she downed the last of her coffee. "What would I do without you?"

Don't even think about it. That town dump? Basura. I don't socialize with every piece of trash, you know.

"Yes, you are picky." Chuckling, she crept back into the cottage. Everything was still. Opening the dishwasher, she began to empty it. The plates clacked together. She'd break some of her precious Fiesta dishes if she weren't careful. She'd also wake up Ryder. So she crept back to bed. Sliding into the warmth of their bed, she watched him sleep. Ryder often slept on his tummy like a little boy. His hair was messy; his sculpted lips, slightly open. Stubble accented his jawline. Asleep or awake, the man was a hunk. And he loved her. Phoebe fell back to sleep, warmed by that thought. When she woke up, he was gone. She got dressed quickly, determined to have a day without worrying.

Instead of singing along to his radio, Ryder was quiet outside.

He was razoring some of the windows, prying off small drops of paint. Ryder was always good with finishing touches. Branson Motors was known for being good at details.

But today he was quiet. Too quiet. The silence felt strange and nausea stirred in her stomach.

Their conversation at the harbor had riled up all sorts of crazy feelings. She wanted Ryder so bad. *This Ryder.* The guy who'd been working on their house the last few weeks? He was the man she wanted in her life. Someone who could be playful with her, yet sympathetic when she did dumb things like try to paint the house on an old ladder. But how could she be sure this Ryder would last forever?

If there was such a thing as a relationship contract, she wanted one. She wasn't good at taking chances. Not anymore. An idea formed in her head. Crazy, but maybe there was a way to bring her peace of mind.

Chapter 20

When Diana pulled up in her yellow Volkswagen that morning with Maisy, Phoebe made her way outside. Brushing her hair from her eyes, she hoped her crazy thoughts would stop. She didn't want to think about Ryder anymore. Her friend was a welcome distraction. The air felt hot and dry, and Phoebe fanned herself with a hand. The tall grass tickled her left leg. She'd shifted back to her denim mini skirt and a pink T-shirt. "Hey, lady!" She gave her friend a broad wave.

Diana and Maisy exploded from the yellow bug, stormy looks on their faces. What had Phoebe gotten herself into? But she kept smiling. Diana definitely needed her help. Her good friend was not a happy camper today.

"Maisy, you remember Phoebe," Diana said.

Folding her arms over a chest that would be shapely one day, the teenager grunted. "Hi."

Oh, my. "I like your hair, honey. Did Jan do that for you?"

Maisy's face lightened a little as she smoothed the green streak with nail-bitten fingers. "Yeah. She did." Phoebe wanted to hug her. Growing up, she wasn't the girl that boys would send texts to in class. She was the last to be picked for any team because she couldn't move fast enough. But her willingness to laugh at her mistakes earned her friends as she grew older.

"Well, I appreciate you coming over today to help me weed."

Maisy glanced at Phoebe's cast. "No problem. Diana said maybe I could go to the beach. I've got my suit in the car."

"Of course you can! We'll go together. You just take that suit into the kitchen."

By this time Diana was giving eye signals. Phoebe wanted a few moments alone with her friend. "What is it?" Phoebe asked when Maisy had disappeared into the house, the door whapping shut behind her.

"She's talking about going home."

"What?"

"Do you believe it? Says she wants to go back to Florida, but of course her mother's not there."

"Where is she?"

"Who knows?" Diana threw out her hands. "Either she's in Florida or out sailing around the Caribbean. Delinda's not good with details. What if Maisy just takes off one day. Runs away to find Delinda?"

"Poor thing." Phoebe couldn't imagine how that uncertainty would feel. "But why? She's only been here a month or so."

"She says it's boring. It's hot. Nothing's going on."

"And Florida's going to cure all that?"

The conversation ended when Maisy reappeared. Phoebe walked Diana to the car, but they never had a chance to say another word. Giving her friend a supportive hug, Phoebe opened the car door and Diana slid inside.

"Newlyweds should be happy," Phoebe reminded her friend.

"Right." Diana threw her a determined smile. "See you this afternoon, Maisy," she called out as she backed down the driveway. Maisy had come to stand beside Phoebe. Watching the bright yellow car disappear, the girl looked lost.

An uncomfortable silence fell over them. But Phoebe was having none of that. "Come on, Maisy. Let's see what I've got in the garage to help you." Phoebe led the way into the earthy, cool darkness. Rooting around, she pulled out a couple of gardening gloves. One was pink and the other was flowered. She waved them in the air. Not alike but still a pair. "Success! At least we have a left and a right."

"Does that hurt?" Taking the gloves, Maisy was studying the cast.

"Not unless I do something stupid, which is pretty often."

Maisy burst out laughing, a rusty cackle that sounded like it hadn't been used much lately. She was pretty when she smiled.

"You have such nice thick hair," Phoebe said reaching out. But Maisy ducked. A cold hand clutched Phoebe's heart. She drew back her hand while her mind swirled with suspicion. "Well, will you look at me? Just grabbing anybody's hair. I'm sorry."

"No, that's all right." But it wasn't. Phoebe could see that.

Picking up a plastic basket, she handed it to Maisy. "Here you go. Every weed you see, just yank it out and throw it in here." But her eyes still searched the jumbled shelves. Grabbing a green piece of foam, she handed it to Maisy. "This pad will keep your knees from hurting when you weed."

Tossing the gloves in the bucket, Maisy stood there, bucket in one hand and pad in the other. Something was missing. "A hat. You'll need a hat or you'll get sunburned. Follow me." And Phoebe headed back to the cottage.

"You don't have to fuss about me," Maisy said, bumping along behind her. "I'll be fine."

"It's no trouble at all." When they reached the back door, Phoebe took the basket and pad from Maisy's hands and placed them on the stoop. "Follow me."

Inside the sunny kitchen, Maisy glanced around as if it were on the cover of *House Beautiful*. "Cool place."

"Thanks. It's not much but I like it," Phoebe said.

"It's nice when a place looks lived in. My mom and me, well, we never live anywhere long enough to even put pictures up." Here she motioned to the vintage South Shore posters. The colorful illustrations pictured the train decades ago.

Another wave of sadness washed over Phoebe. No wonder the girl was withdrawn and difficult. She never knew what was coming her way. "Why don't you take a seat on the porch and I'll grab some hats?"

While Maisy meandered onto the side porch, Phoebe made her way back to the bedroom. One of Ryder's shirts hung on the bedpost. Coming closer, she ran a hand down the chambray fabric and lifted a sleeve. Breathing in Ryder's scent, she felt her stomach tighten. Yep, it sure smelled like him. *Warm. Sturdy. Sexy.* She couldn't go there. She let the shirt fall. Ryder was sure being quiet today, and his silence made her uneasy.

Remembering why she'd come in here, Phoebe opened her closet and grabbed a couple hats. Ryder traveled light. He'd hung some shirts in here, but they were gone. She froze.

Turning, she scanned the room. His navy duffle bag was open on a side chair. She pressed the hats to her chest. Her heart had stopped. Was she having a heart attack? Maybe. But when she pressed her hand tighter on her chest, she felt something. She was still okay, but not for long.

"Phoebe?" Maisy called from the hall, her steps approaching. "You still here?"

Oh, goodness. "Yes, honey. Sure am. Just choosing my hats. Go out to the porch. I'll be right there." Swiping at her eyes, she somehow made it back into the kitchen. She found Maisy on the porch, studying the table.

"You working on this table?"

"Y-Yes." Geez, she could hardly talk. Her heart was back with that navy bag. "It's my summer project. Pretty pathetic, right?"

"Hmm." Maisy's fingers traced the ragged hearts on the wood. Thinking back, Phoebe remembered how dreamy she'd felt that day.

Holding out the hats with shaking hands, she asked, "Which one, Maisy? The plain straw or the black with the green ribbon?"

"Oh, the black." After cramming it on her head, she went over to the mirror near the door. "What do you think? Do I look older?" Maisy turned her head to the other.

"Yeah. I guess. Do you want to be older?"

"Of course I do. Are you kidding?"

"What's the hurry?"

"I get to drive. Maybe I'll have a boyfriend." She began ticking off things that had once seemed important to Phoebe too.

"Oh Maisy, boys and cars just bring more trouble."

The girl threw Phoebe a weird look. Teenagers always thought being sixteen or so solved everything. They had no idea.

But Phoebe's mind veered away. *What to do. What to do.* Ryder was leaving.

Feeling that her lungs might just burst, Phoebe pushed open the screen door and walked into the sunshine. The day that had seemed so beautiful now felt too bright, too harsh. Like a bad movie.

Maisy trailed out behind her. "Which ones are the weeds?"

Pressing a hand to her heart, which had started to beat again, Phoebe said, "Well, I guess anything that's not a flower is a weed."

"Wow." For a second the girl looked overwhelmed and Phoebe felt terrible. The yard had been too much for her. The cottage was too much for her. Maybe Ryder was right. She should just sell it. How could she live here if he was leaving?

Just then Ryder rounded a corner and stopped when he caught sight of them.

"Ryder, you remember Maisy. Will's niece?"

His hand shot out. "Right. We met on the Fourth of July. I'm Ryder."

Suddenly shy, Maisy shook his hand. "Hi." Phoebe didn't blame her. Ryder was an eyeful. A green T-shirt clung to his torso, with a damp patch headed south in a V. And then there was that wicked pirate headband he wore. But his smile? Strung a little tight today.

He was leaving. Her heart felt like a rock inside.

"So. What are your plans?" He glanced from one to the other.

"Maisy's helping us with the yard."

"Weeding." Maisy glanced around. This was one big job.

Eyes widening, Ryder jumped right in. "Maisy, I'm here to help Phoebe this summer. But I guess I've been so wrapped up in the painting, I clean forgot the lawn." He glanced over at Phoebe like he was inviting her to chime in.

"Yeah, we just never got around to it." Her eyes met Ryder's and they tangled. His eyes roiled with heat. Afternoons spent lolling about in the pink bedroom probably spun out in both their minds like a film, the kind that made you breathe heavy.

But Maisy was here so it was back to business. "While you start with the weeds, why don't I just get that lawn mower going?" His eyes clicked to Phoebe. "You do have a lawn mower?"

"Yes. Somewhere. Probably in the garage."

Turning, Ryder sprinted toward the garage like he was escaping the scene of a crime.

Phoebe struggled to organize her thoughts. "Maybe you could start around the house. In the shade?"

"Sure thing." And Maisy was gone.

Before long the mower roared to life, and Ryder was cutting diagonal strips into the wild yard. Circling the house, Phoebe found Maisy kneeling in the shade, pulling plants from the dirt. If she got a daisy or two, she didn't seem to notice. "Doing a great job," Phoebe told her.

Then she saw it. The neat pile of supplies at the back corner of the house. The rollers and brushes, as if he were finished. And he wasn't coming back. Tears blinded her.

But Maisy was there. Phoebe couldn't fall apart right now. The girl's life had been dramatic enough without imposing Phoebe's screwed up mess on her.

Getting to her feet, Phoebe stumbled inside. Her early morning promise to Fernando took flight. The lawn mower roared as Ryder took on the long grass, strong arms vibrating a bit. She sank into a chair on the porch, unable to tear her eyes from him. She loved him wildly, more than ever and that terrified her. If this didn't work out, then what? Sure, right now Ryder was being wonderful, attentive and sweet. But what about next month and the month after that?

What if he turned to another Trixie?

She had to do something. After a thorough search of the cottage, Phoebe came up with a pad of paper and began to jot down her points. Everything she wanted Ryder to promise. If he signed this contract, maybe then she'd feel better. Maybe this awful worry eating at her would go away.

When she was finished, she tucked the pad in a drawer. Then she pried open her can of paint and dipped in her brush. She half-heartedly swiped a few hearts on the top surface. But her eyes weren't on the table, No, they were on Ryder. Just then he looked up, as if he felt her eyes on him. With a wink, he waved. Casual and cool. The man she loved.

But when her stomach growled, Phoebe tapped the top back

onto the red paint and went inside. She rinsed out the brush and left it on the ledge above the sink. Then she started to make sandwiches. By the time the motor went silent, lunch was ready. "Come and get it," she called out from the back door.

Walking toward her with that stride she'd know anywhere, Ryder held a bunch of daisies and black-eyed Susans. "Not much but kind of pretty. Courtesy of Maisy's work."

"They're beautiful." When had he ever thought to give her flowers? "I'll just put these in water. Can you call for Maisy, please?" Taking a vase from the cupboard, she filled it with water. While she was arranging the flowers, Ryder and Maisy came in. She put the flowers in the center of the kitchen table. "They're beautiful Ryder."

Tipping her chin up, Ryder kissed her. Phoebe blushed, not missing the look Maisy gave them. Made her wonder how much she saw at home. From what Diana had said, Will's sister was a real trip. And she was still haunted by the expression on the girl's face when Phoebe lifted her hand earlier in the garage. That was definitely a trained response, and Phoebe didn't like it one bit.

Having company for lunch kept her from asking Ryder questions. Her stomach heaved and she could only eat half her ham and cheese. While they cleaned up afterwards, Maisy drifted out to the porch.

"What's this supposed to look like?"

"Your guess is as good as mine." Wiping her hands on a towel, Phoebe came to stand at the open french doors. "I have a lot of unfinished projects."

Was Ryder one of them?

The teenager circled the table, studying the legs and the tops. She looked puzzled and Phoebe didn't blame her. "I don't know what I was thinking, Maisy. Really I don't."

Maisy looked up. "But it could be really neat. You know, full of seashells, fish and stuff. Maybe some clouds."

"You have a great imagination, Maisy." Phoebe rubbed the back of her neck. The heat buzzed in her head. "Isn't it about time to go down to the beach?"

Ryder peeked in. "Did I hear beach?"

"Yeah, I guess. This July heat is getting to me."

Questions pulsed in her mind. But Phoebe couldn't ask them. Then her fears would be real.

Before long they were all in their suits, towels slung around their necks. In her bag, Phoebe had sun lotion and some grapes. Ryder piled three chairs into the canvas wagon they'd always used on beach days. They started out. Maisy was clearly excited. When they reached the top of the stairs, they grabbed their chairs and left the wagon.

"You stay right here," Ryder told Phoebe. "I'll take this stuff down."

Of course, she could have made it down but the cast was clumsy. Sand ended up in it, making the itching worse. Families had set up their towels and tents down near the water, and the three of them quickly found a spot. She didn't miss the curious look on Maisy's face when Ryder carried her over to where Maisy was setting up the chairs.

"Sure wish this cast was off," Phoebe said, looking at the waves.

"Next week, right?"

"Can't wait." But would he be with her?

She didn't want to go there.

Ryder's shadow fell over her. "Do you mind if I go out into the water? I hate to just leave you here."

"Of course not. Go. Scoot." But when she waved her hands at him, she felt terrible.

Don't go. Don't go. The words echoed in her brain.

Doing a shallow dive, Ryder emerged and shook back his long thick hair. Then he threw her that wicked smile before setting out for the sand bar.

"Your Ryder's really something," Maisy said from the chair next to her.

"That he is, but he's not mine."

Maisy snorted. "Of course he is"

Phoebe followed Ryder's every move. "Do you like your mother's boyfriend?"

Maisy appeared to think that over. "Oh, Ray's not so bad. He likes my mom. I kind of hope this one lasts." When Maisy made a face, for a second she was like a mother who hopes her kid doesn't mess up again.

Now that made Phoebe chuckle. She adjusted her hat and began to slather herself with sunscreen. She didn't want to pry but Maisy continued on.

"I mean, it's not like my mom's boyfriends are like Ryder." She stared after him with awe reserved for Olympic swimmers. Ryder was doing a slow crawl parallel to the shore. He swam the way he danced, with total control and sexy rhythm. Phoebe loved watching him and, apparently, so did Maisy.

"What do you mean?"

Maisy shrugged. "I guess this isn't nice to say, but my mom picks up losers. At least the last one was, before Ray. Ryder's so cool and he's crazy about you."

"You think so?" Butterflies circled in Phoebe's stomach.

The girl snorted. "I know so. The way he looks at you? You should have seen him picking those flowers. They had to be just right."

"Aw." Maisy's words warmed her.

"I don't need a stepfather, but if I did, I'd sure choose Ryder. He's awesome."

"Yeah. Right. I guess every woman between here and Texas thinks so." Her troubling doubts resurfaced.

"Like you've got anything to worry about." Picking up a stone, Maisy winged it toward the water. "He adores you. Bat shit crazy, as my mother would say."

"Well now." Delinda must be a very colorful person. Phoebe tried to imagine Will using that phrase but her imagination failed her.

With dreamy eyes, Maisy watched Ryder swim. "Some day I want a boyfriend just like Ryder."

"Oh, you'll have one, Maisy," Phoebe rushed to give her hope. Anything to erase all the pain and uncertainty from her face. Didn't every woman in the world want to find the right man? And how did she know he was right?

"Hey!" Suddenly, Ryder was standing there, the water giving his skin a wet sheen. More than one woman glanced over. "Coming out, Maisy? The water's great."

"Um. Sure. I'll be right there."

Ryder's glance slid to Phoebe. "Wish you could come too. The water's beautiful. Finally got warm enough."

"Next week." She looked down at her cast.

"Right. Next week." Turning, Ryder stared at the horizon.

While they were talking, Maisy had managed to slide out of her baggy shift. Okay, she was not skinny but she looked fine, although the bathing suit was probably three years old. "Go on in and cool off." Phoebe shooed them away with her hands.

But watching the two toss Frisbees in the deeper water, where Maisy was apparently comfortable, Phoebe wondered about Ryder's expression when he'd said "next week." Like they wouldn't have one. Not together.

Sitting in the hot sunlight, she shivered.

Things were so complicated.

Chapter 21

Maisy had gone home and they were alone. Phoebe stood out on the porch, not knowing what to do. The two of them had eaten chicken salad from the refrigerator, but they'd both picked at the food. She wasn't hungry and neither was Ryder. Heck they'd hardly spoken. She tucked the contract under one of the cushions.

Ryder was inside, filling the dishwasher. A whippoorwill called somewhere deep in the woods. The night felt sad. No happy chatter filtered from the road. Even the lake had fallen silent. When Ryder walked up behind her, she smelled his soap but it brought no comfort. He didn't wrap his arms around her. Feeling sick at heart, she turned to see storm clouds gathered in his eyes.

"What is it, Ryder?"

"Aw, Pheebs." Taking her hands, he tugged her over to the futon. "Come on. Let's sit down."

Yep, not good at all. When Phoebe perched on the edge of the futon, she heard the crinkle of paper. Ryder looked away and she held her breath. What was the use? Maybe she'd been a fool to think they could repair the past.

"Don't worry. I saw your bag," Phoebe finally said. "I know you're leaving."

The eyes he turned to her were full of pain. She'd never seen him like this. "Here's the thing, Phoebe." He set down the words as if they were hot coals that might burn.

"I love you. So bad it hurts." His voice cracked.

"I love you too, Ryder." Somehow she got that out. "I don't want either one of us to hurt ever again."

Elbows resting on his knees, he looked worn out. "I've changed and I'm asking you to love me now, this man sitting right here. Not the idiot I was before. Can you believe that?" Desperation flooded his eyes.

"Yes, I can see that. I believe it. I believe in *you*, Ryder. You're the sweet man who's taken care of me these last few weeks. The guy who plays checkers with me at night. The man who'll sleep in a pink bedroom." She was relieved to see his lips curl into a smile, even though it was a sad smile.

"I don't want to be your handyman. Don't get me wrong. It's been great, being here with you. Kidding around and well, loving you." Here his voice cracked.

"Oh, Ryder..." Her arms jerked. How she wanted to hold him.

But he pushed them away. "Nice words but I see something different in your eyes. Dammit, Phoebe. You're like a dog that's been kicked once and can't trust anymore. And I don't blame you."

By this point, they were leaning toward each other but felt far apart. When had she ever felt so uncomfortable?

A soft, sad smile touched his lips.

"Don't say that," she whispered. "I do trust you."

He gave a frustrated growl. "I don't think you do. And I can't stand it. Can't stand you doubting me. Makes me wonder what I'm doing here."

When Ryder fell back in his chair, the pain on his face seared clear through to her heart. She couldn't lose him. Not again. Desperate, she tugged the pad of paper out from under her. It wasn't easy and she ripped it in the process.

"What's that?" he asked.

She handed him the contract. "Please read this. If you just sign it, why then, I'll know. I'll know we're going to work things out this second time."

Looking puzzled, he ran his eyes down her list. She had to make him see. "This could solve everything, Ryder. If you agree to this in writing, it would be as binding as a marriage contract." She flinched at his reaction. Instead of feeling the peace that Phoebe felt writing those points, Ryder looked furious. Her chest felt so tight. She could hardly breathe.

Ryder was seething. By the time he got to the end, his nostrils flared. When he threw the pad onto the sofa, she lost all hope. Standing up until he loomed over her, Ryder put his hands on his hips. "If this is what you think of me, Phoebe. If you think I'll agree to every small detail of how our day should go, then you have no trust in me, and I have no business being here. Are you also going to tell me when I should brush my teeth? What time I should be in bed?"

"Ryder, I—"

For a big man, Ryder could sure move fast. Her heart broke as she watched him stride to the door, where his bag sat waiting. "I'll make plans with someone to take care of this kitchen. The floors, the cabinets. Whatever you want." He gave the room a dismissive look.

Her own anger flared. "Oh, great. You're going to make me sell it, aren't you? You're going to kick me out of my home—"

When he pointed a finger at her, she stopped. "No, Phoebe Hunicutt. Stay here as long as you like. Remember how we were here together, every minute of it. And then ask yourself if I've changed."

Frantic now, she had to clarify things. "But Ryder if you sign the contract, we won't even have to get married again. We'll just have this understanding."

His face turned pale. "That's just frigging great, Phoebe. So if one of us gets pissed about something, we can just walk away? Is that what you want? An escape hatch?"

"No, that's not what I want." How could she make him understand? "That's not it at all."

When Ryder ripped open the door, she thought he'd tear it right off the hinges.

What had she done? "Don't go, Ryder. Please don't go. Don't leave me." She hobbled toward him until she stood in the doorway.

Marching through the darkness, he didn't even turn around. When had it started to rain? A fine mist coated her skin as she stumbled after him. Sobbing, she didn't feel the rain. Didn't feel the ground squishing beneath her bare feet.

When he reached the Harley, he turned. But she couldn't see his expression, only the hollow of eyes. Were those tears on his cheeks or just the rain? Twisting, he crammed his bag into the back, swung one leg over and snapped on his helmet. Then he roared off.

Phoebe was left there, sobbing and empty.

"This is all my fault," she told Fernando, staggering past him back into the cottage.

You got that right.

The darn bird wouldn't even look at her.

~.~

Ryder nearly killed himself driving up Red Arrow. At first he didn't have his lights on until a car honked at him. Crouched over the Harley, he felt like he was crashing through an invisible wall of pain.

And he blamed himself.

Phoebe was trying to protect herself...from him. He gave a harsh laugh, thinking back to the days when he thought he was a stud muffin, as his sisters had called him back then, and not in a nice way. Stephanie and Lisa had tried to knock him down a peg or two. But his dad was right. The two had spoiled him. He'd grown up thinking the earth revolved around him.

But tonight? If he couldn't be with Phoebe, then what was the point? When the double truck came up in the left hand lane, it just made him mad. Crouching lower, he opened it up. Knowing this was dangerous as hell, he passed the truck on the right just as the guy started to change to the right lane. Was she worth dying for? Right then, he thought yes. What did he have to live for anyway?

But his dad's ugly mug came to mind. He eased up. Yeah, Stanley would never get over that one. Ryder couldn't do that to his dad. It was going to be hard enough telling his father that their plans hadn't worked. The mission had failed.

The garage was dark when he pulled in. Everyone had gone home, and the only light was the one beaming over their sign. When he drove around back, the motion detector clicked on floodlights. First he opened the back door and then rolled up the wide garage door before wheeling the Hawg inside.

For the first time ever, the smell of the shop didn't feel like home. He stood in the darkness and sniffed. No, that prissy pink cottage had become home. Home was the mismatched kitchen that now had to be switched out by some other guy. Home was that porch with the tongue and groove ceiling, and the table Phoebe wanted to paint, not that she ever finished anything. But he'd had hopes. They'd had fun at that table. They'd sat there and played checkers. Strangest foreplay ever, when he'd said "King me," and Phoebe had carefully placed another chip on his with her neon green nails. The nails he knew would be making grooves in his back that night.

He didn't even want to think about the half-pink bedroom and the fancy white metal bed frame. He'd kind of gotten used to them. The loss deepened into despair. He'd imagined them making their babies in that bedroom. Their family, together. Throwing back his head, Ryder howled with loss. His anguish echoed from the cinderblock walls. He had to get a hold of himself.

His father had left everything in a corner, including his one-man gym. No way was he hauling all this back upstairs. Not tonight. Now he set up the gym, piece by piece. Enjoying the clang of metal on metal, he welcomed every bruise when he missed a juncture and pinched his hand. When he finally got the equipment into position, he stripped down to his shorts and wrapped a bandana tight around his forehead.

Then he ran through his routine at a punishing speed, again and again, taking a break only to hydrate. Getting into the zone, he worked his body until his palms were peeling under the gloves, and every muscle in his body screamed at him to stop.

The night sky was lightening to gray when he dragged himself upstairs.

~•~

The following day Phoebe called Diana. "Can you drive me to the doctor tomorrow? I have to get my cast taken off." She was sniffling.

"Sure, but where's Ryder? Hey, are you crying?"

"He's gone and yes, I'm crying."

Her friend gently extracted the story from Phoebe in fragments, like slivers of her heart. It took a while for Diana to get it. Phoebe had to keep doubling back. If she couldn't make her friend understand, then how had she expected Ryder to know how she felt?

"A contract, huh?"

"Am I totally stupid? I spent the whole night after Ryder left straightening my cupboards."

"I guess sometimes it's hard knowing what to do." Diana wasn't answering the question. "What time should I be there to pick you up tomorrow morning?"

"Nine thirty." So she *was* totally stupid.

After they hung up, Phoebe took a seat on the porch and turned to Fernando.

"Well that was great." Snatching a tissue from the side table, she blew her nose. "I can't even explain this to my close friend."

Matters of the heart sometimes cannot be explained.

How did this bird get to be so wise?

"I did a half ass job." She'd have to put cream on her nose. It was that red. "I don't explain things right. Me and my stupid contract."

Yes. You have a point.

"He didn't like it."

Trust me, no man would.

"Oh great. Now you tell me." Leaving the porch, she wished Fernando were a real bird, the kind you could cover with a towel so he'd shut up. Maybe if he were a female flamingo, then he'd understand. Where was that darn yellow tablet? She ripped through the cottage, yanking cupboards open and pulling out drawers. But she never found it.

That night she hardly slept. The bed felt so empty.

In the morning she was up before dawn. Down on the beach, she walked and walked in her cast, picking up stones and then skipping them across the waves that were just starting to build. Everything here reminded her of Ryder. The shoreline where they'd sat and talked about nothing in particular. The dunes where he'd spread out the blanket. Even the grass that he liked to work in his mouth.

His mouth, his lips. The way he sang off tune. Ryder.

Life felt empty when she dragged herself up the stairs. Thank goodness the cast was coming off today.

Of course Diana grilled her the moment she got in the yellow VW. "Do you have a cold?" Diana stared her red nose.

"No. I've got the blues."

Diana put the car in reverse. "Maisy will be heartbroken. She wouldn't stop talking about Ryder. I think Will was a little jealous."

"Diana, I don't want to talk about it, okay?"

"Okay." But her friend kept checking on her in the rearview mirror.

Thank goodness Dr. Swanson was on schedule. But one look at her when he entered the room and he stopped, her chart in hand. "Do you have a cold or something?"

"No, it's nothing." But his nurse gave Phoebe a sympathetic look. Sometimes women just knew. Thankfully, the conversation turned to the weather.

Half an hour later, she was back in Diana's car, surprised that she didn't feel more relieved. The cast had dragged her down for six weeks. But with Ryder there, it hadn't felt that bad. No, he'd carried her down to the beach. Emptied the dishwasher so she wouldn't have to bend over. All the sweet things he'd done came back now, cold comfort.

"How does your leg feel?" Diana asked as they drove back to Gull Harbor.

"Like it hasn't been used in a while." She stared down at the toes Ryder had painted neon green and flamingo pink that night. The color was a bright contrast to the pale leg that hadn't seen the sun all summer.

"How did you ever manage to polish your toes?"

"Don't ask," Phoebe said, digging in her purse for another tissue.

"Okay, I won't." Silence. "But he did that for you? Really?"

"Yes. Yes, he did." The list was long of Ryder's wonderfulness.

"How totally cool. And hot."

Phoebe turned on the radio.

When they reached the cottage, Diana pulled into the driveway where Ryder's black truck still sat. Stanley or Mick would probably have to drive Ryder down here one day. Phoebe sure didn't want to be around when that happened. How could she ever face Stanley?

"Are you okay here alone?" Diana asked.

"Of course. I'll be fine." Sliding out of the car, Phoebe balanced on both feet. She felt curiously light. The whole world felt strange. Strange and awful, without Ryder.

Getting out of the car, Diana came around, her eyes on the cottage. "This looks terrific. No wonder Maisy wants to move in. She told us our condo was totally boring."

"He worked hard on it." The lawn looked so tidy from when he'd cut it. "Maisy did a great job with the weeds."

"She enjoyed being here."

Phoebe jammed her key in the lock and pushed the door open. Diana followed her into the kitchen that now felt so empty.

Looking around, Diana said. "So what's your plan?"

Phoebe glanced over at the unfinished table on the porch and knew she'd never finish it. "Guess I'll go in to work. Give Jen and Carly a break." But she shrank from the questions people were sure to ask.

"Don't worry. People aren't talking about you."

"Yet." Phoebe threw Diana a crooked smile. "No, I'll just finish things up here." She had no idea what.

"Okay. See you tomorrow night for book group?"

"Right. See you then. And thanks, Diana. Thanks a lot."

Diana gave her a tight hug at the back door. "Things will work out. You'll see. You two love each other. Whatever it is, you can handle it."

Phoebe wished she had Diana's certainty.

Later that evening, after choking down half of a frozen pizza, she went into her therapist's office. "Is this how it's going to be, Fernando? People will feel sorry for me. They'll have questions."

On the other side of the screen, Fernando didn't blink an eye. *Curiosity is a very human thing.*

"So birds don't have it?"

Her metal sculpture fell silent.

Another man letting her down.

But Ryder hadn't let her down. Not this time. So what was this all about? Trust. And her lack of it.

The following evening, she drove herself to Diana's house. It felt good to be behind the wheel again, but it sucked that the car still smelled like Ryder. When she reached Diana's, she made herself get out. Although she hadn't read the book, that never had mattered in the past. Not with this group.

"Hey," Diana said when she answered the door. "Everything okay?"

"Fine," she said brightly, stepping inside.

"Hey, girl." Kate looked up from the bowl of guacamole. "Don't mind me. I'm pregnant and raging hungry."

But no amount of joking could lift Phoebe's mood.

"So your cast's off, huh?" Kate kept eating.

"Right. You like my two tone tan?" As long as they were discussing her tan and not her heart, this evening might be doable.

Chili and Sarah piled in not long after that. Soon everyone had a margarita in hand. Since she was driving herself home, Phoebe was sticking to water tonight.

"How is the leg?" Chili asked.

Phoebe looked down.

"What? *Que pasa?* You look at your leg like it is some new thing you did not know you had."

"Fine, I guess." Everything felt off. Everyone's eyes were on her, and Phoebe felt their questioning weight.

"Want to discuss the story?" Diana asked. "Tense right, this mystery?"

Ah, a diversion tactic. Phoebe sent Diana a grateful smile.

"Not as tense as it is in this room," Kate said slowly, her eyes circling between Phoebe and Diana. "What's going on, Phoebe? You're usually so cheerful. How's Ryder?"

No one moved. Did anyone even breathe? Chili's glass hung in mid-air.

"Gone." The word sounded as empty as she felt.

"What happened? You were so happy, no?" Slowly, Chili set her glass on the coffee table.

Talk about being a buzz kill. Her friends stared at her. "It's just that. Well, I'm not sure..."

"Oh, Phoebe." Sarah's eyes warmed. "You don't have to tell us. Not until you're ready."

"I think she is ready." Leaning forward, Chili twisted a length of her dark hair. "So what happened? He looks at you like you walk on the water."

Phoebe's laugh was high and nervous. "Really?"

"Really. Cole and I both liked him." Kate held up her hands. "But you don't have to share until you're ready."

"But sharing the weight of your sorrow might help you." Chili would not let this rest.

"In the past we'd had an issue." Surely they'd understand when she told them. And then maybe they'd have some suggestions. "Another woman."

"Bah! Is that what broke up your marriage?" Chili said with disgust. "Another *chica?*"

"Yes, but that's in the past. He's changed."

"She is out of the picture?" Chili sat waiting. In fact they all were.

"Oh, yes. Over and done with. Ryder and I, well, we had such a nice time together this summer." Her voice had become choked and she cleared her throat.

"So what's the problem?" Kate asked.

"I just want to be sure this time. I mean, I don't want it to happen again." She turned to them for answers. "How do you know?"

Kate shrugged. "You don't. Not really. I mean, will Cole's ex come to town some time and steal him back? I don't have an answer for that."

"Snowball's chance in hell, Kate," Diana said with certainty.

"But how can you be sure?" Phoebe felt so confused. "How do you know?"

"You don't," Sarah said softly. "But your heart knows. What is your heart telling you?"

Oh, Fernando would love this.

"My heart isn't sure." Pressing a hand to her chest, Phoebe felt her heart racing. "That's why I asked him to sign a contract."

"Contract?" Kate gave her a blank look.

"Oh, *mama mia*," Chili murmured.

Horror filled Kate's face. Even sweet Sarah looked taken back by this admission.

"No, you didn't," Diana murmured.

"Yes, I did." And with that, the contract that had seemed like the best idea in the world looked ridiculous. Who did she think she was?

"You have a right to do whatever makes you comfortable," Sarah said, nodding in sympathy.

"But I'm not comfortable at all. I'm jumping out of my skin." She was practically bouncing on the sofa.

"How did he take it?" Kate wanted details. "I think Cole would be insulted."

Shaking her head, Phoebe remembered the slamming of the kitchen door. "That's putting it mildly. He was furious."

Thumping a fist to her chest, Chili exploded. "*Que hombre.* Of course he was! You are trying to hog tie him with the rope."

The mention of the rope made Phoebe cry harder.

"You love him, no?" Chili asked.

"Yes, of course I do." Great. Now she had hiccups.

"Do you trust him?" Diana peered into her eyes. "That's really it, isn't it? This is a matter of trust."

Curling into a tight ball, Phoebe tried to shield herself from her own feelings. "I trust the Ryder I came to know this summer. And I don't know how I'll live without him. How will I ever do it?"

Reaching over, Kate took her wrist. "If that's what it comes to, you will. You will live without him."

"But I don't wah-ah-ant to," she wailed.

By this time Diana had tears running down her cheeks and so did Sarah.

"We will always be here for you." Sarah set aside the book that no one had finished or wanted to discuss. "But how can you fix this?"

There followed a ridiculous list of proposals from wrapping herself in plastic wrap and appearing at his door to just sneaking into his bed. Things got crazy. By the time Phoebe drove home that night, a million solutions circled in her brain. She could hardly sleep. What was she going to do? When she opened her cupboards the next morning, she saw the edge of her yellow pad under some platters. This was the first time one of her messes ever gave her a solution to anything.

Chapter 22

It had been a while since Phoebe had driven a truck. Didn't matter. Today she was a woman with a mission. Good thing traffic was light on Red Arrow Highway. Every time she shifted, the truck jerked and bucked. Ryder would kill her if he could hear his gears grinding. But he wasn't here. She hit the accelerator and drove.

When she reached Branson Motors, the sun was bouncing off the green sign, and all three bays were open. The whining of a drill filled the air, along with bursts from an air pump. Choppers sat in the sunlight, waiting to be taken inside. Business as usual, but she hadn't planned on all this activity.

No matter, she was here. A nervous wreck when she got dressed that morning, she couldn't decide what to wear. The July weather was so breathlessly hot. Finally she grabbed her little white skirt and the flag top. By the time she reached the garage, her hands were glued to the steering wheel with sweat. She had no idea how to work his air conditioning, not without running off the road. Wiping her hands on her skirt, she pulled onto the grass in back and got out. Her right leg buckled once in awhile. But after a couple steps, she got her balance. What she was about to do might be bold, but Fernando had agreed this was the only way to handle it.

She was risking everything.

Ten minutes from now, she might be driving back down that highway, her whole world destroyed. No matter. What was that saying? Nothing ventured, nothing gained? She had to try.

In her imagination she pulled on her big girl pants. Then she walked in. At first no one noticed her. Mick was working over a Harley, along with a couple other guys. Ryder and Stanley stood talking in the glassed-in office. Papa was waving his hands while he bent Ryder's ear. Ryder leaned against the counter with his head down, like he'd heard all this before.

When Mick saw her, he turned the music down. The change in volume must have alerted Papa and Ryder. Their conversation stopped. For one wild second Phoebe wanted to run. But she had to try to fix this. For her, there was only one man. Only one life and that was with him.

Okay, she would have preferred to talk with Ryder in private, but that wasn't going to happen. So she sucked it up and stood there shaking. He'd come into the main garage with Papa right behind him. "Phoebe?" Ryder looked like he couldn't believe his eyes.

"Yes." What was that? Her voice was so small, she could hardly hear herself. "Now look here Ryder." She ended up shouting because Mick may have turned the music down but not off. "I love you. That's just the way it is. I love you like crazy." She held up the pad of yellow paper. "And I don't blame you for being mad about this."

His eyes went to the yellow pad. Ryder stopped dead in his tracks, and Stanley ran right into him.

With one good yank, Phoebe tore the contract from the pad. How foolish she'd been, thinking this could give her a secure future. She had to do that for herself. Ryder's jaw dropped as Phoebe ripped the paper again and again. Finally she tossed the bits of paper into the air. The pieces fell over them like confetti, and Ryder wore a big smile. Stanley just looked confused.

"Kind of a grand gesture, isn't it?" Ryder said, taking her in his arms. He picked a couple pieces from her hair. Gosh he felt good.

"You're kind of a grand guy." She smiled up at him. "Will you marry me?"

"Yes." And he kissed her. "As long as you never write another contract."

"You got it. As long as you..."

His eyebrows lifted.

"Nothing." She snuggled under his chin. "Just be you, okay?"

Stanley broke into applause, so of course the others followed. Phones flashed and she figured they'd end up on the cover of the next issue of *The Beacher*. So what.

"I can't live without you," she whispered.

"You don't have to," he said before kissing her again. "No more talking about the past. Just the future."

Whipping out his hankie, Stanley wiped his eyes and hitched up his jeans. "Now this," he said to no one in particular. "This is mission accomplished. You bet."

"Oh, Papa. Come here." Phoebe waved him over so he could

be part of a group hug.

"So you're taking the name back?" Hope gleamed in her father-in-law's eyes.

"Wouldn't have it any other way."

"Phoebe Branson." After a quick hug, Stanley disappeared back into the office mumbling her new name.

Now, she liked the sound of that.

Epilogue

From the window of her bedroom, Phoebe watched family and friends gather in their backyard. Diana and Carolyn had worked hours on the trellis arching over the new walkway and leading to the fire pit. Ryder had hired a stonemason to reconstruct the pit and it was beautiful. The bluish gray stonework added a rustic touch to the pink calla lilies, banked by white roses adorning the pit. Maisy had worked her tail off planting bright pink gerbera daisies in the flowerbeds that led to the patio. Phoebe could hardly believe this was the same yard she'd ignored all summer.

The garden wasn't the only thing that had been improved by Maisy. To Phoebe's amazement, she'd also taken on the porch table, which now had a beach theme complete with shells. Phoebe was thrilled that the teenager would be in Gull Harbor for a while. After begging her mother Delinda, she'd been allowed to stay with Will for the upcoming school year. Phoebe hoped that went well. Diana still had her doubts, but the whole family agreed that a stable structure was what Maisy needed. Will's parents were seriously considering relocating to Gull Harbor and leaving Indiana behind. So many good things had happened this past summer.

Pulling the white dimity curtains closed, Phoebe was relieved that this day had arrived. At Ryder's urging, they decided not to delay the wedding. Oh, it hadn't been easy convincing her parents. Concerned by her surprise call, Cal and Lorna had jumped in their car the minute Phoebe gave them the news. She hadn't let her folks in on what was happening in Gull Harbor. Stanley was way ahead of them, and bless his heart, he helped reassure them when they arrived for their three-day visit in early August. Now they were back for the wedding, and Phoebe's mom adjusted the shoulder length veil for the fifth time.

Diana stuck her head in the door. "Are you ready?"

"Just about. Come on in and close the door." Phoebe waved her inside. She didn't want Ryder to get a sneak peek. He'd already made one trip to the bathroom across the hall, despite her scolding that seeing the bride before the ceremony was bad luck.

No white dress for this second-time bride. Phoebe wore an outrageous pink dress that fit like a glove and was the color of Fernando. Diana, Carolyn, Sarah, Chili and Kate had all chosen a dress in some shade of pink. They'd scored big time at Secondhand Rose. Phoebe had left her card with the new owner, asking her to call when anything pink came in. Esper had been as good as her word, and they were all outfitted. Kate's dress looked more like a tent than a dress because her baby was due any minute.

"Yep, all set," Phoebe told Diana, taking one more spin in front of the mirror. "Has Ryder cleared the area?"

"They just went outside." Diana fanned herself. "Wait until you see your groom."

Phoebe grabbed Diana's hands. "Oh, Diana. Is he handsome?" She could only imagine.

"Smoking hot."

"Now, now," her mother clucked. "The bride is supposed to be the center of attention on the wedding day."

Over Lorna Hunicutt's head, Phoebe exchanged a look with Diana. Sometimes mothers did not understand.

"Hey, what's going on in here?" Carolyn eased through the door, closing it firmly behind her. "Oh, my goodness. Look at you!"

Phoebe did a quick pirouette and nearly slid right out of her sling back heels. "Do you think I'll be able to dance in these?"

Carolyn shrugged. "Kick them off. I've seen that dance floor. We'll probably all be barefoot later."

"I'm so glad the weather has cooperated." Phoebe smoothed a hand over the silk that tucked in all the right places.

"Only you could wear that dress and not be arrested," Carolyn murmured.

A knock came at the door. "You girls ready in there?" Kate called out. "You better hurry or I'm going to have this baby right here!"

"We're coming. We're coming." Phoebe kissed her mother. "Mom, go join Daddy. I'll be right out."

"Oh, sweetheart." Her mother gave her a kiss. "I'm so happy for you."

"Then stop worrying," Phoebe whispered before pushing her mom out the door.

And then there were just the three of them, beaming at each other. "Are you ready, Phoebe?" Diana asked.

"As ready as I can be." Phoebe glanced at the pink walls that Ryder had finished painting in August. If these walls could talk, what stories they'd tell.

When they reached the kitchen, two of the catering staff were busy at the counters. Phoebe loved the new look of her kitchen, not that she intended to do much cooking. That was one thing that hadn't changed. She was back at work and picking up dinner on the fly. In the two months before the wedding, Ryder had finished the flooring and installed new white cupboards. Sometimes when she came through the door, she hardly recognized her own house.

"Has Brody arrived?" she asked Carolyn as they left the kitchen. Carolyn's nervous flush told Phoebe the man had arrived.

"Yes, and this time he's arranged his schedule so he can stay for two weeks."

The sun was slipping behind the tall pines when Phoebe walked outside. She was glad they'd decided to be married in their own yard and not down on the beach. After all, working on the house had brought them together again.

Carolyn signaled to the organist and the wedding march began. The group of fifty family and friends was small, but everyone who mattered to them was here. When Phoebe looked down the aisle formed between the white chairs, her breath caught. Ryder was so handsome in a gray tux that matched his eyes. His steady gaze drew her forward. Next to him stood Stanley, his best man. He'd wanted to wear his jeans, but Ryder put his foot down. Phoebe hadn't seen Stanley in a suit since their first wedding. Even Fernando wore a white collar and black bowtie. Ryder had put her lawn decoration right next to the arched trellis for the ceremony.

"You look beautiful," Ryder told her when she reached him.

"Thank you. So do you."

"Just don't fall."

"Hey, no chance." Taking his arm, she held on tight.

The music stopped and the minister began. When the time came for their vows, a hush fell over the crowd. Second weddings weren't new for this group. Some of Phoebe's friends hadn't gotten it right the first time. But for Phoebe? She knew this second time was forever.

Their vows made reference to second chances, patience and love that endures. She felt Stanley's eyes on them the entire time. Then they exchanged the wedding bands that had "forever" etched inside, along with the date. When the minster said, "You may now kiss the bride," she caught Stanley's eyes over Ryder's shoulder. Her father-in-law winked.

"Oh, Ryder," she whispered. "I'm so happy. Is this for real?"

"This is for always." His kiss carried that promise.

The guests had been given bags of shredded yellow legal pads. When the recessional started and they turned, everyone showered them with the stuff. How they laughed because only Phoebe and Ryder knew just how that contract went down. Phoebe was still finding bits in Ryder's hair when they danced to the first song two hours later.

"Guess that's all we have left of the contract, Mrs. Branson," Ryder whispered.

"Yep. And that's all we'll ever need."

His arms tightened around her. For their first dance they'd chosen an old Sinatra favorite, "The Second Time Around." For them and a lot of her friends, the words had special meaning. They did have their feet on the ground. This time they knew what it took to make a marriage work. A good partnership was more than moonlight and kisses, although that sure helped.

"This time we're taking time to have fun," Ryder said as he spun her around the small dance floor.

"Did you have anything in mind?" She batted her lashes at him innocently.

When he whispered his reply, excitement made her knees weak. "I didn't know you'd seen that movie."

"Oh, yeah, babe. Several times."

For them? The second time around was definitely the best.

THE END

Other Books by Barbara Lohr

Windy City Romance series

Finding Southern Comfort

Her Favorite Mistake

Her Favorite Honeymoon

Her Favorite Hot Doc

The Christmas Baby Bundle

Rescuing the Reluctant Groom

The Southern Comfort Christmas

Windy City Romance Box Set: Bks 0-III

Man from Yesterday series

Coming Home to You

Always on His Mind

In His Eyes

Late Bloomer

Man from Yesterday Box Set: Bks I-IV

About the Author

Barbara Lohr writes heartwarming contemporary romance, with a flair for fun. In her *Windy City Romance* series the women are based in Oak Park, Illinois, a western suburb of Chicago. However, these girls get around. Readers enjoy jaunts to Tuscany, Guatemala and Savannah. The *Man from Yesterday* series is set in Gull Harbor, Michigan, where close high school friends welcome newcomers with equal warmth. The charming small beach town actually exists but under another name.

Family often plays a role in Barbara's stories. "No woman falls in love without some family influence, either positive or negative." Dark chocolate is her favorite food group, and yummy food often figures in her work. Barbara lives in the South with her husband and a cat that insists he was Heathcliff in a former life. Sign up for her newsletter by going to her website. Friend her on Facebook or connect on Twitter! She loves to hear from readers.

For more information on the author and her work, or to sign up for her newsletter, please see:

www.BarbaraLohrAuthor.com

www.facebook.com/Barbaralohrauthor

www.twitter.com/BarbaraJLohr

A Word from the Author

Many thanks to Romance Writers of America, a group whose members are generous with their knowledge base. The loops and forums of writers who address writing and publishing issues are invaluable to me.

To my readers, thank you! Your appreciation and support warm my heart. To my growing Read and Review team, love you guys! Keep responding to my newsletters and be sure to enter my giveaways. I sure appreciate your interest and hope to continue to write books that take you on "journeys of the heart," as one of you mentioned.

Thanks to Kim Killion for covers that package my work perfectly. I look at those covers and think, yes, my characters could walk right off that page. And the same to Chris Hall, my editor. After untold hours of working on a manuscript, your suggestions and insight are invaluable.

For my daughters Kelly and Shannon, keep those reading lamps on over your beds. For us, reading has always been a tie that binds. My grandchildren Bo and Gianna bring me such joy and of course pop up in Mama B's novels. To my husband Ted, words aren't adequate to thank you for your love and support, especially when my computer crashes and you provide tech support. May we have many more wonderful years together with trips to Leopold's for ice cream.

www.ingramcontent.com/pod-product-compliance
Lightning Source LLC
Chambersburg PA
CBHW071239190726
48292CB00007B/2363